Signs of Attraction

Signs of Attraction

LAURA BROWN

AVONIMPULSE

An Imprint of HarperCollinsPublishers

An excerpt from *Change of Heart* copyright © 2016 by Tina Klinesmith.
An excerpt from *Montana Hearts: True Country Hero* copyright © 2016 by Darlene Panzera.
An excerpt from *Once and For All* copyright © 2016 by Cheryl Etchison Smith.

Avon, Avon Impulse, and the Avon Impulse logo are trademarks of HarperCollins Publishers.

EPub Edition JUNE 2016 ISBN: 9780062495570

Print Edition ISBN: 9780062495587

AM 10 9 8 7 6 5 4 3 2 1

To Kari,

*My cheerleader. You believed in this story when
I lost faith. You loved my characters and helped me
shape them into who they needed to be. And you
pushed me forward when I would have held back.
It's because of you this book is what it is.*

Acknowledgments

THIS NOVEL HAS been quite the journey for me. I am so fortunate to have had many eyes on it at different stages, all helping me arrive at this final, incredible point. From early readers to late, each one of you has made a huge difference. Thank you for everything, Josie Leigh, Adrienne Proctor, Alice Bell, Cara Bertrand, Vanessa Rodriguez, Karen Mahara, Heather DiAngelis, and Mom. Your feedback was invaluable.

Kari, Heather, and Vanessa, you rock at ripping apart my novels and helping with ideas on how to put it back together—or just listening to me babble. You've held my hand through this amazing journey, and I feel so blessed to have you by my side.

To writers I've met and interacted with on Twitter and Facebook, you all are amazing and talented and full of support and encouragement. I'm so grateful for your friendship.

I had the amazing fortune of entering *Signs of Attraction* into writing contests, even more so for being picked for the final agent round. Thank you, Sharon Johnson, E. L. Wicker, and Elizabeth Briggs. Not only did you choose me as a finalist, but you also provided feedback on my first chapter as well as tons of support. And a special thanks to SC for not only running a diverse contest but also choosing me as a finalist.

To my agent, Rachel Brooks. Thank you for falling in love with Carli and Reed. You challenged me to bring them to the next level, and I'm so thrilled I get to work with you. You deserve a superhero cape with your name on it!

To Elle Keck and the entire Avon Impulse team. Thank you for loving this story as much as I do and embracing all the diverse elements presented. You not only gave me a chance but helped put hearing loss front and center in a romance novel. I feel so fortunate to be an Avon writer and to work with all your talent.

To my husband and son. I know it hasn't always been easy to handle the time commitment writing takes. I love you both, and you've helped me achieve this goal, even when distracting me from my computer.

Chapter One

Carli

THE MINUTE THE professor opened his mouth, I knew it would be a long semester. The muffled sound struck a vein deep inside my skull, vibrating tension destined to trigger one of my frequent headaches. I slid my hand under my long brown hair, scratched my cheek as a decoy, and then ran my finger over the microphone of one hearing aid. Static rang loud and clear, confirming my suspicions. My hearing aids were fine.

The professor was the problem.

His booming voice ricocheted an accent off the walls of the small classroom. An accent I identified as...not from around here. Dr. Ashen's bushy mustache covered his top lip. Students shifted. Pages turned. Pens moved.

I flicked my pen against a random page of my thick book. Words spilled from his bottom lip, and I couldn't understand one fucking sound. Survival skill 101 of having a hearing loss: blend in. I'd grown skilled at blending, almost mastering the task of invisibility. No cloak required. Take that, Harry Potter.

I always, always, *always* heard my teachers. Until now.

Big Fuck-Off Mustache + My Ears = Not Happening.

Dr. Ashen glared my way. He tapped his textbook and went right on speaking.

I couldn't see his book; tapping it didn't help. Moron. I rolled my eyes and landed on my neighbor's book. I scanned the words, hoping something, anything, would match. Nothing did. What a waste of a class. I shoved my book and slouched in my seat. No way could I keep up. No chance in hell.

With a sigh, I focused on two women standing by the dry-erase board, both dressed in black, heads close as they chatted. They looked much too old to be students, but considering this was an undergrad/grad class, anything was possible. Perhaps they were assistants to Dr. Ashen. They looked to be following him about as much as I was, but that didn't mean they weren't his assistants. They could've heard his spiel one too many times before. I wished I'd heard him at least once.

One of the women wore the coolest glasses with tiny gemstones in the corners. If I ever needed glasses, I wanted those. Chic Glasses Lady glanced at the clock and said something to the other, who had long brown hair in perfect ringlets. If my hair had curls...I shouldn't be shopping for fashion styles in my linguistics class. They moved to get their bags as the door opened.

You know those corny movies where the love interest walks in and a halo of light flashes behind them? Yeah, that happened. Not because this guy was hot, which he was, but because the faulty hall light had been flickering since before I walked into the room. His chestnut hair—the kind that flopped over his forehead and covered his strong jaw in two to three weeks' worth of growth—complemented his rich brown eyes and dark olive skin, which was either a tan or damn good genetics.

Not that I paid much attention. I was just bored.

And warm. Was it warm in here? I repositioned my hair, thankful it not only covered my aids but also the sudden burning of my ears.

Dr. Ashen stopped talking as Hot New Guy walked over to the two women, shifted his backpack, and began moving his hands in a flurry of activity I assumed was American Sign Language. Chic Glasses Lady moved her hands in response while Perfect Ringlets addressed our teacher.

"Sorry. My car broke down, and I had to jump on the Green Line," Ringlets said, speaking for Hot New Guy.

Car? In the middle of Boston? Was this guy crazy?

Dr. Ashen spit out an intense reply. Chic Glasses signed to Hot New Guy, who nodded and took a seat in the back of the room.

For the next two hours—the joy of a once-a-week part-grad class—I watched the two interpreters. Every half hour or so they switched, with one standing next to Dr. Ashen. They held eye contact with one spot near the back of the room, where Hot New Deaf Guy sat. I'd never seen ASL up close and personal before. My ears, faulty as they were, had never failed me, at least not to this degree.

From the notes the students around me took—pages of them, according to the girl on my left—this class was a bust. I needed this to graduate. Maybe my advisor could work something out? Maybe—

Beep. Beep. Beep.

Dammit. To add insult to injury, my hearing aid, the right one, traitorous bitch, announced she needed her battery changed. Right. This. Second. And if—

Beep. Beep. Beep.

I reached into my purse, rummaged past lip gloss, tampons, and tissues, and searched for the slim package of batteries. I had no choice. If I ignored the beeping it'd just—

Beep. Beep. Beep.

Silence.

Fuck. My left ear still worked, but now the world was half-silent. And Dr. Ashen was a mere mumble of incomprehension.

I pulled out my battery packet only to find the eight little tabs empty.

Double fuck. No time to be discreet. I tossed the packet onto my desk and stuck my head in my bag, shifted my wallet, and moved my calendar. I always had extra batteries on hand. Where were they?

A hand tapped my shoulder. I nearly shrieked and jumped out of my skin. Hot New Deaf Guy stood over me. It was then I noticed student chatter and my peers moving about. Dr. Ashen sat at his desk, reviewing his notes. All signs I had missed the beginning of a break.

Hot New Deaf Guy moved his fingers in front of his face and pointed to the empty battery packet I had forgotten on my desk.

"What color battery?" asked Perfect Ringlets, who stood next to him.

"I…Uh…" The burning in my ears migrated to my cheeks. I glanced around. No one paid us any attention. Meanwhile I felt like a spotlight landed on my malfunctioning ears. Hot New Deaf Guy waited for my response. I could tell him to get lost, but that would be rude. Why did my invisibility cloak have to fail me today? And why did he have to be so damn sexy standing there, all broad shoulders and a face that said, "Let me help you"?

He oozed confidence in his own skin. Mine itched. Heck, his ears didn't have anything in them, unless he had those fancy-shmancy hearing aids that were next to invisible. The kind of hearing aids I assumed old dudes wore when their days of rock concerts gave them late onset loss. Not the kind of aids someone who had an interpreter at his side would wear.

At a loss on how I was supposed to communicate, or where my jumbled thoughts were headed, I waved the white flag and showed him the empty packet like a moron.

He nodded, twisted his bag around, and found the batteries I needed.

I glanced around the room again. No one looked at us. No one cared that a hot guy holding out a packet of hearing aid batteries threw my world off-kilter.

This class was going on the List of Horrible Classes. Current standing? Worst class ever.

He tapped the packet and signed. A few movements later, much like a speech delay on a bad broadcast, the interpreter beside him spoke.

"Go ahead. Sharon says this guy has a thick accent. Must be hard to hear."

This could not get any more humiliating. I glanced at Perfect Ringlets, who I hoped was Sharon, and she nodded.

"Thank you." I took out one battery, pulled off the orange tab, and popped it into the small door on my hearing aid before shoving it back in my ear. Hot New Deaf Guy still hovered over me, wearing an infectious smile, a smile that made my knees weak. I handed the packet back. "You don't wear hearing aids, so why do you have batteries?"

He watched Sharon as she signed my words while putting the batteries away. "I work at a deaf school. Most of my students have hearing aids and someone always needs a battery. I keep a stash on hand," he said via the interpreter.

"That's nice of you."

He smiled again. I wished he would stop. The smiling thing, I mean. Every time he did, I lost a brain cell. "My name's Reed." He stuck out a hand when he finished signing.

I looked at his hand, a bit amazed at how well he could communicate with it.

Not an excuse to be rude. I reached for his outstretched hand. "Carli."

Sharon asked me how I spelled my name. Reed looked at her instead of me. When I touched him, a spark of some kind ignited and dashed straight up my arm. A tingling that had nothing to do with my ears, or his ears. His eyes shot to mine and I froze. Unable to move or do anything human, like pull my hand back. All I could think of was the fact that I'd never kissed a guy with a beard before.

I broke contact before I turned into a tomato. "C-A-R-L-I," I said to the interpreter.

He signed something to her that she didn't speak to me. Then she walked away and he squatted next to me. Soft jeans flexed over his knees, molded to his sturdy frame. He reached for my notebook—still blank—and pen. Even with the beard, he had a soul patch beneath his full bottom lip. My own bottom lip found its way into my mouth and my teeth clamped down. I tried to stop but couldn't. A hot guy was taking an interest in me. It wasn't a common occurrence.

Why don't you have any communication accommodations?

He wrote in scrawly, messy words across an angle on my notebook. Close to me, so close if I leaned a little our shoulders would brush.

I shrugged, careful not to brush him, and seized the pen.

What would I have? I don't sign.

He laughed, the sound low, guttural, and without restraint. A bit jarring since not a single other noise had come from him. As he wrote, I glanced around again. Still, no one watched us. I swore eyes bored into the back of my head but couldn't find any proof.

You could have a CART provider.

I wanted to write *what the fuck is that?* but figured it might be boorish. Instead, I stared at him, slightly less boorishly.

He laughed again, the sound no longer low, but free, without any societal restrictions. It hummed in a quiet manner across my veins. He started scribbling again.

CART, I forget what it stands for. You know those court stenographers who type everything in court?

He looked up at me while I read. I nodded. I'd seen some frumpy librarian-type woman positioned near a judge in images before.

The university provides that to Deaf and Hard of Hearing students. You should take advantage of them, especially in a class like this.

He capitalized *deaf* and *hard of hearing*. I had no idea why. Everything about this conversation contradicted with my upbringing. I wanted to squirm, allowing only my foot to tap a jittered dance. I'd never spoken to a deaf person before. I'd never had one sitting in front of me, full of a normalness I never possessed. I picked up the pen.

I can handle things on my own.

Motto of my life. My father all but had it engraved over the front door: handle it yourselves. Next to that? Perfection is never overrated.

Reed studied me with intense eyes. My breath caught as I resisted the urge to lean in closer. I tried to look away, really I did, but found I couldn't.

I'm sure you can. But getting help to hear is being independent. Without Sharon and Katherine, I wouldn't be able to take this class. And without CART, neither will you. I can get it set up for you. Give it a try. What do you have to lose?

He reverted to studying me intently as I read his words. I looked at him and wondered how to respond. This was so completely out of my comfort zone, yet he had a point. Without help, I was dropping this class.

Dr. Ashen made a loud noise. Startled, I looked up, creating a chain reaction when Reed glanced over to the interpreters. He quickly scribbled something on my paper before heading back to his desk.

I took a deep breath, ready for the last hour of the class. If a God existed, my inability to hear the professor was only due to my hearing aid battery dying.

Nope. Was it too late to convert to atheism? I understood the spittle from Dr. Ashen more than any of his words. I turned my attention to the interpreter. Chic Glasses Lady, Katherine, stood nearby, out of spittle range. They must have learned fast. Her hands moved smooth and easy, her face full of expression.

I knew I wasn't going to hear anything for the rest of the class. My head ached, and I was done pretending for the day. Instead, I focused on Katherine's hands, fluid movement from one sign to the next. The beautiful motion transfixed me.

Something deep inside me shifted. I had no clue what she said. But I felt it. Her words made sense on some level.

I knew exactly one sign, *I love you*, and that wasn't about to help me. I spent the rest of the class watching her, no longer hearing Dr. Ashen.

When I finally looked at my paper, Reed had written a phone number down, plus *text me if you want to talk*.

Students around me wrote notes. The interpreter signed. Dr. Ashen continued saying nothing I could infer. And I really didn't want to delay my graduation. I didn't come this far in my quest to be a teacher to fail now.

I pulled my phone out of my back pocket and plugged Reed's information into a new text message.

Me: How do I get this CART thing?

Chapter Two

Reed

THE LETTER ARRIVED on my twenty-third birthday. A stained, wrinkled, off-white envelope I equated with a bag of flaming shit. It lay on the passenger seat, burning a stink hole into the latte-colored fabric as I drove. The smell a clear indicator that nothing good waited inside.

Only one reason remained for the adoption agency to contact me. I gripped the wheel as I swerved to avoid hitting a pothole. My stomach swerved just to be an emotional bastard.

The letter had to come from my birth parents. Two adults who gave me up at the age of three without looking back. Two adults who nearly destroyed my life. Two adults I had no desire to ever meet.

At the red light, my car idled, the rumble of the motor filling the car and everything inside. I gripped the wheel tighter. The letter stuck out its tongue, taunting me. *Don't you want to know why you were deserted? Maybe they feel bad. Maybe they need a kidney.* I exhaled, eyes on the red light. Fuck it. I grabbed the offending piece of shit and tore it open. A folded letter fell into my lap, addressed to the agency. A straight slit indicated it had been opened and passed along.

The light turned green, and I tossed the letter back to the passenger seat. City congestion crippled traffic to a slow crawl. Gas. Brake. Gas. Brake. The letter a beacon to my peripheral vision. I snatched it and looked down at the return address of the original letter.

Juan Suarez.

A name. A name belonging to any random male in any random part of the world. No, the name didn't mean a damn thing to me.

The handwriting, on the other hand, meant something. The same loopy, messy scrawl as mine.

My car lurched; the wheel shook. I pulled my eyes back to the road and the pothole I'd hit head-on. The car teetered and tottered. I eased off the gas, but the whole damn car trembled. A thump, thump rattled my veins. Dammit.

A pedestrian waved at me. Yeah, yeah, I got it. The car's making sounds now. Well, deal. I pulled over to the side and exited the car. I rounded the back, finding nothing out of the ordinary until I came along the front passenger tire. Flat with dented metal.

I kicked the tire, just to be sure. Still flat. Someone stood next to me, probably talking the way hearing people did. I didn't have time to play nice. Not today. I whipped out my phone and set up a text to my roommate.

Me: Tire flat. Help please.

I checked the time. I was already late for my first day of classes. If I didn't arrive in twenty minutes, the interpreters would leave. Not acceptable.

While I waited, I pulled my books from the backseat and stuffed them into my workbag, along with the pile-of-shit letter.

Val: Again? ;-p

My roommate, keeping my ego in check since 2002.

Me: Pothole. Either hit car or pedestrian.

Or be distracted by messy handwriting I could duplicate.

Val: Pedestrian. Always pedestrian.

Me: Help? Yes. No.

Val: Yes. I help. Car where?

I gave her the location, then hightailed it out of there. One small bonus: I got an extra run in.

I should've been distracted by the letter in class. Instead I got distracted by Carli. A lot better than staring at my own handwriting as I took notes. The loops reminded me of Juan. My gut told me he was my birth father.

Not the birthday gift I had hoped for.

But Carli…It had been a while since anyone caught my attention. She had brown eyes so full of emotions I wanted to name every single one. And pink cheeks against pale skin, all without the need for makeup. I liked making her blush, more than I should. Toward the end of class, my phone vibrated, pulling me away from studying whether her hair hit her shoulder blades or below. Normally I ignored my cell, but Val could have a status update on my poor tire.

Only the text displayed a strange number I hoped was Carli.

Unknown: How do I get this CART thing?

Yeah, definitely Carli. Much better birthday gift.

Me: I'll take care of it.

AFTER CLASS I made my way to the chain pizza restaurant my friends and I frequented. Located on the outskirts of campus, it served as a good place to meet up. Furthermore: good food and alcohol.

Due to class, and Val having to deal with my car, I arrived first. Two hostesses stood at the wood podium, both new. I waited for the two girls dressed in black to look up, and then I held up four fingers. They continued to stare at me, one saying something. I tried to catch a word on her lips, but the chewing gum made it near impossible.

I leaned over their desk and pointed to a pen and paper. They continued talking. I pointed to my ear and shook my head. Finally, I lip-read something.

Girl One poked Girl Two in the ribs. "...deaf."

If only a face palm was an acceptable interaction outside of the Internet.

Girl Two led me through the bright restaurant, decked out in neon signs. She stopped at a corner table. Score. I scooted into the booth. With my back to the wall, I had optimal view of the entrance. Then I pulled out my notes while I waited.

I thought of Carli as I looked over my scribbles. Her paper had been blank when we chatted, and I hadn't caught her writing anything the rest of the class. Good thing she took up my offer. While I was thinking of CART, I sent an e-mail to Nancy, a provider I had used in my English classes.

Then I stared at my notes. If Carli continued in the course, she'd need to know what she'd missed. I snapped a picture of my notes with my cell and sent them her way.

A shadow covered my phone. I looked up to find Willow, hands on hips, long brown hair braided and draped over one shoulder.

She removed one hand. "*Whatcha doing?*" I packed up my books, and she sat next to me. She pulled me into a hug, standard greeting in the Deaf World. "*Happy birthday.*"

"*Thanks. And to answer your question: I'm helping a new friend.*"

Willow's eyes tried to break free of her sockets. Before she collected herself to harass me, as I knew she would, the other members of our group arrived.

Willow and I scooted out of our side of the booth to greet everyone properly. Tanner gave me a hug/pat on the back, while Val gave Willow a hug and kiss. As always, Tanner was stuck on the girl-on-girl action. Being Val's roommate for longer than the two-plus years they'd been dating, I was more than used to it. Though I will admit, walking in on two girls making out was much better than walking in on a guy and girl.

We all settled back into our seats. Only Willow forgot the be-nice-to-the-birthday-person memo. *"Reed's helping a new friend."*

Val's hand landed on the table with enough force that I felt the vibration. Eyes on me, she signed, *"When's the last time he picked up a new friend?"*

"Shit," Tanner signed before grabbing a menu.

"Beth." Willow bounced in the seat, the movement traveling from her end of the booth to mine.

I fisted my hands and gave the table one swift pound. *"It's my birthday. We are not talking about Beth today."* I preferred we didn't talk about her again, ever. But two years was not long enough for Val and Willow to let it go.

"Tell me about the new friend," Val signed.

Clearly my birthday meant nothing to these assholes. *"Her name is C-A-R-L-I. She's hard of hearing, no support services. Her hearing aid battery died during class."* I spelled out her name since ASL sign names were not related to their English counterparts. They were their own breed, awarded to members of the community.

Val and Willow gaped at me, mouths open. Tanner, on the other hand, raised his hands up to the sky. *"Finally! He goes after a hot girl again."* He studied me as only an asshole would. *"Where does she fall on the hotness range?"*

I shook my head. *"The last time I answered that, Val stole Willow."*

Val blew me a kiss. *"Not my fault she swings both ways."*

Willow gave both of our shoulders a squeeze. *"I'm still open to the three-way."*

Val and I recoiled. We'd been friends since elementary school, closer to siblings than anything else. We were comfortable enough with each other to live together, not have sex.

"You horny bitch," Tanner said.

"Yes, I accept that label. Go on." Willow flailed a hand dramatically.

The conversation halted there, as the waitress came over. Val, an interpreter student, slipped into her role. Both Willow and Tanner watched Val like I did, even though they were Hard of Hearing. They didn't always need her, and I hadn't a clue why they heard in some situations and not others.

I didn't use Val to place my order; I pointed to what I wanted on the menu. She helped me when needed, and in turn I used her only when absolutely necessary.

"Hotness range. Answer. Now." Tanner leaned forward, elbows on the table. Staring me down.

I thought of Carli. Those large brown eyes with a swirl of captivating shades. Her long brown hair as it dipped into the V of her shirt, against ample cleavage. I signed the outline of a curvy body, my hands itching to feel the warmth of the real thing.

Tanner turned to Willow and Val. *"How long has it been?"*

"Two years. Since Beth," Willow signed.

"Where's the damn alcohol?" I signed small, seen and ignored by the assholes I called friends.

"*Two years.*" Tanner leaned back. "*In that time no new friends. No dates. No sex. Nothing. You sure your dick hasn't shriveled up and fallen off?*" For added emphasis, he let the "dick" bounce on the table.

Two sets of eyes were on mine. Only Willow dared glance lower. I should've offered to show the fuckers my penis remained intact. Instead I signed, "*Back off,*" before I thought about it, realizing too late the hole I'd dug myself.

Val's eyebrows shot up. "*Wow. She's special.*"

Tanner's dick jokes had been going on for over a year now; they knew I'd beat his ass later. It'd been a while since I welcomed anyone new into my world. Same amount of time since I felt protective over anyone. And who could blame me? Sticking up for Beth kicked me in the balls.

I wanted Carli to be different. Needed it, really. My crazy radar had failed me before, and it could very well fail me again. Still, I couldn't spend the rest of my life avoiding new contacts because of one gross error in judgment.

Our drinks arrived, and I gulped down a third of my beer. "*My car fixed?*" I asked Val.

"Yeah." She eyed my drink. "*I guess I'm driving?*"

I patted my pockets. "*I don't have the keys. And it is my birthday.*" I gave her my best puppy-dog eyes.

Willow raised her glass. "*Happy birthday. May twenty-three be a good year for you.*"

We all clanked glasses.

"*New age. New girl. Good start.*" I wanted to yell at Val again, but the sincerity on her face stopped me. She wasn't poking me, not anymore. "*You deserve it.*"

I swallowed more of my beer. The look in her eyes could mean only one thing. I'd left the envelope in the car. And she'd known me long enough to know what it meant.

WE CLOSED DOWN the restaurant, as usual. It was a Deaf thing. When you can't communicate with the world at large, you hold on to the ones you can communicate with a little bit longer.

I expected Val to bring up the letter during the car ride. I kept one eye on her, in case she removed her right hand to sign. She didn't. She let the car remain dark and focused on the road. Her tune didn't change when she pulled up to the two-family house we called home. We climbed the side steps to our second-story apartment. I said good night, before she got any ideas, and made my way into my bedroom.

I dropped my bag down by the door and kicked off my shoes. Physically and emotionally exhausted, I stripped down to my boxers and fell face first onto my bed. The soft brown comforter enveloped me, and I almost closed my eyes right then and there. But I didn't. I had something left to do.

I grabbed my cell from my pants pocket and checked my text messages. Before I got to my mother's, I froze at one I didn't expect.

Carli: Thanks. You're a lifesaver.

A smile took over my face. One class with this girl and the rules I'd set in place two years ago faded from sight. I couldn't deny it felt good to help someone again. I couldn't deny it felt better helping *her*.

Me: :-)

The next message belonged to my mother. We'd celebrated a few days ago, but I knew the drill.

Mom: Happy birthday, baby boy. I didn't give birth to you, but I know you were born at 10:43 p.m. It took three more years for you to enter my world, and I'm grateful every day. I love you.

The next text would be the hard one. It had been two years, but it wasn't getting easier.

Mom: And from Dad: make a wish, hold it close. A new year begins. Pick a new goal. You have 365 days to make it real.

I blinked back the tear threatening to fall down my cheek. Didn't matter that I was alone. Dad taught me not to cry. He taught me a lot of things, half of which went out the window when he died.

Each year since then, I had to make a choice: Did I pick a goal? The past two birthdays, the answer landed firmly in the no column. It had been 100 percent yes before his death, before the betrayal.

But this year I had a goal. Carli. I wasn't sure what it meant. I could want her friendship. I could want to help her understand our linguistics teacher. My gut rejected both of those notions, suggesting a more personal reason for my fascination.

It had been two damn long years. But hours after class, her pink cheeks still came to mind, clear as the text in front of me.

This year, my wish? Carli wouldn't be anything like Beth.

Chapter Three

Carli

NAIL BITING TURNED into a competitive sporting event as I tried not to think about this CART thing. And how embarrassing it was to need this assistance. I envisioned all sorts of awkward, larger-than-life, and—hopefully—unrealistic scenarios this would create. To the point where I had CART = a fire-breathing dragon.

Outside the linguistics classroom, the hall light still flashed, flickering yellow light down on the wooden door and off the white tiled floors, creating the perfect spot to film a gritty horror movie complete with screaming co-eds and bouncing boobs.

One would think that with the amount of money we paid in tuition, they could fix a faulty light bulb. And perhaps my nerves turned me into a bit of a bitch as I stood in the alternating shadow and light. Time to get out of the flashing.

After a deep breath and further contemplation of the horror movie—zombie students, definitely zombie students—I forced my legs into action. And froze once inside the room. Reed had already arrived. I almost didn't recognize him. Or rather, I shouldn't have recognized him, not with a smooth jaw with only a light hint of stubble. He looked different, stealing my breath more than before. Yet I knew it was him. Beard or no beard still equaled Reed.

He sat at a corner desk next to an older lady who had a laptop set up and was facing his way. Her hands moved swiftly as she pressed on keys from some small device nestled between her legs. Complete words popped up on the screen as she continued pressing down. It reminded me of an awkward piano player. When she finished, Reed reached forward and typed a response.

I didn't see what he wrote, not that I was close enough to read the words. My traitorous eyes traced his jaw, where so much hair had been just last week. He looked younger. A part of me wanted to ask why he'd shaved. Another part of me wanted to throw out his razor so he wouldn't do it again.

I shook those crazy thoughts aside and walked over to them. He looked up and smiled as I approached, and damn if my knees didn't wobble a bit. Maybe I didn't need to confiscate his razor after all.

Carli? the older lady with short white hair typed onto the laptop.

I nodded. "Hi."

Reed leaned in to type on the laptop.

Reed: This is Nancy. She's a CART provider. If this works out for you, I'll show you how to get it set up for the school to pay.

I looked back and forth between the two of them. "Who's paying you now?" I asked Nancy.

She smiled and pressed on her keys, my words appearing on the screen. Then she continued pressing keys as she spoke.

"Reed's an old friend. He asked if I was available and explained the situation. Best for you to try CART first. Since I'm available and on contract with the school, we can work it out if it helps."

It was kinda cool to listen to her voice and read her words on the screen. I didn't have to mentally fill in the gaps of any words I didn't hear.

Reed: I'll let you two chat.

He moved to grab his bag, and a wave of panic hit me. He was leaving me? Alone with this strange technology and a clear label that I wasn't like the rest of the students?

"You're leaving?" I asked before I could stop myself.

Nancy transcribed.

Reed scratched the back of his head as he looked at me. His intense scrutiny made me feel somewhat exposed and vulnerable.

Reed: I'm used to sitting in the back, but I can join you.

He moved over one seat and pulled out his notes. The now-familiar scribbles made me smile. I set up my own belongings, then took my purple pen and leaned across to his desk.

Thank you, I wrote on a corner of his page. He read my note, then locked eyes with mine and smiled.

There went my knees again. His presence made me feel better about needing assistance hearing. Heck, he made me feel. Period. And that wasn't a good thing. Reynoldses didn't feel.

I pulled my attention back to Nancy, and she talked a bit about CART and how she needed to have words in her computer dictionary. If the word wasn't in the vocabulary, it might come out wrong.

Mind-boggling. Learning about this was mind-boggling.

Dr. Ashen arrived, and before he even put his bag down, he started speaking. Sharon, perfect ringlets pinned back, moved next to him and signed for Reed. My ears still couldn't make out a thing Dr. Ashen said. The mustache prevented me from lip-reading anything but spittle.

I pulled my eyes away from the flapping mustache and focused on the screen. Nancy busied herself with awkward piano movements and words popped up in front of me. Coherent words. Full sentences that made actual sense.

Students around me took notes, and for the first time, so did I. As Nancy typed I managed to look down at my paper, scribble what I needed to remember, and look back at the screen, catching myself up with the words still available to me. Even with my head down, I didn't miss anything. Pretty amazing with a teacher I couldn't understand a single word from.

An hour into the class, Reed slid a folded note over to me. My heartbeat rose to a gallop. What was this? Middle school? As far as I could tell, he was a graduate student, slipping me a note. It made me feel sort of warm and fuzzy. I unfolded the paper.

Any better?

I held in a laugh. Before responding I looked up at the laptop. Interrupting Dr. Ashen, Nancy had written:

Nancy: Don't let Reed distract you from your learning.

This time I didn't manage to keep the laugh in, but I think I kept it soft enough. Reed, however, looked over and saw Nancy's tease. He snorted, shook his head, and turned his attention back to the interpreters.

Much better. I owe you some coffee.

I slid the paper back over to his desk and returned my attention to the laptop. I didn't fail to catch Nancy's smirk. Okay, so maybe I was flirting a bit. But I really did want to thank him. This class had gone from the one I understood the least to the one I understood the most. Who would've guessed?

I was deep into scribbling notes while trying to keep up with Dr. Ashen's lecture—I had no clue how fast he talked, no wonder I didn't understand him—when the paper slipped under my arm. I startled and turned to Reed. He faced forward, but the curve to his lips was probably for my benefit. I glanced at his interpreters. Great. We had an audience. What did they think about what was going on? What did I think? What was even going on?

I opened the note in my lap.

After class?

I put the note back on the table. At this rate I wasn't going to pay any attention to the pretty words being typed for my benefit. If only my heart would settle down into my chest.

After class I told Nancy she was a lifesaver. She nodded toward Reed, who chatted with his interpreters, and told me to make it official. Nancy packed up her equipment and set it on a rolling cart most people used for luggage. Reed appeared next to me, stuffing his belongings into his bag. He smiled. I had to lock my knees. He should need a license to unleash that thing. He clenched two fists, rotating one on top of the other in opposite directions.

Oh, smart. I was about to have coffee with a guy who couldn't hear, and I couldn't sign. What was I thinking?

That he was hot and saved my butt in Dr. Ashen's class. I owed my future teaching career to his help, assuming I never had students as difficult to understand.

He grabbed the paper we had used for notes and pointed to the word *coffee*. I nodded and he pulled out a pen.

There's a coffee shop around the corner, unless you have some other place in mind?

I shook my head. My contribution to the conversation consisted of yes/no answers. I supposed I could shrug for maybe. Woot, a total of three words I could say to the guy. With a point to the door, we set out, walking in silence. It was weird. We didn't know each other and couldn't communicate.

Well, there was one way we could communicate that wouldn't require any talking at all…No, mind on target. Coffee. Even though I already hit my caffeine limit for the day. And needed dinner. Oh yeah, this was smart.

Well, there was one way we could communicate
that wouldn't require any talking at all. (No, mind on
target once. Even though I already turned on my engine
for the day and needed dinner. Oh yeah, hit was
sweet.

Chapter Four

Reed

CARLI STARED AT her feet, conversational avoidance
behavior. If only she knew we were communicating just
fine. Communication didn't have to be verbal. It could be
visual or physical. To prove it, I pointed to the door, and
she fell into step beside me.

Steps have a rhythm, a poetry to the motion. Some are
fast and hurried, in an oh-shit-I'm-late type of scenario.
Others are slow and at ease, a Sunday don't-have-a-care-
in-the-world motto. Carli's steps faltered every few feet.
Not in a comic falling-over way. No, her faltered steps
indicated a hesitance, an insecurity.

I caught her eyes and smiled. I didn't want her feeling
resistant around me. She took a breath and smiled back.

My own steps faltered.

If nothing else, she threw me off my game.

I turned into the small, dimly lit coffee shop. A mirrored wall opened up the area, enhancing the maroon cushions and bohemian feel. The barista gave me a double take, then pointed to her lower face and gave me a thumbs-up. When my teaching job was on break, I tended to let the whole shaving thing lapse. But now it was up and running again, and for some reason I decided my professional look was beard-free. I scratched my hairless cheek as she handed over her pen and paper. I'd been known to survive on caffeine, the record at thirty-six hours before I crashed. I wrote down my order, added a winking smiley face, and handed the paper back.

She gave me a wink and went about prepping my order. When I blew on my coffee, Carli pointed to a muffin. She was a little closer to my world than she thought. I covered up my smile by taking a too-hot sip. If I didn't stop making this a habit, I'd never taste food again.

Oh well, my tongue was already burnt, so I took another sip. I continued with our lesson—one I'd bet my shiny new Blu-ray player would go over her head—by pointing to a table by the window. She nodded and I set off, passing by the other tables full of people with moving mouths and stationary hands clutching drinks.

I slid into the booth and grabbed my notebook and pen, placing them on the glass table. I wrote a note and slid it across to Carli as she unwrapped her muffin.

How did you like CART?

She popped a piece of her muffin past her plump lips. My blood pumped hard. I wanted to feel that movement against my lips, my skin, my…I sipped my coffee, and the taste skipped right over my raw taste buds. A reminder my tongue was burnt. No kissing. Not tonight.

Huh. I wanted to kiss someone. And not just someone in the large, grand ocean of availability. This person across from me. My heart doubled its efforts and my stomach thought maybe the coffee was too hot. How long had it been since I'd felt this way?

Beth.

I burned the thought right out of my head. If only I could burn the girl from my memory. Relief washed over me as Carli slid the notebook my way.

It was amazing. I didn't know what to expect, but I went from not understanding Mr. Scary Mustache at all to following everything. I don't think I've ever followed that much of a class.

Scary Mustache? Is that what happened when a mustache grew too long? I raised my eyebrows and tapped the name on the paper. Good thing I hadn't left one when I shaved.

Dr. Ashen. Can you lip-read him?

For a moment I was almost relieved the comment had nothing to do with kissing. My tongue had this funny idea she could help relieve the numbness.

She grabbed the paper back before I could fully focus. Damn. Here I was, making a fool out of myself. Stop thinking about her lips.

Do you lip-read?

I wanted to lip-read her. To the point where I almost asked her to say something and I'd try to understand it.

Focus, idiot. Lip-reading. Not kissing. Not Carli's lips. The act of lip-reading for communication purposes.

Some. I think it helps to combine lip-reading with sound, easier for you than me.

She read the note and her eyes locked with mine. A small part of me hoped the conversation would sway to lips and not reading. Hers were pink with something glossy, even after eating a third of her muffin. How many kisses would it take to remove entirely?

And I was being a dick. She had taken her first step into my world, and all I could think about was her lips and kissing. Then it hit me. She wasn't staring at me because of the thoughts rolling around in my head. She hadn't interacted with others who had hearing loss. I took the paper back.

Do you have any friends with a hearing loss?

She shook her head, and my heart broke a little. What a lonely life, to be so different and so alone. Time to forget about her lips.

Well, you do now.

Her smile warmed me more than the coffee. She needed a friend, not some guy looking to ease his burnt tongue in her mouth.

Thank you. I didn't think there were many young people with hearing loss.

She really was a fish out of water.

Our numbers are small, true, but we stick together. The Deaf Community is tight. I'll introduce you.

She read my note and turned her gaze to her muffin. I scared her and she didn't know the not-so-pure thoughts rolling around in my head. Wrong time to suddenly resume interest in the opposite sex.

I laughed at myself. What a time to decide to be normal again. I reached for the pen and paper.

Don't worry. It's not a death sentence. We don't bite. I can introduce you to someone who's like you.

She sent me a smile, distracting me once again with her lips and thoughts of what that smile would feel like pressed against my skin.

And you're not?

I hadn't scared her off. Not yet, at least.

I meant someone Hard of Hearing, who can hear with hearing aids. Hearing aids gave me headaches, not language.

Something new crossed her face as she wrote.

I have headaches most of the time.

I forgot about her lips. Was she closer to my nonhearing than I thought?

Then take them off.

She shook her head.

Can't hear enough without them. And it doesn't make a difference.

I tapped the table. Something wasn't right with this picture.

How bad is your hearing loss? I don't mean to be nosy, but unless you have significant loss, the headaches don't seem normal.

She frowned at my note.

Moderate. I guess. No one really talks about what I can't hear.

Moderate. The picture she presented definitely didn't make sense.

Sorry you have headaches. Have you always had your hearing loss?

She nodded. Then grabbed the pen and bent over the paper, blocking it from my view.

Since we're doing twenty questions: favorite movie?

The smile grew on my face before I could help it. Conversation swerve, excellent execution from one hard-of-hearing girl with pink glossy lips.

Dead Poets Society. *A bit cliché for a teacher. You?*

She read my note, body relaxed and at ease. I hadn't realized how tense our previous topic had made her.

Mine's Penelope.

Oh God. Willow's favorite movie. Good thing I enjoyed it, because she wanted to watch it All. The. Time.

My friend loves that movie. The girl w/ a pig nose, right?

Carli nodded. I shifted the conversation to other movies. After the *Penelope* reference, it came as no surprise she was into chick flicks—Willow would love her. I wrote down a few of my drama and high-action favorites.

She slid the notebook back my way, with a grin I swore bred evil.

So you go for explosions and scantily clad women?

Busted. I caught the last drop of cooled coffee on my numb tongue and shrugged a shoulder. Nothing wrong with explosions and scantily clad women.

We continued chatting as the sky grew darker outside. When I focused on the café, I noticed the crowd had diminished. Without meaning to, I had dragged her into Deaf Time.

As a small token of thanks for sitting here this long to write back and forth, I collected her items and tossed them in the trash for her.

When I turned, I caught her checking me out. She darted her eyes to her bag as I stood, feet sprouting roots and turning my legs into tree trunks. It was mutual. What I felt was mutual. And damned if that didn't make me feel like an insecure thirteen-year-old. Even if I needed this, badly.

I grabbed the notebook and scribbled down *thank you* before showing her the sign and pointing to the paper. She smiled and nodded. On instinct I moved in to hug her, like I would've after any other meeting like this. Except she wasn't part of the culture, and my need to touch her wasn't friendly at all.

I balled my hands into fists and stepped back. Something flashed across her face, and I realized she was closer than before I moved toward her. She would have let me touch her. I nearly switched tactics, again, before thinking with the head not in my pants. Instead of a hug goodbye, we waved at the exit of the coffee shop and headed in different directions.

For two blocks I contemplated turning around and hugging her anyways. Just to feel her body pressed against mine, even for a second.

Then I took in a breath of the cool city air. I might be trying to help Carli, but so far, she was helping me. For the first time since Beth, I felt alive.

Chapter Five

Carli

MY HEAD SWAM after the strangest coffee meeting of my life. Well, more of a stabbing swim, thanks to my headache's appreciation of my late caffeine addition. I'd never communicated about hearing loss with another person. And it felt...strange.

Yup. Strange. I planned on sticking with *strange* to classify my evening. At least my "date" was hot and filled out a tee shirt quite nicely.

I took a deep breath as I walked down Beacon Street—not the cleanest air, mind you. For the past three years, Boston had been home. The cold air settled into my bones, and I pulled my jacket tighter. Didn't matter that people passed me in short sleeves. I was destined to always be cold. Even though it was late, cars still lingered on the street as students and other city dwellers lined the walkway.

At the brownstone I called home, I trudged up the three flights of stairs to my apartment-style dorm I shared with my BFF. I entered and let my bag and jacket fall to the floor before dropping myself onto the teal couch in our living room. A vanilla scent hung in the air, courtesy of my roommate and her candle addiction. Our dorm had a nice living space and open kitchen area, plus two bedrooms and a shared bathroom. Heaven in campus living. Heck, more affordable and nicer than anything off campus anyways.

"How was that cat thing?" D asked from the kitchen as my body sagged into the couch. D was short for DD, which was short for Deirdre Deborah. Hey, we all had our own parent issues. Lord knew I did.

"CART, not cat. It was cool. I got to read what Dr. Ashen said, rather than try to understand the un-understandable."

"I don't think that's a word."

"Bite me. I'm a math education major, not English." And my ears would do well not to get in my way again.

"You don't want me biting you. What about Hot New Deaf Guy?"

I rolled my head back on the couch. "His name is Reed."

D pulled her dyed-red hair into a messy bun and secured it with one of the three multicolored pens on the wicker coffee table. "Yet no mention of the biting."

Without warning, my mind traveled back to the end of our coffee meeting, when I stood scoping his nice ass. I fixed my hair around my face in a desperate attempt to hide my burning cheeks.

"Where does he fall on the Carli scale?"

Yes, I had an odd obsession with math most of my life. "Holding steady at eight."

D's black-lined eyes opened wide. "Never, in the three years I've known you, have I heard of an eight."

I picked up my bag. "And what does that say about my inner psychosis?" She was already thinking it, courtesy of her psych major, so might as well get her to fess up before she went into full psychiatrist mode.

"Either this guy really is hot, or you need to get laid."

"Is that your professional opinion?"

D doubled over in laughter and I escaped to my bedroom. I considered my muffin as my dinner, and the caffeine had me sufficiently jittery. But more than that I felt…unsettled.

It was well past time for some comfort. I changed into lounging clothes, letting the soft fibers soothe me. My ears were itchy, as the hearing aids turned earwax into a wet mess. I pulled them out, and the air tickled my damp ears as I cleaned the lingering wax off my molds. Tinnitus rang in the almost silent room, thanking me for that last bit of coffee. Quiet was never truly quiet when my ears rang on their own.

I set up my work on my bed. Four books and corresponding notebooks each got their own prime spot. I gave each the most attention I could give it. Once my brain wandered, it was time to put the book aside. I stretched before picking up the next book. D thought my study habits were insane; she didn't get how I could comprehend everything. To me it felt like I spent hours on each subject, but I was told it was minutes. I didn't question it. It was how I learned. The only way I knew how to process information.

Not that my father agreed with my self-assessment. To him, my study habits were one more area where I was impaired. As an elementary student, I began studying in my room, away from the rest of the family, away from his disapproval.

Tonight as I paused after working on linguistics, thoughts of Reed filtered in. I brought my hand up to my face, copying his movements from before we left. "*Thank you.*"

Intrigued, I rolled onto my back and picked up my phone. I searched for ASL, amazed at the sheer volume of sites I hit. Though I shouldn't have been surprised; was there anything one could search for and *not* hit a million random sites?

Maybe...

No, Carli, mind on target. The first site I clicked on housed a visual dictionary. I scrolled through, clicked on *thank you*, and got confirmation that was the sign Reed showed me.

What else had he shown me? *Coffee.* I found the sign and it looked similar to what I remembered.

For the next hour, with way more concentration than normal, I searched through the dictionary, soaking up each word like a sponge. My hearing aids were off and yet I understood videos. Sure, the videos were just of a man or woman performing one sign over and over again. But it was still cool.

I also spent a decent amount of time with the alphabet, forming my hands to match what was on the screen.

At the end of the hour I lay sprawled on my back, watching my own hand.

C-A-R-L-I, C-A-R-L-I, C-A-R-L-I.

R-E-E-D.

Chapter Six

Reed

THE STAINED, WRINKLED, off-white envelope floated
down, covering the page of my Psychology of the Deaf
textbook. Ironically, it covered the early childhood section.

I pushed the book into the center of the kitchen table
and looked up at Val.

"I wondered when you'd stop hiding this."

I wanted to snatch it and put it at the bottom of the
same drawer I shoved the letter. Or burn it. Burning it
would work.

Val pulled out the wooden chair and sat opposite me.
She studied my face, choosing her words carefully, no
doubt. *"How are you doing? Between the letter and the
new girl, I can't tell."*

I shrugged and flicked the envelope off my book with
the capped end of my pen. *"I'm fine."*

Val leaned her elbows on the table. "*Liar.*"

I dropped the pen into my book and closed it. "*What do you want?*"

"*Truth.*"

"*The new girl's name is C-A-R-L-I.*"

She didn't sign anything. She stared me down, round brown eyes never wavering from mine.

"*I don't want to talk about it.*"

"*Too bad. What did the letter say?*"

"*Don't know. Didn't read it.*"

Her eyes warmed. I didn't want to see the concern. Not in regards to this. "*You have to.*"

My eyebrows shot up. "*Really? I need to read a letter maybe connected to my birth father? Twenty years too late. I think not.*"

"*What if it's important?*"

My eyebrows shot up even farther. I signed nothing.

"*Right, right. Sorry. My bad. But aren't you curious?*"

I shook my head and pushed the chair back, the wood strained against the linoleum. I didn't make it far before she caught my arm.

"*I know this is bothering you. I can't imagine it's easy to suddenly receive a letter from your birth father. But holding it inside won't work.*"

"*I have nothing to say.*"

My phone vibrated in my back pocket, and I grabbed it, ready to kiss whoever provided me with this interruption. Even Tanner. When I saw Carli's name, I couldn't stop the grin.

Carli: How are you going to watch the video for class?

Unfortunately Val read the screen as well.

"Wow, she really does think like a hearing person. She doesn't know about closed captioning?"

I ignored Val.

Me: What do you mean?

Carli: Do you use interpreters?

Damn, Val was right. How could she not know of captioning? Or did she not realize the video had them available?

Me: It has captions.

"You really have a project set up for yourself with this one," Val signed.

It wasn't about the project. Not with Carli. It was about something more than the project. Sure, she could benefit from what I could show her. But more…I liked her.

Me: Have you used captioning before?

Carli: No.

Me: I can set up your TV if you want. Do you live on campus?

I had to stop by the library anyways and could use a break from all this weekend studying.

Carli: Yes.

I shouldn't have smiled, not with Val still watching me. But resisting was pointless.

Me: Want me to come show you how to set up captioning?

As I waited for Carli's response the sensation of two lasers digging into my skull set in. Sure enough, Val's eyes were locked on me.

"Is she a project or a date?"

Good question. What was Carli?

"*A friend.*"

Val's lips curved. "*Are you ready to fuck the rules?*"

I slipped my phone back into my pocket and tried to walk away, but Val grabbed my arm. "*What has being cautious done for you?*"

I glanced at the wrinkled envelope on the table. "*Protected me from shit like that.*"

Val didn't let go.

"*My problems with Beth came after the fucking.*" I yanked my arm free, but Val stomped on the floor.

"*Fine. Fine. You win. I just want you to start living. A part of you died with your father.*" I pointed to the envelope, but she kept signing. "*Not that father, your real father. The one who raised you.*"

She collected the envelope and left me alone. Points to Val. When she was right, she let it be, never needing the confirmation. And dammit, she was right.

Of course, she didn't realize Dad taught me to be cautious. Or rather, not to be stupid. He was convinced my birth parents were teenagers who got themselves into trouble. As a high school teacher, he'd seen teenage pregnancies and heard statistics that products of teenage pregnancies were more likely to become teenage parents themselves.

I carried his warnings under my skin. Ready to scold me the minute my hand made it up a girl's shirt. It made me cautious, a point Val and Tanner loved to drive home. Caution was somehow an abnormal trait. Didn't matter; it was who I was.

And speaking of cautious, a certain girl in my linguistics class wasn't too keen on having me in her dorm.

Me: OK, silence. I get it. I can explain it. But each TV is different. Search for captioning when you get the chance.

Carli: Sorry. I didn't hear my phone.

Me: Did you want some help with the captioning?

It took her a few more minutes to respond, but when she did, it was worth it.

Carli: Sure. I'll text you when I'm back on campus.

I put my phone away and turned back to my textbook. The words blurred in front of me. I ran my thumb down the page in an attempt to pull my attention back to the words. Failed. Screw work. I wasn't getting anything done anyways.

In need of an outlet for my energy, I changed into shorts and a tee shirt and set out for a run. I ran until the shirt clung to my back and my breaths came in fast puffs. I ran until my phone vibrated. Over on the grass, I steadied my breathing and pulled out the phone.

Carli: I'm home. I live in South Campus, off Beacon St.

And I was dripping in sweat.

Me: Be there in about an hour, that OK?

Could I shower that quickly? Must remember she's not on Deaf Time.

Carli: Sure.

Too late. I picked up my pace and made it back to the house. After a quick shower, I bumped into Willow in the kitchen carrying a bowl of popcorn.

"*Want to watch a movie?*" she asked, chewing and therefore not moving her lips for a change. "Penelope *is on.*"

I barely resisted rolling my eyes. "*Can't.*" I almost signed I had a date, but I didn't. Not really. Not an established one.

Willow smirked. "*Helping a poor, lost, hard-of-hearing girl?*"

I turned to the living room and narrowed my eyes at Val. She threw her hands in the air. "*I barely said anything.*"

"*Bullshit.*" I stuffed my wallet into my back pocket. Before I left, I asked Willow what channel *Penelope* was on.

"*Why?*"

My lips curved against my will. "*C-A-R-L-I likes that movie too.*"

Chapter Seven

Carli

I PACED MY bedroom as I waited for Reed to arrive. My stomach fluttered, and I counted the butterflies. When I started in with the X-to-the-power-of, I knew I was in deep trouble. Instead I focused on cleaning my bedroom, or at least making sure my bra no longer hung on the doorknob (it did; I took care of it).

The waiting made me insane, so I pulled out two of my textbooks and got to work. In the middle of round two of bouncing between subjects, my phone buzzed.

Reed: I'm here. Someone was leaving and held the door open.

I almost dropped the phone. For thirty seconds I turned into a girly girl. I ran to the mirror, smoothed my brown hair artfully around my shoulders, wiped off a smudge of makeup, and caught myself before I pushed my breasts up.

A knock at the door caused me to jump. No time.

I opened it, and Reed smiled at me, one of those dazzling smiles. And every bone I had turned to jelly. I let him into the dorm, grateful my jelly bones still remembered how to work.

Reed looked around, taking in our small living space with campus-provided couch and chairs. He moved to the television, but I grabbed his arm and pulled him back. He looked at me, large eyes full of questions. I shook my head and walked to my room, keeping my hand on his arm.

Which had nothing to do with the hard muscle I held. Honest.

The television in the living room belonged to D. She claimed she needed it out of her bedroom in order to study, but she did most of her studying in the living room. Didn't matter to me. Whatever worked for her.

In my room I let go of his arm and pointed to my personal flat-screen. Reed nodded, though I caught something flash in his eyes. Disappointment? Did he think I brought him in here for something else? Because...I was tempted.

He made a motion with his hand, which just had me eyeing his biceps. *Pay attention. He wants the remote.* By the time I grabbed it, I caught Reed eyeing the books on my bed. He held up two fingers and raised his eyebrows in question.

I shrugged, not knowing how else to explain myself. I wasn't good at explaining myself, even in English.

He got to work on my television, and two minutes later, I had a black rectangular box at the bottom of the screen with white letters flashing across. The shimmer in his eyes said he was damn proud of himself, as he should have been. Not only had he figured out the captioning but he also had my knees weak. Again. Then he gestured to the screen.

What were the odds *Penelope* would be on TV? A laugh escaped me as I collapsed onto my bed, eyes transfixed. Penelope wore a scarf, covering the lower half of her face, making lip-reading impossible. I never quite knew what she said. I had my guesses, and they didn't match the words being displayed.

The scene ended and a commercial came on. I tore my eyes away and looked up at Reed and the big smile on his face. At a loss for anything else to say, I signed, "*Thank you.*"

His grin widened. It should be illegal to be as handsome as he was. A tough square jaw riddled with a day's worth of stubble, brown hair that flopped onto his forehead, and the biggest eyes I had ever seen. He glanced around my bed, grabbed one of the notebooks and a pen, then looked at me with those eyebrows raised, signing, "*Write?*"

"*OK.*" My hand shook as I tried to remember the alphabet.

He paused, taking in the fact I'd now signed twice to him, no doubt, and then began scribbling in a fury.

I was going to ask how you liked the captioning, but now I want to know why you didn't tell me you knew the ASL alphabet.

I grabbed the paper back from him.

I didn't. I looked it up. There are some cool online dictionaries.

He blinked at me, then laughed. With a shake of his head, he pointed to the word *captioning* on the paper before handing it to me.

I shook my head. My hand would cramp if I kept writing. Time to pull out the big guns. I put the paper and pen back with my books, then grabbed my laptop and opened up a blank document.

Me: The captioning is really cool. I always assumed Penelope's spoken words were different in that scene.

I wondered how many other things I had misheard and feared the answer was *a lot*.

Reed took the laptop and it hit me how…intimate this was. We sat on the edge of my bed, thigh to thigh thanks to the regulation twin. Heat radiated off him, warming my thigh as it sent little electrical heat elements in all directions. When he moved, his arm brushed mine—more heat. His head dipped as he typed, and a whiff of citrus shampoo tickled my nose. Would it be wrong to push him back and thank him in a different manner?

Reed: Now you can read and not have to guess.

The words broke through my lust-filled haze. Guess. I'd been guessing my way through life. Huh. My solid world rocked on its foundation as I saw things in a new light. How much of what I thought to be true wasn't?

What else was I hiding from myself? My headache increased as a knot formed in my stomach.

A hand on my arm broke my internal chaos.

"*You OK?*" Reed signed.

I nodded and took the laptop back, pulling myself together. Time for a distraction.

Me: Were you born deaf?

Reed angled the laptop but kept it on my lap. Each touch of the keypad caused the warm machine to press against my thighs.

Reed: Yes.

He turned the laptop back to me. The action increased the intimacy of the moment. If he moved his head a few more inches, our lips would meet. As it was, his breath brushed my cheek, and I couldn't stop the shudder of need that traveled through me. I pulled myself together.

Me: Did you always know ASL?

His face hardened, ever so slightly. He took the laptop from me.

Reed: ASL was my first language. I was adopted at the age of three. My mother wanted kids and didn't care what package they came in. She dealt with a fussy three-year-old who couldn't communicate and took the time to figure out why. When my hearing loss was diagnosed, we learned ASL together. She never once judged me for my lack of hearing.

Me: No father figure?

Reed paused with his fingers over the keyboard, airborne above the letters, eyes on the screen. I almost took the laptop back, but he started typing.

Reed: Dad was there too.

He hovered over the keys again, as though he had something else to type, but in the end he handed the laptop back to me.

Me: What happened to your birth parents?

He shrugged.

Reed: Don't know. It was a closed adoption. Mom got limited information. We suspect the struggle with my hearing caused them to give me up.

My heart broke. I had no idea what kind of kid Reed was, but the adult sitting next to me didn't deserve to be abandoned.

Reed: Don't look so sad. My mother is my mother. I wouldn't want it any other way.

When Reed didn't mention his father at all, my curiosity piqued again, but a loud noise came from the television, and I looked up. Instead of watching the actors' lips, I read the captioning. And realized, again, how much I missed.

Me: I really need to thank you for this.

Reed leaned into me, shoulder to shoulder. I pressed against him, unable to stop myself.

Reed: For pressing a button?

Button? My head snapped toward his, and all at once we were way too close together. Our faces were inches apart. His eyes had gold specks in them. This close, there was no mistaking the enlarging of his pupils as he stared back at me.

He kept his eyes on mine as he reached behind me and grabbed something. My heart hammered so loud it drowned out all other noise. His warm hand lifted mine, and I couldn't help the shudder. Then something cold landed in my hand.

The remote. And, what do you know, there was a button labeled *CC*. Closed captioning.

When I looked back at Reed, he smirked at me. I shoved his shoulder, and he let out a loud laugh.

Reed: No need to thank me. You planning to take an ASL class?

The laptop sat on his lap, and I crinkled my nose as I read. Without thinking, I leaned across his lap and typed.

Me: Who would I sign with?

He leaned back and held out his hands, giving me a puppy-dog look I was sure he perfected as a kid. My cheeks felt way too warm.

Me: Sorry, I didn't mean that.

Reed: I can teach you and see if you can audit ASL 1. My advisor is one of the ASL teachers.

I bit my lip. What did I want? I had no idea. The foundation rocked again, my feet scrambling for purchase. How had so much changed since meeting Reed? It seemed absurd. A deaf guy showed up in my class, and all of a sudden I contemplated learning sign language.

Reed: I don't mean to be forward. Forget I "said" anything.

I laughed and took the laptop back.

Me: It's not that. It's just…a lot. But yes. I think I'd like to learn.

He took the laptop from me and closed it.

"Hey," I said, hands out at my side. A single eyebrow rose high on his forehead, his entire face dialed to Tease.

My heart kicked, and I reached for the laptop. Two could play this game. I snatched it back, only to have his other eyebrow join the first. He gestured for the laptop. I shook my head and clutched it to my chest. He got his hands around the side, one hand grazing my stomach. I quivered but kept my grip firm, even as he tried to pry it from me. Wasn't happening. I leaned back to get away from him. And ended up flat on my back, with him on top of me and the laptop wedged between us.

Reed stopped wrestling. He stopped moving. Only his eyes moved, taking in every bit of me he could see, which wasn't much with our position and the laptop. His gaze traveled from my eyes to my mouth, and I licked my bottom lip before I could stop myself.

He took a deep breath, let go of the laptop, and got off me. In fact, he got off the bed. The absence of his body heat left me cold and confused. What the hell? He closed two fingers down to his thumb, then held up the *N* sign until he saw something in my face that must have shown my recognition, followed by the *O* sign.

N-O. No.

Ouch. Well, I shouldn't have been surprised. After all, I was damaged goods. At least, Dad always told me so. I blinked at the sudden burning in my eyes and copied his sign and mouthed the word. He nodded and grabbed the notebook.

Probably not a bad sign to teach you.

He paused and took in my face. I put on my best blank look, perfected from years of not showing my boredom when I couldn't hear. But somehow he saw through the façade. He brushed a thumb over my cheek. Once again his eyes traveled down to my mouth. Only this time I didn't lick my lips. Nope, I kept them in a straight line. This guy had to be the most confusing male I'd ever met.

With a shake of his head, he returned to the notepad.

I'm sorry. Now, pay attention.

It took a little while for me to push the mystery of Reed out of my mind. He proceeded to point to different objects around my room and show me the signs. I had no idea how much of this I'd remember, but it was seriously cool. Made me think of high school when I taped note cards around my room with Spanish words on them. It would be harder to do this with ASL, at least until little video note cards were available. Huh, video note cards. Now there was a concept. Could I figure out the formula to—

My phone buzzed with an incoming text.

Reed: Hit your limit?

I didn't think so, but considering I just went on a mini mental vacation, I guessed I had.

Me: Sorry, my mind wandered.

He pointed to me and swiped two fingers down his chin before following it up with spelling out the word.

"*C-U-T-E*."

He thought I was cute? We were in my bedroom, and he thought I was cute. I hoped there was enough air, because my lungs threatened to suck it all up in a matter of minutes.

My phone buzzed.

Reed: I should get going. See you in class on Thursday?

Did I dare ask him to stay?

Me: Sure. Thanks for all your help.

Stupid chicken. I was never the forward one. Wasn't going to be any different with Reed. With his odd behavior, we might never lock lips.

Reed: I had fun. Hope it was helpful for you.

I didn't know what to say. He introduced me to a whole new world. I managed to nod. He leaned forward, and I held my breath, not sure what he was about to do but hoping it involved his lips. And mine.

He gave me a quick two-second hug, waved, and jogged down the steps. A part of me wanted to yell after him to come back. The other part of me realized the ineffectiveness of calling after a deaf man.

"Hot, hot, hot, hot," D exclaimed.

I jumped, squeaked, and held the door tight against me. I hadn't even heard her come home, never mind witness the awkward hug.

"Are you sure he's only an eight on the scale?"

I closed the door and let my mind wander. "No longer an eight. Nine." And a half.

D jumped in place. "Is this the first nine you've set your hot little sights on?"

I nodded. No one had been more than an eight before. I was in trouble.

Chapter Eight

Reed

IN THE SMALL Deaf Studies department, I found my advisor's office door open. Gina sat at her desk, short blond hair fanning over her face as she poked at her keyboard. I reached into the office and flipped the lights off and on several times. She pushed her hair back as she looked up and smiled.

"Hi, what's up?"

I stepped in and closed the door behind me.

"Do you have availability in your ASL I class?"

She blinked. Not because I shocked her. Her furrowed eyebrows warned me a comeback brewed in the dark recesses or her warped brain. *"Why did I waive your ASL requirement for the Deaf Education program if you feel you need to take ASL I?"*

I took the cushiony brown chair on the opposite side of her desk. "*I have a new friend. Hard of hearing. Doesn't know ASL but is interested in learning.*" At least, her willingness to learn the other day indicated as such. A class would be an ideal environment for her.

Gina crossed her arms, soaking me in before signing, "*Girl?*"

"*Is it important to know?*"

"*Yes.*"

I sighed. The problem with being part of a small community: everyone knew your business. Whether you wanted them to or not. On this one, I blamed Willow. "*Yes. A girl.*"

Gina flashed me some teeth with her grin. "*Welcome back. I've missed this version of you.*"

I shifted in my seat. "*You have availability?*"

She turned to her computer and clicked a few times. With her eyes on the screen, one hand on her keyboard, she signed with the other. "*Yes. Tuesday and Wednesday, 4:30–6:00 p.m.*"

I pulled out my phone and noted the information down. "*Tell me about my new student.*"

I didn't know a whole lot about Carli, but I shared what I did. Gina's smile grew the more I talked.

"*She sounds special.*"

"*Maybe.*"

"*How are your students?*"

I grinned—couldn't be helped. "*Good. I've got a smart group.*" I had six students in my third-grade class at a Deaf school. Full of energy and a lot of fun.

"I'm sure they're thrilled to have a Deaf teacher."

They were. I wasn't just their teacher; I was a role model. Not a small deal when most of the world was hearing. *"They are."*

"Feeling good as the teacher instead of the student?"

For the next twenty minutes, we chatted about my course work and how to keep the students on track. When I finally left, I had a few new ideas for my students. And a class to convince Carli to join.

I sent my first text as I left the Deaf Studies department and jogged down the stairs from the third floor.

Me: Do you have classes T and W 4:30–6?

Carli: Whhyyyyy?

Me: ;-) My advisor teaches an ASL class those nights. She has room if you want to join.

Carli: I don't have classes then. Not sure I can handle another one.

Me: Then audit the class.

I all but held my breath as I waited for her response, my heart trying in vain to pump without oxygen.

Carli: You could teach me instead.

The air flew out of my lungs. Thoughts of teaching her scrambled my brain, as it led me right back to her bed and wrestling over the laptop. She had felt good underneath me. If it wasn't for the flash of Beth warning me to back off, we might be having a different conversation today.

Me: Scared of a class with a Deaf teacher?

I wasn't the right one to teach her, not with the way I wanted more from her.

Carli: Now I am. How am I supposed to learn with a deaf teacher?

Me: How did you learn anything with me? Check it out tomorrow. If you like the class, stay. If you don't, leave.

My screen turned black as I waited for a response. I had no idea what ran through Carli's mind. I could only cross my fingers. I walked down one more flight and made it to the first floor before she responded.

Carli: I'm in. Tell me where.

And now I stood in the stairwell wearing an inane grin on my face.

Me: I'll meet you, introduce you to Gina.

MY PLAN THREATENED to explode in my face like a fucking bomb. Work and traffic delayed my mad dash to campus. I ran up Comm Ave in an effort to be somewhat on time. Gina wouldn't mind if I was late; she knew I was coming from work. But Carli might not get that. I contemplated stopping and sending her a text, but figured I'd be there faster if I didn't. Besides, don't text and run. Right, Dad?

As the building came into view, I spotted a girl standing by the bottom of the steps. Carli glanced at her phone, then out into the traffic. The wind blew her hair into her face, and she brushed it back. The strands slid from her fingertips, falling back across her face. I wanted to feel her hair through my own fingers, as I tugged her head so I could reach her lips.

I almost slowed so I could watch her.

But then she turned and caught me. And completely checked me out, those brown eyes trailing down my body to my shoes and right back up again, a slight smile tugging at her lips. I didn't know whether to slow down and let her look, or speed up and take her. One thing was clear: I hoped she liked what she saw.

I reduced to a walk when I got close. "*Sorry,*" I signed as I worked on catching my breath. I grabbed my phone, and it took me extra time to get my message across in a way autocorrect could comprehend.

Me: Sorry I'm late. Student issue.

I put my phone back in my pocket and gestured for Carli to follow me. Still on a high from the run, I jogged up the steps to the second floor. When I found room 204, I pointed to the number before opening the door and heading inside.

"*Sorry I'm late,*" I signed as Gina turned my way. Eleven students also turned my way, eyeing both Carli and me.

Gina looked at her wrist, which held no watch, and back at me. "*You're not late enough for me to teach Deaf Time.*"

"*Next time I'll be later.*"

She grinned, and I gestured to Carli before going over what I knew about her again, including that she knew almost no signs. Gina ripped off a piece of paper and wrote a note before handing it to Carli.

Once Carli read it, Gina turned to the board and wrote in a green marker. She introduced me and Carli, then told me to see her in the hall. I waved to Carli, boosting up my smile with the look of terror in her eyes, and followed Gina.

"*Why late?*"

"*Traffic.*"

She crossed her arms.

I blew out a breath. "*One of my student's parents didn't show up.*" I had to leave the student with another teacher in order to make it here. Unfortunately, this wasn't the first offense.

"*That's awful,*" Gina said, her eyebrows creased in worry. "*How's the student?*"

This was the part that got me most. "*Used to this.*"

Gina squeezed my shoulder. "*This is the hard part of teaching. And it doesn't get better.*" She turned to her door. "*Now I'm going to go torture your girlfriend.*"

"*She's not my girlfriend.*"

"*You're the worst liar.*" She slipped back into her classroom before I could respond.

I shuffled out of the building, taking time to recharge from the hectic afternoon. The hustle and bustle on the streets soothed me. I slowed down as everyone else sped up, my day finishing as theirs struggled on. A moment to gain perspective in a world determined to toss me around.

I headed toward the library. Instead of doing some research for my psychology class, I ended up in the kids' section. Why couldn't someone have written a book titled *Why Mommy and Daddy Don't Like Me?* Rejection came in all shapes and sizes, from giving up your child for adoption to forgetting to pick up your damn kid from school.

Or killing yourself in a way that looked accidental.

I looked up at the off-white ceiling. *That's right, Dad; I'm talking about you.*

As if on cue, in that weird I-know-you-like-you're-my-actual-blood thing, my phone vibrated in my back pocket. A video call from my mother.

I grabbed a chair at a small table and answered the call. I held the phone out in my left hand and signed with my right. *"Hi, what's up?"* I asked.

"Val says you have a new girl?"

Did Carli and I miss the memo we were dating? *"I met someone who is hard of hearing and needed help."*

My mother brushed back her dark curls. *"Hot?"*

Only my mother could tease me like this while I sat in the middle of the library. *"Yes, she's hot. OK? I admit that she's hot."*

"Wow, you really like her."

"You finished being nosy?"

She shook her head. The overhead lighting of the nurse's room danced across her dark cheeks. *"Never. I am your mother; it's my right to be nosy."* Her cocky smile faded. *"It's nice to see you come back to yourself."*

"Because I said a girl is hot?"

"It's the smile on your face, in your eyes. It's helping someone out again. You forgot who you were, inside. That teaching spirit you got from your father."

"Last I checked I work as a teacher."

"I would have been surprised if you changed course. But outside of your work, when was the last time you did this?"

We both knew the answer: Beth. Val and Willow had already beat me over the head with it. *"You finished?"*

"Fine. Yes, I'm finished. Is it wrong to want to see my only child happy?"

I focused on the creases around her eyes and the bags under them. *"You OK?"*

She gave me a sad smile. *"It's still hard. I keep expecting him to walk through the front door. I miss him."*

I didn't respond, not right away. I found it impossible to miss someone unforgiven. *"It's been two years. He's not coming back."*

"I know." The front of her scrubs rose and fell with what must have been a deep my-son- needs-help breath. *"Just promise me one thing."*

I scratched the back of my neck before answering. *"Fine. What?"*

"Let this girl in. Don't push her away because of Dad or Beth."

I had no intentions to tell her about either. *"Don't you have work to get back to?"*

She smiled, but it didn't reach her eyes. *"I love you."*

"I love you too."

We ended the call, and I sat there for a while longer. Why couldn't everyone just let me be?

I LEFT THE library early, determined to be on time for a change. Carli wasn't expecting me, but I wanted to check on her. I certainly didn't rush to campus to see her for two minutes and then desert her.

Me: How's it going?

I leaned against the railing, squinting out at the setting sun.

Carli: Not bad.

Class must be over. I angled myself away from the blinding sun to the main entrance of the building. The doors opened, and Carli stopped when she saw me. The door swung back, her reflexes the only thing saving her from a nasty headache. She managed to get on the other side without further attempts at hurting herself. She blinked, either due to the sun or me, and pulled out her phone.

Carli: What are you doing here?

I shrugged. The unease from my conversation with Mom? Gone.

Me: I dropped you off into a strange land, had to make sure you survived.

She held out her hands and angled her head to look at herself. I let my gaze join hers and roam over her curves, on display in her jeans and V-neck tee shirt. Tight V-neck tee shirt. My heart kicked up a few notches. I forced a laugh, to keep myself in check, and put my phone back in my pocket.

Carli's thumbs flew over her screen, and my phone vibrated. I shook my head. She blew out a breath, and the hair by her face flew in multiple directions. She pointed to my side, in the direction of where I'd shoved my phone. I shook my head again, this laugh coming easily.

She was stubborn; I'd give her that much. She tapped her phone and held it in front of my face.

Well, I was stubborn too. In ways she couldn't yet imagine. I pushed the phone away and slowly signed, "*Walk.*"

She stared, not an ounce of amusement on her face.

I raised my knees, walking in place.

One of her hands moved in a shaky manner. "*W-A-L-K?*"

I tapped my nose, then turned and began walking. She fell in step beside me. Victory. It tasted good. So good I bumped my shoulder into hers. "*You're cute but stubborn,*" I signed.

Carli stopped walking. It took me two steps to register her shoulder no longer brushing against mine. When I turned, her thumbs were flying over her phone again. Her hair had created a snarl around her face, and her shoulders were stiff. This time I pulled out my phone when it vibrated.

Carli: I spent the day in three different classes, trying to listen and process a lot of important information, then the last 1.5 hours trying to understand a language I don't know. Brain fried.

And now I felt like a prick, especially when she rubbed her temple out of exasperation. Before I responded, I pulled her into my side, then let go when she fit perfectly. Not too much, not too little. Like Goldilocks and the damn baby bear's bed.

Me: Sorry. Are you going to stop going to class?

Carli: Not yet. Will depend if I burn out in a few weeks.

Me: Perhaps I owe you some coffee this time around.

Carli: I may need coffee to stay awake during Dr. Ashen's class.

Me: If you start to nod off, I'll get you caffeine.

She looked up at me, and time seemed to stop. No cars moved, no people walked, no breeze blew. Just her and me and the sidewalk. Her eyes glowed amber in the light. Then she shook her head. Cars moved, people walked, wind blew. The spell broken.

I contemplated different ways of reclaiming that magic as we walked the rest of the way to her dorm without communication. I came up empty. I didn't know what had caused it the first time. For all I knew, it was a fluke.

At her dorm she bounded up the steps, but I stayed behind. Was there really something between us, or had it been too long for me? I hoped it was real. I needed her to be real.

She turned and I continued to take her in. *Please be real.* She took a step back to me as if in answer to my question. And I…well…

I chickened out. A big fat ugly chicken.

Me: See you tomorrow. Have a good night.

Something flashed in her eyes. And I knew in that moment she felt what I felt. Whatever simmered between us was real. I imagined climbing the steps and taking her in my arms. Those curves that fit so well against my side would feel better front to front. I wanted to feel her, all of her, in ways I hadn't wanted in far too long.

"*Good night,*" I signed, then followed the words up on my phone. She copied me, and when her hand touched her mouth, I almost leaned in and touched her myself, with my lips.

My feet held firm, and I waited until she entered her building before starting the walk back to my car. Stupid.

Well, I had two choices. I could either continue to be lonely and stuck with my hand for any sort of pleasure. Or I could man up and ask her out the next chance I got.

I pulled out my phone and set up a text message, but I was smoother than that. Next chance. Not now.

Chapter Nine

Carli

I BLINKED MY dark room into focus, my breath ragged as if I'd woken from a bad dream. I remembered no such dream.

I was about to curl back under my blankets when my phone buzzed, rattling the plastic drawers next to my bed. My clock bounced from the motion. 1:51 a.m. I picked up my cell and found the reason for the commotion: five messages from my sister.

Matti: There are nice people in the world, right?

Matti: I mean, there has to be, but why is our world so full of fucking a-holes?

Matti: Not you. You're not an a-hole.

Matti: But we all have the potential, don't we?

Matti: You're probably asleep, being the good little girl you were beat into being.

I sighed. Drunken Matti. Older than me by 349 days. She always got melodramatic long before she reached the bottom of the bottle and had been that way since the bottle contained formula.

Me: You OK, babe?

Matti: No. I'm not OK. Do I look OK?

Me: Can't see you, sis.

Matti: R any of us really OK?

Me: Where are you? If the bar's in the city, I'm on my way.

Matti: Home. Nightmare.

Nightmares. Matti was always riddled with them. She'd wake up gasping, drenched in sweat, and never, never tell me why.

I eyed my hearing aids, already off for the night. With a sigh, I toggled my cell's volume up as loud as it would go and tapped my sister's name.

She answered on the second ring. "You didn't…call," her voice slurred as I strained against the high-pitched ringing of my tinnitus to understand.

"Yes, I did. What was the dream about?"

"I'm shaking my head no…familiar…sight."

Yup. Matti's typical response. At least it helped me fill in the gaps in my hearing. I strained further as she began speaking again.

"You live in…rest of us can't. Hold…baby sister. Hold tight."

My heart kicked into a frenzy. I couldn't figure out what she was talking about, but that could have been the alcohol as much as my hearing. Still, the concept was familiar, the whole conversation familiar. My three sisters were connected—bonded, even—over something I didn't understand. Some piece of information I somehow missed, as the youngest who couldn't hear. I always felt left out, the ugly duckling, the poor little hearing-impaired youngster. They acted like they were doing me a favor by keeping secrets and pushing me away. It hurt more than they could ever know.

"Then go talk to a sister who understands, because obviously I'm too much of a cripple to get it."

"No, no, no, no." Matti's voice grew louder and softer, an indicator her drunk level had arrived at Crazy Gesture. "It's not that. Forget I said anything."

"Drink your mysterious fears away, and go cry on someone else's shoulder. Me? I'm going to sleep. I have class in the morning."

"I'm sorry. Get...sleep."

I disconnected the call and nestled back under the blankets. My heart refused to calm down. Try as I might, I could never decipher Matti's code. And I believed she wanted it that way.

Story of my youth. Matti waking up scared, me unable to calm her down, then me going to bed unsettled while Matti sneaked off to another sister's bed.

I turned off the light and closed my eyes. Only I saw an ashen-faced Matti dripping in sweat from fear. I could never go to anyone for my own comfort, to right the odd shifting of my world that occurred every time.

I didn't know what possessed me, but I sent a text to Reed.

Me: I'm jealous you're adopted. My family is driving me to drink.

Now my heart hammered for a different reason. I put the phone under my pillow and squeezed my eyes shut. My pillow vibrated with an incoming text.

Reed: If I didn't have work in the morning, I'd join you.

Dammit. Why did I wake him?

Me: Sorry to wake you. I needed to text someone.

Reed: No problem. If I was asleep, I wouldn't have felt the text. If you still need a drink tomorrow…

Me: No, no. I'm good. Matti, the 3rd sister (I'm #4 and the baby), had a nightmare and woke me up.

How pathetic: *my sister woke me up with a bad dream*. What was I? Five? I buried my head in the pillow.

Reed: That sucks.

I laughed. And the earlier apprehension faded away.

Me: You were just what I needed. Thanks for being awake.

Reed: Anytime. You won't disturb me. I keep my phone off me when I don't want to be interrupted. But I've upgraded to a meal. Think you'll be hungry after class tomorrow?

Holy shit. Did he just ask me out? At two in the morning?

Me: Define this meal.

What could I say? I was bold at two in the morning, in a dark room, being warmed by the light of my phone and the words of a hot guy.

Reed: ;-)

Me: You have to give me more than that.

Reed: Man. Woman. Dinner.

A burst of laughter had me clamping a hand over my mouth.

Reed: Otherwise known as a date, by the non-cavemen species, which I can't guarantee I am not. You can practice the half-dozen signs you know.

Me: As long as you don't toss me over your shoulder, I'm in.

Reed: As stated above, I make no guarantees. But I do need a few hours of sleep before my kids run all over me tomorrow. Good night, Carli.

Me: Good night, Reed.

I fell asleep wearing a silly-ass grin, dreaming of a man too alluring for his own good.

I'D FORGOTTEN HOW hard it was to pay attention in class when my crush was in the room. Never mind sitting next to me. My hands were clammy, my stomach in knots, and my throat felt like it had survived a cat attack. Dr. Ashen lectured while I read Nancy's words. The sounds floated through the room, my ears unable to grasp onto them.

He talked about glottal stops and the different sounds of the alphabet, so my lack of comprehension had epic bad timing. A double *T* sounded like a *T* in my own head, but apparently was more a *D* in actuality. Dr. Ashen kept repeating the sounds, but my ears refused to process any of it. I had a long list of things that I planned on forcing my roommate to say when I got back to our dorm.

I ripped off a small corner of my notebook paper.

How are you following any of this?

I slid the note under Reed's elbow. He didn't look at me but put down his pen and grabbed the offending piece of paper. With eyes darting between the interpreter and the note, he read.

I forced my attention back to Nancy's laptop, failing to wipe the silly grin off my face. The words sped across the screen, and I was lost forcing my brain to comprehend when the note landed next to my hand.

I do my best, and Dr. Ashen is taking that into account. I've never heard words, so these differences are fascinating but impossible. My roommate's hearing and has been trying to explain these to me, but…?

I tucked the paper under my notepad and waited a few minutes before responding.

I've heard words and still can't decipher most of this. And I can't understand Dr. Ashen. All I have are the sounds in my head, and they don't quite match up to what is being discussed.

When I slid the note back, I brushed against the fine hairs on his arm. A warmth zinged through me at the contact. Even with a sweater on, I shivered in my boots. Meanwhile, he radiated heat through his short sleeves. My nipples tightened at the contact, my body thawing. For a full minute I contemplated curling up with his warmth—naked would be ideal—before snapping myself out of it. Stop it, Carli. Focus on glottal stops that make no sense.

I realized I wasn't the only one feeling the zing when the note came back and Reed's hand lingered on my wrist.

Make sure you talk to Dr. Ashen. He needs to know this is a problem for you.

This note passing + reading CART = complicated. I made it work by writing fast and then catching up what I missed on the screen.

I can't understand a word Dr. Ashen says. How am I supposed to talk to him?

We really needed to stop passing notes—this was going to get obvious soon. At least Nancy had stopped smirking at me.

Call him over at the end of class and have Nancy type.

And Reed was henceforth known as Captain Obvious. A good match for my Clueless Girl. Even in my own head, he got the better superhero name.

At the end of class, I did just as Reed had suggested: I asked Nancy for help.

"Is that why you two were passing so many notes?" she teased.

I couldn't help the blush. It was the truth. We were discussing the class. But we were also about to go out on a date. I refused to let my mind wander and called Dr. Ashen over before taking a deep breath.

"I'm doing my best, but I'm having a really hard time hearing the differences you are describing. They all sound the same to my ears."

This was not easy for me to say. I didn't talk about hearing loss. Ever. I played like I was hearing, changed my hearing aid batteries discreetly, and bluffed whenever possible. It was the way I was raised.

Dr. Ashen leaned over the table but not in an imposing way. His moustache twitched as he talked. At least no spittle hit my papers or me. His voice grew a little clearer one-on-one, but I still would have been lost without Nancy.

On your homework, let me know where you are guessing and where you feel confident. I will take this into consideration. I'm not here to fail you for not being able to hear, but I do want you to at least grasp the basic concepts.

With a smile he stood up and returned to his desk, where another student waited with a question.

"Feel better?" Nancy asked, while flexing her fingers.

I nodded. "Yeah." I moved to put my book and notes in my bag, to find them missing. Reed stood beside me, wearing his infectious grin, with both his bag and mine on his shoulders.

I put my hands on my hips but couldn't help the smile.

He held up one hand, sporting the *R* shape, and shook it back and forth. I hadn't learned that one yet and gave him my best blank stare. Very slowly, he finger-spelled.

"*R-E-A-F-Y?*"

No, that didn't make sense. I must have gotten the *F* and *D* mixed up again.

I nodded and followed him, willing the growing ache in my head to take a chill pill. Long days of classes, trying to understand complicated material, and hours of staring at a computer screen weren't a good combination. And now my eyes were getting extra strain as I would either have to read or remember signs to understand Reed. But then he smiled at me, and the ache in my head and the strain on my eyes didn't seem to be a big deal at all.

SENS OF ATTRACTION

Chapter Ten

Reed

CARLI AND I walked a path filled with visual noise. People wore all kinds of clothing, assaulting my peripheral vision with a kaleidoscope of colors. I focused on the teal sweater of the sweet-smelling woman beside me. For the first time in a long time, I wanted. This. Here with her. The anticipation of what might come. A chance to be fucking human.

At one point I brushed Carli's hand, her pale skin an addictive smooth texture. I wanted to feel more, find out if the same smoothness would continue. Her eyes caught mine, an invitation present in them, sending thoughts of naked skin straight to my dick. An invitation I nearly jumped on. Yet caution lurked in the recesses. I breathed a sigh of relief. She wasn't like Beth. Not even close.

At the grill, I paused. The location served more alcohol than food. I eyed my date. Too late, I realized I didn't know her age. As a senior she should be twenty-one, right? I pulled out my phone.

Me: You're 21, or older, right?

She nodded, and I breathed in relief. Her fingers brushed mine as she grabbed my phone.

Carli: Yes. 21. You?

I put the phone in my back pocket. "*Two. Three. Twenty-three,*" I signed.

Her eyebrows drew together.

I laughed, I couldn't help it. I repeated the sign and she continued to stare at me. *Come on, Carli; you can get this,* I thought. Only she didn't. I pulled my phone back out.

Me: The sign for 23.

Carli: You're going to give me a headache.

I gripped her shoulder and guided her into the restaurant, where moonlit dusk ruled. Each table had pendant lights over it—if not, I wouldn't have come here. I liked seeing my food, but I needed to see my date.

And then there was the whole communication thing.

At the hostess station, a woman mouthed something. Carli turned to me, and I shrugged. I almost held up my hand to signal *two*, but Carli angled her right ear into the hostess and managed to communicate.

Of course, her communication ended the same way mine would've, with her holding up two fingers.

The hostess grabbed two menus and two sets of silverware before turning and marching off into the restaurant. Carli followed, and I reached out my hand, ready to place it low on her back, imagining the feel of the curve beneath my palm. Her pace kept her out of range. I shoved my hand into my pocket instead. Instead of focusing on what a fucking wimp I had become, I concentrated on the motionless patrons of the restaurant. Hands in laps or on the table. I liked the animated talkers, the ones who threatened to take an eye out with a fork. At least with them I had a hint of the conversation.

We sat down across from each other at a narrow booth, our knees brushing as we both slid in. I kept my legs out farther than I needed to, our legs still touching as we sat, the contact a slow awakening to the person I used to be. The menus dropped to the table as the hostess's mouth flapped some more. I almost labeled her an idiot, until I realized I hadn't signed and Carli had spoken. Poor lady probably had no clue she wasted words on us.

At least, she wasted them on me. I looked at Carli to see if she understood, but she just shrugged. I smiled and flipped through the menu. I planned to order a beer, but I scanned the cocktails page and found the drink Willow ordered the last time we were here. I had stolen half. There were times I wished it was okay for a dude to order a fruity drink.

I turned my menu around to Carli and pointed to the drink, giving her a thumbs-up. She raised her eyebrows, so I shrugged. A smile played at her lips as she turned back to her own menu.

When the drinks arrived, I grinned. She'd ordered my suggestion. Only now I wanted some. Would it be rude to steal a drink from a girl I hadn't kissed?

Yes, yes it would. Unless I kissed her now…

And now I wanted a kiss more than the damn drink. I wanted to feel Carli. No alcohol, no pretense, just lip to lip. I shook my head and pulled out my notebook and a pen. We started off talking about linguistics class and CART. The more Carli drank, the more her filter loosened. I liked her loose. Especially when she slid a certain note my way.

If this is a date, I should ask about anyone else you may be seeing. If this isn't a date, then you keep your secrets.

Her cheeks pinked, and she tried to grab the paper back. I was quicker, or less buzzed, and doubly glad for it.

Yes, this is a date. And no, I'm not seeing anyone else.

I made sure to touch her hand when I passed the paper back, my fingers lingering on her knuckles. The point of no return had been crossed. About damn time. Why had I taken so long?

Tell me about your last girlfriend and why you broke up.

That's why. I scratched the back of my neck, trying to put into words the whole Beth shit storm in a way that wouldn't scare Carli off.

Last girlfriend was two years ago. A hearing student in the Deaf Studies program. I dumped her when a friend caught her talking about me like a fucking charity case.

I really didn't want to screw this up too soon. It had been way too long, almost as if I had waited for the brunette with soft brown eyes across from me. She caught my hand and squeezed. I had the urge to clasp tighter and pull her in for a kiss.

Her loss. Partly why I don't date much with my ears.

Our food arrived, and Carli turned her attention to her lasagna, but I ignored my burger. She appeared to communicate well in spoken English. Why would her ears stop her from dating?

Why?

She read my words for much longer than necessary, a crease forming on her brow. As though I had poked a balloon and the air deflated. I didn't like seeing her this way, especially when she had already given me so much. I collected the paper and wrote another note. Then I passed it her way while I ran a hand down her arm and tangled our fingers together.

Their loss.

Her eyes locked in on mine, our hands still clasped, a key sliding into the slot and turning. And somehow she stole a little part of me. Had this woman received praise? Been told how valuable she was? I didn't know. But it had become my mission.

I walked her home after the meal. The city lights twinkled instead of the stars, hidden out of view. Nighttime promises circled around us, reducing the crowded streets to the two of us and the question of how to end the date. I held her hand as we walked silently together, my warm palm to her cold one. Would her lips be cold? If so, I could work a little magic and warm her right up.

When we arrived at her building, I stopped but held tight to her hand, needing her touch. My nerves were ready to go back to the two-year lonely existence. Her palm against mine was enough to prove the rest of me was not. I continued the silence as the air heated up around us. I wanted this moment to be her and me with no reminders of where we differed.

Her eyes shined in the yellow streetlights. Open and receptive. My heart picked up to a jog as I leaned in. She tilted her head, angling to meet my mouth. Every part of me screamed to pull her to me and devour her at once. I didn't. I held back. Worth it when my lips connected with hers. She tasted of alcohol and chocolate. I wanted a deeper taste, badly. My hand tightened on hers, and she opened her mouth, swamping me with need. I wanted to know if the magic would continue when I took all of her. Tonight.

I wasn't that guy, never had been. It had to be the years causing this, those two lonely years. I pulled back. When Carli opened her eyes, the same need burned. In that moment I knew it wasn't the years. Whatever I felt, she felt too.

My dick was on board for some more exploration, and I hoped like hell she didn't look down. Because I was two seconds away from fucking all rational sense and taking her against her front door. But I still wasn't that guy. I took a step back. Her smooth fingers slipped from my grasp.

"*Good night,*" I signed.

Her hands shook as she responded. "*Good night.*"

She stared at me awhile longer before heading up her stairs. Once she disappeared from view, I turned and sat on a concrete step. A smile stretched my cheeks, and my heart still trampled the pavement at a fast pace. I looked up at where the stars should've been, wondering if it was too late to follow her.

Then one star came into view, winking among a murky midnight blue sky. I thought of Dad, and for the first time, my smile didn't fade.

Me: I had a good time.

Without waiting for a response, I pushed myself back to my feet. Hands in my pockets, I made my way back to my car.

Chapter Eleven

Carli

THE FOLLOWING SATURDAY I lay belly down on my bed with my linguistics work in front of me. Next to me, Reed copied my pose. Elbow to elbow we worked on diagramming sentences. To my surprise the deaf guy was better at this than me. English had always been my weak spot. $2(45 + 53) / 4(66 - 59) = 7$, easy. Noun + Verb = Sentence, not so easy.

In full teacher mode, he crossed out my diagramming and reworked it on the page, putting me to shame. I glanced at my notes from class, and my eyes caught on a quote. *We have a biological predisposition to learning language.* I grabbed my highlighter and marked the note in pink. Then elbowed Reed and pointed to the quote.

He put his pen down and read the note. While he read I scribbled on a clean piece of paper.

Perhaps that's why you're kicking my ass at this even though you didn't have language until you were three.

A smile crossed his bitable lips, and he began writing.

I believe it's true that we all want to learn. Deaf kids without language are starved to communicate. The old theory that ASL is a crutch is a bunch of bull. Give a child a language, any language, and he or she can use that language to learn others. Mostly it takes work and patience. My parents had both in abundance.

As for you, you're looking for the equation, and the grammar equation doesn't make the same sense to you as math does. That's OK. Many kids with a hearing loss gravitate toward math because it's visual.

And here I thought I liked math because my father did. Though I supposed Reed had a point. Math was easy to follow along without sound, in contrast to my other subjects.

My dad's an engineer. One of my sisters is an accountant. I'm the only one who can't hear. Explain that, Mr. Teacher.

Reed snorted.

"*Fine,*" he signed. Then he mimed bowing down to me, which was a mini head nod from his position.

I pushed his shoulder, and he went with the motion before righting himself. I was pretty sure he did that only because he wanted to. The man oozed strength; a light push from me wouldn't send him spiraling.

He pointed to me, made the sign for *love,* then changed both hands to the letter *M* and had them brush each other. "*M-A-T-H.*"

I love math. Yup, that was true. I copied his signs and nodded. When I met his eyes again, they were hot on mine, and I got lost in them. We were alone in my room, the door closed since D studied in the living room. Suddenly it felt very private in here. We hadn't had much time together in the past week. My headache had been up to turbo level on Thursday, so we hadn't gone out after class. Reed had walked me home and gave my throbbing head a kiss good night. And for an hour afterward, my head was quiet.

Now the silent room filled with my heart drumming in my ears. I let my gaze travel down to Reed's lip as I licked my own. When I forced my eyes back to his, he was no longer looking in my eyes. He was looking at my mouth. I inched forward, just a bit. He held still, holding strong at the top of the Most Confusing Guy List. Anyone else would have been all over me by now. Reed held back.

I inched forward again. If he didn't kiss me, I'd kiss him. A surge of power came over me at that concept. Maybe it was time for a change. I gathered up my courage and began to move, only to have Reed finally break.

He crashed into me, his lips on mine, one hand behind my head. Heat surged within me as our lips brushed and our tongues teased. This was what I had wanted. Much better than…than…I couldn't even remember what we had been doing.

I shifted to face him and ended up flat on my back, with him on top of me. His warmth spread through me, eradicating any lingering chill. I wrapped my arms around him, holding him close. Fingers itched to explore his body. Every inch of him pressed against me, and there was no doubt in my mind this was a fit man—and I wanted more.

He held one hand to my head. The other slipped under my back, large hand sprawled out. I squirmed, wanting more of him, needing more of him. He pressed our bodies closer together, accentuating a definite bulge behind his fly.

As I contemplated how far I wanted to go and quickly laughed at myself for having any modicum of self-control, he pulled back. In fact, he pulled himself completely off me and the bed, much like he had when we were wrestling over the laptop a few weeks ago. What the hell? He stood, breath heavy, bulge apparent, and ran two hands through his hair. Hair I must have messed up without even realizing it.

"*No,*" he signed, unable to get his breath under control. He grabbed the notebook. While he wrote, I stayed sprawled on my back, 100 percent confused. He was as into this as I was. I felt it. I had visual proof. Why the rejection? Again. Before the hurt overpowered the heat, he handed me the notebook.

I'm sorry. I didn't mean to take advantage of you.

I blinked at his words, somehow even more confused than minutes ago. I had been two steps away from removing my own clothes and announcing I was on birth control. If either of us was taking advantage of the other, I was the culprit, not him. Before I could grab the pen, Reed began packing up his stuff. I waved for his attention. He ignored me. I grabbed his arm, and he froze.

"*Stop,*" I signed, then grabbed my phone.

Me: You didn't take advantage of me. Why are you leaving?

My heart sagged heavy as I watched him read and waited for his response.

Reed: I have to. Trust me. Thursday? Dinner?

Me: I don't understand.

If he didn't like me, why was he here in the first place? I pulled my knees into my chest, hands clutched. Unsure if I was confused or hurt. *Confurt*, a messed-up word for my messed-up emotions. Reed let out a breath and sat down next to me.

Reed: I'm sorry. I just…need to take things slow. Thursday?

Well, how could I argue with that?

Me: Stay. Let's finish work. You were still ripping apart my diagramming. How am I supposed to put it back together?

He glanced at the paper he'd demolished but not finished correcting. A hidden conflict played out in him. The only thing not hidden was the bulge lingering in his pants. A bulge I really wanted to help him with, despite his odd behavior.

"*Sorry, you right.*" He put down his stuff and went back to work, remaining seated this time around. I still got a kiss good-bye when he left, but it was cautious, controlled. More than anything, I wanted this man to lose control. I wanted to feel all of him, whatever lurked beneath that surface. A part of me warned that I should be worried about his reasons for holding back. But the truth was that I trusted him. More than I should.

Chapter Twelve

Reed

ON WEDNESDAY, TANNER had a rare weeknight free and demanded dinner in the city. Willow was already crashing at our place, so we played rock, paper, scissors for designated driver. I lost. The girls hugged and kissed each other like they won the lottery. I headed out to my car without them and gunned my engine. It got the girls into the car and earned me the label of *asshole* for the night. I pointed out that *designated asshole driver* might not be a good thing.

I sipped my Coke as the three of them drank their beers, or fruity drink in Willow's case. I gestured for her drink. "*Come on. One sip?*"

She rolled her eyes. "*Fine. I always lose my drink when you drive.*"

I grinned as I took more than a sip, stopping only when Willow slapped my shoulder and reclaimed her drink.

"*Delicious.*"

"*Bastard.*"

Tanner tapped his fingers on the table. "*Maybe I'm wrong. But this man here looks awfully perky.*"

I rested my elbows on the table.

"*He has a girlfriend,*" Willow announced.

Tanner's eyes shot up. "*How can you have a girlfriend if your dick is shriveled up?*"

I clenched my fists into two tight balls before forcing myself to sign. "*You want to fight?*"

Tanner grinned. "*It's true? You do still have a penis?*"

"*You finished?*" I signed one-handed, sharp and intent, the tension settling into my rigid fingers.

"*Fine.*" Tanner's shoulders sagged. "*I'm just happy you're finally having sex again.*"

Val shook her head. "*Have you met him?*" she asked Tanner.

"*Since high school, sweetheart.*"

"*Then you know the answer to that.*"

I rubbed the kink in my neck. "*Are we finished with my love life?*"

"*No,*" Willow signed with both hands for added effect.

"*Two years.*" Tanner banged his head on the table. "*Fuck her already.*"

My jaw ached as I ground my back teeth. *Fucking asshole.*

"*Wow,*" Val signed, one hand on Tanner's arm. "*She's different.*"

Tanner leaned back in his chair, not giving a damn his neck and my hands were about to meet. "*Good. Have sex.*"

I rammed my clenched fists on the table. Judging by the looks I got from our neighbors, I rammed too loud. "*Enough. Is your own sex life that lacking?*" I locked eyes with Tanner.

Willow laughed. "*Shit.*" She looked at Val. "*We're the only ones getting any.*"

Tanner took a swig of his beer.

I relaxed my hands. "*Well, what do we have here? Man with big mouth talks a lot but says nothing.*"

"*Blow me.*"

"*You wish.*"

"*Poor men,*" Willow signed in both our directions, shaking her head. "*Your lives are just so…dry.*" She elongated the sign with one hand, while the other brought her drink to her lips.

Tanner scowled. I leaned back, thought of Carli. After two years in the desert, life didn't feel dry. It was rich, full of ferns, trees, and waterfalls. And a beautiful woman with amber eyes.

"*Why are you waiting this time?*" Val asked, all good humor vacant from her face.

Life. Experiences. Habit. Yet my hands didn't move. I stared into her brown eyes, conveying things only a life-long friend could process.

"*Can you do it? Can you drop the act and just be yourself?*"

I raised my eyebrows. "*Myself is a horny bastard?*"

Willow and Tanner doubled over in laughter.

Val did not. "*I understand why you're so cautious— really, I do. I was there; you'd be foolish not to be cautious.*"

But I see the passion in you. And I see that flame burning for her." She paused, took a sip of her beer. "*No, I take that back. Let me meet her. I didn't screen Beth well enough.*"

"Val," I caught Willow hissing her name from across the table. The two broke into an English-only conversation. Tanner flicked at his hearing aids in a move that could mean only one thing—he adjusted his volume to listen.

My phone vibrated, and I pulled it out of my pocket.

Carli: I need to attend a deaf event. Since I happen to know a deaf guy, I figured this shouldn't be too hard...

You could come here right now and listen to my roommate fight with her girlfriend over why we haven't had sex yet. On second thought, scratch that with a heavy red pen.

Me: Not sure hanging out with me is going to match the assignment.

I put my phone down on the table. Val and Willow were still talking, but Tanner readjusted his hearing aids. "*They finished?*" I asked.

"*New topic. I'm not interested.*"

My phone buzzed. Carli sent a picture with details on an assignment to attend a Deaf event. At the bottom, Gina had handwritten that hanging out with me and my friends would work.

Thrown under the bus. And liking it.

Me: Well, I better not let you down. I'll see what I can work out. I still need to introduce you to more people like you.

Carli: Don't you mean us?

Her words warmed me from the inside out. I did nothing to prevent the silly grin.

Me: :-) Good girl. But no, I mean you: Hard of Hearing, wears hearing aids, and can communicate in spoken English. Stay tuned. According to Gina I have two weeks to pull something together...

I put my phone down, and three pairs of eyes stared at me.

I locked eyes with Val. *"Wanna have a party next Saturday?"*

"Why?" Val elongated the sign straight down to the table.

"You wanted to meet C-A-R-L-I, right?"

"Yes," she signed slowly, not trusting me.

With a sigh, I loaded the picture of her assignment and turned it around.

Willow threw her hands up in the air in a silent wave. *"Matchmaker Gina. Love it!"*

"You want to plan a party in a little over a week?" Val asked.

"You can screen C-A-R-L-I."

"But food, beer, cleaning."

Tanner slapped the table. *"B-Y-O-B. Make lover boy clean. Done. Party. I'm in."*

I narrowed my eyes. *"Leave her alone."*

He raised his hands in surrender and rocked his chair back.

"Come on," Willow signed to Val, eyes darting to me and my not-so-typical behavior.

"Fine." She ran a hand through her hair as Willow and Tanner Deaf clapped. *"I have one requirement."* She

leaned forward and locked eyes with mine. *"Let go of the past."*

I mimed cutting the cord. Willow and Tanner began a new conversation, but Val continued staring at me. The message was clear. She wanted me to cut the cord for Carli, not her. To let go of everything that had held me back.

I didn't know if I could. How does one wake up one day and change 180 degrees? It didn't happen that way. The key here? I wanted to try. For Carli.

Chapter Thirteen

Carli

SATURDAY, I TOOK the Red Line into Cambridge then caught a bus to take me one town over. Social media entertained me during the long trip. I even took a few quizzes to pass the time—my Disney soul mate is Tarzan. Not sure how I feel about that one. Once I got off the bus, I smoothed down my skater skirt over my leggings. I stretched up onto my toes, my ballet flats allowing me ample movement. The cold breeze caused me to shiver, but I also sweated due to nerves. What had I gotten myself into?

I clutched my bag to my shoulder as I walked the streets of Somerville. I crossed another busy intersection and saw a house up ahead with gray chipped siding and a lot of cars out front. Panicked through and through, I thought of canceling on Reed and taking the long trip back home. But my legs propelled me forward.

I traveled down the cracked asphalt driveway and climbed to the second floor to Reed's apartment. The door to the kitchen stood open. People milled about. Sounds filtered through the storm door. Hands moved in animated chatter. Unlike the parties I usually attended, no music played.

I swallowed the lump in my throat and was about to text Reed when someone waved me in. The screen squeaked as I opened it, and voices crowded my ears. I still couldn't pick out a single word, but without the heavy bass I at least stood a chance.

A pretty woman with short curly hair and golden brown skin waved me in and smiled at me. "Are you Carli?" she asked, hands moving along with her voice.

"Yes," I managed in both languages.

Her smile grew. "I'm Val, Reed's roommate. Nice to meet you." She held out her hand when she finished signing and shook mine. Years of uncomfortable-social-interaction training allowed me not to flip out, at least on the outside. On the inside I was a monkey rattling her cage and flinging her poop. Why hadn't Reed mentioned his roommate was female? Was that the reason he held back? Were they an item? Oh God, was this destined to be the most awkward handshake in history?

"How did you know it was me?" I asked. There, I managed a neutral response.

She laughed. "For starters? The scared-shitless look. I remember my first ASL gathering. Feel free to kick Reed's ass over this. Second, you're exactly as he described you."

I glanced down at my attire before looking back up. Was that good or bad? And then it clicked. She introduced herself as his roommate, not his girlfriend. The man could just have a platonic female roommate, right?

Movement behind Val caught my attention. Reed. Worn jeans hugged his legs, and a black tee shirt with some white writing over one pec emphasized his broad shoulders. His hair was messy, and a day's worth of stubble lined his face. I couldn't tear my eyes away from him as the butterflies in my stomach flapped in anticipation.

"*Hi. You OK?*" he asked as he came over, smile firmly on his lips.

I nodded.

He signed something. I caught the word *house* but nothing else.

"*Sorry.*" Was it too late to text him I couldn't make it?

Val poked Reed in the arm. "Be nice to the poor girl. Did you find the house without any problems? Which you obviously did since you're here." Again, she spoke and signed like it was completely natural.

I didn't know the signs for what I wanted to say, so I spoke them to Val. "The directions were fine. No problems." I waited for her to explain what I said to Reed, but she didn't. I shifted and rubbed my toe into the tiled floor. "Um, I don't know the signs for that. Do you mind signing them for me?" This really wasn't going to work. I still wasn't sure of her connection to Reed, and I needed her to help us communicate.

Val grinned. "I'm sure he pays enough attention to your lips that he should be able to lip-read you by now."

Reed poked Val in the side and signed something fast and forceful to her. Above his dark stubble his cheeks pinked, which made my own uneasiness subside. Okay, Val was not his girlfriend. The whole interaction screamed embarrassment, not groveling.

Val laughed and walked off.

Reed shook his head and turned back to me. "*Thank you…*" He signed something else that seemed like he was thanking me for being there.

"*No, thank you.*" After all, this was for my benefit, right?

I got lost in his face, in his smile, until he reached forward, wrapped a hand around my waist, and pulled me in for a quick, scorching kiss. I managed to grasp onto his shoulders for balance, just as he set me back on my own two feet.

He motioned for me to hand over my coat, which I did, only to find him looking me up and down like I was going to be his dinner.

He put his hand to his chest, thumb touching his body, fingers wiggling. I had no idea what it meant, but his facial expression told me it was a compliment. Worked for me.

I followed him farther into the room. The kitchen opened up to a casual living area. A beige couch lined one wall, with other chairs dotted around for the party. The indents on the multicolored rug indicated a coffee table normally balanced the room. The couch and most of the chairs were occupied. People even sat on the floor instead of standing. Around me the place was…loud. Not sound level, though there was a fair amount of speaking. But hands moved. Everywhere. People laughed, loudly. Some people even made non-English noises as they signed. Reed pointed to a girl with long brown hair braided over one shoulder who sat cross-legged on the wood floor. She looked up and smiled as we approached.

Reed signed something quickly to the female then turned to me. He pointed to her. "*Name W-I-L-L-O-W*," he signed slowly, letting me catch up to each letter before pointing to her again and signing the letter *H* twice.

I shook my head, not following him.

He pointed to his ear, then to Willow. She perked up, cupped her hand under her ears, and turned her head. "Like my new hearing aid molds? I went for pink this time." Her voice sounded normal to me, but I looked at her ears, and sure enough, she had behind-the-ear hearing aids with pink molds.

Reed leaned forward and pressed a kiss to my temple. He signed something followed by "*fun*," and then left us alone.

I sank to the floor, tucking my legs under me.

"So tell me, what kind of hearing aids do you have? Any fun colors?"

"Behind-the-ear, no fun colors." I pulled my hair up on the sides, showing off my aids. I wore my hair down 90 percent of the time, partly because I liked my hair down, but mostly because I wanted to conceal my hearing aids.

"Been there. I hid my hearing aids for years. Best thing I ever did was take an ASL class."

"It's hard to hide them, isn't it? Especially when the batteries die."

"Oh my God. Don't they have the worst timing possible? I swear, I'll be in the middle of being proposed to, and I'll have to stop to change my battery."

I threw my head back and laughed. "Or, true story, in the middle of getting it on. Really hard to stay in the mood when your hearing aid is beeping." Never saw that loser again. In hindsight sex wasn't the most opportune time to let him know I couldn't hear very well.

Willow doubled over in laughter. "Oh, yes, to the right, to the...dammit. Stop beeping already."

I followed her over in laughter, liking Willow already. Never before had I chatted with someone like me. There was a connection with her and, by default, the rest of the room.

We were laughing over the dumb looks people gave us when they found out a young woman had a hearing loss when Reed came back over. He squatted down next to me and handed over a hard lemonade. I looked at the drink, then him. He tilted his head to the side, as if to say "so?" I took the drink.

He turned to Willow and signed something. I caught the word *nice*.

"Of course I'm playing nice," she exclaimed, hands flapping at him. "You worried I'm going to share all your dirty little secrets?"

His good humor faded. "*No.*" He pulled out his phone and typed something, phone angled so I could read the screen.

Reed: Don't listen to her. She lies.

I snorted, put my drink down, and grabbed his phone.

Me: Then why have you let me sit here with her for so long?

I handed the phone back, but he had already read what I wrote and held my eye contact.

"*Fine. Later,*" Reed signed. He leaned in and kissed my forehead, lingering in a way that made me think he wanted to be the one chatting with me. Then he turned to Willow, pointed an accusatory finger at her, and walked away.

"Wow, hot," Willow giggled as we both watched Reed exit to the kitchen.

I took a sip of my drink. "And now I really want to know about these little secrets."

Willow laughed, and Val plopped down in between us. "I've been hovering all night waiting for her to say that." She turned to Willow. "Did you see Reed?"

Willow held her hands out at her sides. "I was right here. Hard to miss."

Both ladies had stopped signing. I put my drink down. "If you two aren't about to share some details, I'm leaving."

Val got comfortable, which involved leaning on Willow. "Oh, I'm sharing. It's been a long time since I've seen Reed like this."

"And how is that?"

"Like a love-sick puppy. Haven't seen that since Beth, the bitch. And no offense, Carli, but you're being screened for authenticity."

Time to start drinking. I gulped down some of my tangy beverage. "And?"

"Keep looking at him the way you do, and you'll pass with flying colors."

It was my turn to have red cheeks. And I involuntarily glanced toward the kitchen, looking for Reed.

"Yup, she passes," Willow said.

I took a deep breath and stopped searching the crowd for him.

Val, arms crossed, scrutinized me. "So far so good."

Willow sighed. "Val grew up with Reed, and she's very protective over her friends. Hurt him, especially after what we're about to share, and she'll kick your ass."

I drank some more, even as Val turned to Willow and gave her an evil eye. "So what am I missing? Reed said a previous girlfriend talked about him like a charity case, but I know there's more."

Val let out a breath and checked our surroundings. She leaned forward. "Can I talk soft, and you'll still hear me?"

I shrugged. "Give it a try."

Val dropped her voice down a level. "How's this?"

I gave her a thumbs-up.

"Okay. Beth. They met through a local deaf event and, since they went to the same school, struck up a conversation. She"—Val turned to Willow—"how do I put this?"

"Was a conniving bitch?"

"Oh, that part's a given. But she played dumb with ASL. Like she was just learning, but she was actually pretty proficient. Which meant she could twist Reed's words around. And she did."

"What's the point in that?"

Willow shook her head and grabbed Val's drink. "Beth banked on the teacher in Reed. Before her, he always enjoyed finding people who wanted to learn more ASL. He stopped, until you."

Her words shouldn't have made me feel special, but they did.

"Anyways," Val said, taking her drink back, "I caught Beth in a few stretches of the truth but didn't think it right to tell Reed. Word to the wise: I won't do that again. He's cautious with relationships, as I'm sure you've already seen, so it took them a while for things to heat up."

"She doesn't want to hear this," Willow said, tugging on Val's arm.

"She has to." Val turned back to me. "Seriously, you need to hear this, even if you don't want to. But I'll stop if you don't."

I was more curious than a cat. "I'm not so naïve to think the man hasn't had sex before." In fact, I preferred it.

"Good. Reed and I have been roommates for a while. The place where we lived had thin walls, but with a deaf roommate, I didn't care. Beth finally got into Reed's bed. In the morning I caught her in the kitchen, sobbing." Val shook her head and took a swig of her beer.

"I'll tell this." Willow shifted as she spoke. "Basically, Beth tried to play it that she was drunk, when she had the alcohol tolerance of a frat boy. She pulled a sob story with Val and actually tried to claim he date-raped her."

My jaw fell open. "What?"

Val held up her hands. "Not true. So not true. I've heard less vocalization from porn. Not once did she tell him no. In fact, I heard her clearly request the opposite. No one who says *yes* and *now* that often was being taken advantage of, and I told her so. Her fake tears stopped and she didn't even try to argue with me."

"That's when she went into the charity case," Willow said. "About how a poor deaf guy wouldn't know any better, wouldn't know if she was into it or not unless he could hear. Which is a bunch of bullshit, if you ask me." Willow flipped her braid over her shoulder. "And how she was taking pity on him, since he probably didn't get much being damaged goods."

I clenched a fist, far too used to the *damaged goods* line. "He's not damaged."

Val pointed at me. "I like you. Beth then tried the whole sob story again to Reed when he got up, but I cut her right off. Only now she was signing better than she had the entire time they'd known each other. I told him the full truth, voice off, and she understood every word. Then he kicked her out. It took us two more months to figure out where she learned ASL, which just makes me want to slug her even more."

"Down, girl." Willow placed a hand on Val's shoulder. "I bumped into her around campus. She never saw me, too busy yelling into her phone. I followed her for two blocks as she bitched about her stupid younger brother. Turns out he's deaf, and the family dynamics sounded worse than a soap opera."

"That's horrible," I said, unable to stop the flash to my own family. Only my father was the one who called me stupid.

"Tell me about it. How could she pull that shit with Reed when her own brother—"

Willow clamped a hand over Val's mouth, stopping her rising voice. "Let it go. It's not worth it."

Willow removed her hand, and Val took a deep breath, unclenching her fists.

I turned to look for Reed again. This time I found him in the kitchen, signing with some friends. And all his strange behaviors made sense. I would be a little gun-shy after an experience like that myself. He turned and caught me staring at him. Instead of pulling away, I smiled. Those butterflies fluttered again when he smiled back. He looked behind me at Val and Willow. The smile faltered, and he made his way over.

"Shit," Val muttered.

He sat down next to me, knees raised, studying my face, before narrowing his eyes at Val and Willow.

"She needed to know," Val said in both languages.

Reed shook his head and dropped it to his knees. I wrapped an arm around his shoulders and rested my chin on his arm, wanting to let him know it was okay. It wasn't his fault he had a crappy ex. Didn't we all have at least one?

He picked his head up and looked at me. His eyes spoke volumes, able to read what my own were saying. He moved a hand around my waist, pulled me in, and laid a hot, lingering kiss on my lips.

And everything about him clicked. He was cautious by nature, caused to increase tenfold by Beth. But he didn't want to be cautious with me. Nothing about his kiss said caution, only his reactions to the smoldering heat we created together.

"She's the real deal," Val said when we parted.

Reed reached into his back pocket and pulled out his phone.

Reed: What am I going to do about you?

I picked up my drink and chugged half down. Liquid courage.

Me: Keep me?

He smiled and placed an arm around my shoulders. I couldn't think of any other place I'd rather be than right there, next to him.

Chapter Fourteen

Reed

A FEW HOURS later, I learned something very important: Carli was a lightweight. Worse, a lightweight where everything hit her at once. She held her own for three hard lemonades. One sip into her fourth and her balance slipped away. She laughed, she flirted, and I knew she'd hate me in the morning when her hangover hit.

I hated me already, because any plans I had for the two of us were canceled.

Barely able to keep herself upright, she tried to go home when only Val and Willow were left. Considering the T had stopped running, she wasn't going anywhere by herself.

"*Me home,*" she signed.

I shook my head. "*You're drunk. You're not going home.*" I didn't bother slowing down. I wasn't sure she could understand much in either language at this point of the night. *"Come on. You need sleep."*

I wrapped her arm around my neck and helped her to my room. She hiccupped, a hand over her mouth. I pointed to the trash can, but she shook her head, falling back on the bed in laughter.

My plans for sleeping in the living room vanished. I'd stay on the floor and make sure she remained safe. She reached for her left shoe, grasping at thin air, her foot moving out of the way as she reached, playing cat and mouse. After three tries she gave up, falling back on the bed, tears streaming down her face in laughter. I took both her shoes off.

When she sat up, she checked her feet, then looked around for her shoes. I couldn't stop my own laughter. I pulled out a tee shirt for her to wear and tossed it on the bed.

She nodded and stood, wobbling a bit, before turning around. I kept my eyes on her, afraid she'd fall over and crack her skull open. She grasped the hem of her shirt and pulled it over her head. I needed to turn around, but I couldn't. First of all, she was here, in my room, in the flesh. I knew I was a prick, but I soaked up every inch of her backside. I justified my actions with her continued lack of balance; I couldn't let her fall.

She reached behind her and unclasped her bra, tossing it on the bed. My heart stopped beating. There was no blood left to move. She pulled the shirt over her head, wobbling again. Half of one breast came into view before the shirt blocked it all out. Then she wiggled out of her skirt and climbed into my bed.

That small view nearly killed me. The same pale skin covered her from head to toe and looked as smooth and silky as the few places I touched. I cursed myself for fucking up the night and giving her too much to drink. If not, I'd have my hands on her right now.

I stood still for a good ten minutes, willing my body to relax. When my blood moved normally again, I checked on Carli.

She lay face first on one of my pillows, mouth half-ajar, fast asleep. I brushed her hair back and kissed her cheek. *"Good night."*

I collected the other pillow and grabbed a spare blanket. Once settled on the floor, I stared up at my bed, wondering how different the morning would be from the one I spent with Beth.

But as bad as the Beth shit storm was, the aftermath was worse. I had ignored a call from Dad to be with her. The next one I received was Mom telling me he was dead. I had spent the night with a lie. If I hadn't, if I had answered the call, maybe I would still have my father.

Chapter Fifteen

Carli

THE JACKHAMMERING IN my head woke me up. The shards of pain were so intense I couldn't even move my heavy eyelids. Instead I pushed my head as far into the soft pillow as it would go.

Sure, hangovers were a bitch. My nightly aspirin helped with my daily pain and any hangovers destined to come my way. An aspirin I didn't have because I crashed at Reed's place. I hadn't intended to drink so much. Reed kept handing me another hard lemonade, and I kept drinking. In the light of the morning, as I tried to hold back tears from the throbbing, I added a new equation to my list: my tolerance + Reed = way-too-drunk Carli.

I cracked open one eye. The morning light shone through the thin cloth shades, casting Reed's room in a dim yellow glow. I let one eye adjust and then forced the second open. My stomach lurched and nausea messed with my already overloaded system. I took a deep breath and exhaled through the pain, preparing myself for a long, long morning.

Desperate for a distraction, I fumbled on the night-stand until I found my phone. I turned the screen face-down and clicked it awake, then shifted it up inch by inch to adjust to the bright light.

D: Things heating up with your hottie?

D: OK, it's late. I'm getting worried.

D: Send me a text ASAP to confirm you are not another missing college student!

Me: Alive, drank too much, full living status questionable.

I hit Send, and before I could remove my thumb, I had a response.

D: THANK GOD! I was seriously about to call the cops.

I felt awful for worrying D, but appreciative to have such a caring friend.

Me: Sorry, D.

I put the phone down and tried to lift my head, only to have the jackhammer kick into high gear and my stom-ach roll in protest. Head back on the pillow, I pushed into the soft cushion, desperate for some relief.

A warm hand on my head stopped my squirming. Reed stood next to the bed. He sat down, not moving his hand, which I was eternally grateful for as his warmth soothed the horrible aches. With one hand he pointed in front of his forehead, twisting his hand as he went, then signed, "*P-A-I-N?*"

I closed my eyes and nodded. I hid this from every-one. Sure, Matti and D knew I had frequent headaches, but neither one of them knew how bad it could get or how frequent. Right now, at my absolute worst, I couldn't hide a damn thing.

Pain tangled with my thoughts, with Reed's con-cerned face, and I broke. The tears escaped, and I crum-pled into a tight ball. The bed shifted and Reed held me tight, everything about his embrace a proactive barrier I had never known before. Somehow he found the spot that hurt the most and pressed his lips there. Just pressed, not quite a kiss. With him there, the pain calmed down, and I pulled myself together.

He took my face in his hands, studying me, trying to figure me out, no doubt. Then he held up a finger and left. I wished for the ability to get up and walk away, avoid any further humiliation. But I didn't trust myself to move.

He returned with a glass of water and pressed two round pills into my palm.

"*A-S-P-I-R-I-N?*" I asked hopefully.

He shook his head. "*No, sorry. I-B-U-P-R-O-F-E-N.*"

I let out a breath. Not my usual drug. But I wasn't in any position to be choosy. I pushed myself upright, one pains-taking inch at a time, and Reed helped me. Then I popped both pills in my mouth and swallowed them with the water.

Reed brushed my hair back behind my ear, one side of his mouth quirking, then falling. He grabbed a pen and notebook off his nightstand.

You either can't handle your alcohol, or you weren't kidding about those headaches.

Give the man a million points, because no one had ever seen through me like he did.

"*Both*," I signed, fearful that after everything I learned about him the night before, I wasn't going to be able to hide much longer.

He leaned forward and kissed the top of my head.

Not normal unless this is a hangover.

Tears pricked at the base of my eyes, so I rolled over. He cuddled into my backside. A feeling of safety washed over me. I picked up the paper and pen.

I usually take aspirin before bed to prevent this.

That revealed more than I intended. A tiny door to the Real Carli cracked open, a door I dead-bolted from everyone. I tucked the paper against me to block him from reading. He turned me until I was on my back, and the minute I looked into his eyes, I knew he had seen what I wrote.

His face filled with questions, but he didn't sign. He didn't write. Instead he lowered his head and brushed his lips against mine. Once. Twice. Then sunk into a sweet kiss. Those lips distracted me from my head, from the unease of revealing so much. I wrapped my arms around him and opened my mouth to take the kiss deeper. Probably not my best idea, considering we had both just woken up after a night of drinking.

Reed pulled back. Yup, not my best idea. I was about to put this morning on the List for Worst Morning Ever when he brushed a hand over my forehead. No longer was the look in his eyes full of questions and concern. No, oh no; now heat resided. The hand on my head asked a silent question, one to which I nodded my answer.

Then it was game on. His lips were back against mine in a kiss so far removed from sweet that I might never crave sugar again, because this put even the most delectable sweet to shame. I forgot about my poor throbbing noggin as I wrapped my arms around him and pressed him as close to me as I could get. And still it wasn't close enough.

I wasn't alone in that feeling. Reed withdrew from my embrace and pulled back the covers before sliding inside with me. All I had on was his tee shirt and my leggings, but I would have been fine if I was naked. In fact, at that moment, I would have preferred naked. Instead I accepted the intimacy of being wrapped up with Reed, in his bed, under his sheets. Content to stay in this spot as long as I could.

His fingers slid under the tee shirt, warm against my bare back. I may have whimpered a bit at the contact and squirmed closer to him. As soon as I did, I became aware of two things: we fit together like a puzzle, and his lounge pants did nothing to contain his erection. The hard length of him settled between my legs, and I forgot to breathe.

He broke the kiss, probably because I was about to turn blue, and looked down at me. He removed his hand from my back, which caused me to whimper again. He must have felt me, because one side of his mouth curved, as his hand moved in front of his face.

"B-E-A-U-T-I-F-U-L."

I melted, completely melted, and yanked his mouth back down to mine. This time when his hand slipped under my shirt, his fingers spread across my belly, inching upward. Too slow for my liking. I needed those fingers in more interesting locations pronto, before the pain spoke louder than the pleasure. I wiggled, hoping to nudge him in the right direction. The bastard didn't relent on his snail's pace, but the moment he hit the underside of my braless breast I forgot about moving entirely.

I could focus only on what I felt, what he made me feel, all my energy on his fingers as they inched closer and closer to my nipple. When they reached their target, I bit my lip. All my nerve endings were congregated to that one location, multiplying their asses off until I couldn't contain their numbers any longer.

Body ready to burst, I wondered why we weren't naked already. I opened my eyes to find Reed watching me. His hair fell across his forehead in an uncombed mess. His eyes were dark as night, twin pools of desire. This handsome man was enthralled with me. I almost couldn't believe it. My heart clenched good and tight, threatening to jump ship, switch ownership, and never belong to anyone else again. But no danger signs rang out, most likely because his hand remained on my breast, and damned if any rational thought existed.

I needed to let him know it was okay to continue, but the only complex thought in my head was *more*. Somehow, I remembered the sign for *please*. He arched an amused eyebrow. Stubborn mule. I tugged at his shirt, the same one from the night before, and he removed his hands to pull it over his head. I wasn't thinking with any coherency, because the last thing I wanted was him removing his hands. That was before I got a good look at his body and almost swallowed my tongue. He was lean and trim and fit. While I had never bit a guy before, I had the strongest desire to do just that to Reed.

He grasped onto the bottom of the tee shirt I wore, raising an eyebrow in question. I wasn't as fit as he was, but all sense of self-consciousness was long gone. I nodded, and the shirt I wore joined his on the floor. He skimmed kisses along my jaw, down my neck, not stopping until he sucked a nipple into his mouth.

I arched into him. The now millions of nerve endings centralized in that one area cheered and caused certain other parts to grow jealous. And damp. Then he switched to my other breast, and my body climbed higher and higher. Reed broke my scale in every direction. His kisses = ten, his hands = ten, and I had high hopes for what number other parts of him would be assigned.

When I writhed in need, he stopped.

The cool morning puckered my wet skin, and I opened my eyes to see him writing on the pad of paper.

As much as I want you, I'm not having sex with you right now. Nothing to do with my past that Val and Willow shared, although if I'm honest there is some of that there. More you don't need me pounding into you if your head is pounding on its own.

I glazed over a bit at the pounding, because I really, really wanted it. But the man had a point. I grabbed the paper.

And here I was about to beg you to continue making me forget my headache, even pointing out I'm on birth control. Though considering I left all my meds at home, that one's a moot point.

He laughed at my words, and then kissed me like I was the air he desperately needed.

I can make you forget your headache without pounding.

All my nerve endings did a little jump, and my hand shook when I reached for the pen.

I'd like to see you try.

If only he knew the smile he gave me did half his work for him. He covered my mouth with his again, licking my lips until I opened for him. While our tongues danced a tango, one of his hands slid down my body, again at slow, snail speed. Even though I knew where he headed, I still gasped when his fingers slid beneath my pants and then again when they slid into my panties.

And when they slid inside, my head fell back against the pillow. I could no longer think, only feel. Did I mention this man's hands were a ten? Because that number was much too small—I needed a power of, a large power of. In less than two minutes, he had me flying so high I could've had an out-of-body experience. My body trembled as ripples of pleasure coursed through me.

When I came back down to earth, his eyes were hot on me, soaking in my face and my body. I wanted to give him more. I wanted to give him all of me. With my body sated, I didn't give a damn about my head, which admittedly was out of the red zone. Either the meds worked, or Reed's hands were magic. I reached out and placed a hand on his warm chest. His heart beat wild under my palm. I let my hand slide down his body, getting a little thrill over every bump and ridge along the way.

He let out a breath when my hand slipped inside his pants, and I felt my own hum of pleasure when I wrapped my hand around him and stroked. His hand, still in my pants, relaxed against me, and the moment felt more intimate than if we had sex. Now I was able to watch him as his eyes closed, as his mouth parted with deep breaths. My own body built back up as I continued to stroke and touch him.

Then all of a sudden he grabbed my hand and stopped me. Eyes now open, he shook his head and removed my hand.

I pointed to myself, then to him, trying to say that if I came, he deserved to as well. Either he didn't understand me or he didn't agree, because he shook his head again. Well, I'd flip the switch with my own mouth. I moved my head off the pillow—and the hammering slammed back into me.

Hand clutching the side of my head, I lay flat on the bed. Reed pulled me to him and kissed my head before grabbing the paper.

Don't ruin all my hard work.

I had to laugh.

It was your turn though.

He put the paper down and smiled at me, a full and sure smile. And I realized he may not have had the same amount of fun as I did, but I had given him back something Beth had stolen.

"*Other day*," he signed. Or perhaps that was *another day*?

I nodded and snuggled in, resting my aching forehead against his chest. The contact caused the aching to fade to a whisper.

Please don't include this in your ASL assignment.

I nearly doubled over in laughter.

What? You don't want me comparing you to the hearing guys I've been with?

He put his hands in his hair and rolled his head back. I kissed his chest. He took in my face, and I hoped like hell he saw the tease. When his lips curved, I considered the message received.

My right ear pressed against him, over his heart. The faint beating picked up through the suction of his skin and my ear. It occurred to me that I still wasn't wearing my hearing aids. On a normal day, I put on my aids as soon as I woke up and kept them on until I was alone for the night. Granted, I hadn't made it out of bed yet, but I also hadn't been alone.

Reed brushed my hair back, his fingers skimming the top of my ear. I'd had guys do that before, and their fingers rubbed against my microphone, creating horrible sounds. Here, with Reed, I was me. My ears didn't make much of a difference, not to a deaf guy.

He signed to me and I caught *food*, *help*, and *head*. My stomach understood more than my eyes and grumbled in response.

Reed laughed.

I pointed to my ear and shook my head. He couldn't hear. How could he hear my stomach?

He touched his middle finger to his chest twice. "F-E-E-L."

Oh, great, he felt my stomach rumbling. I dropped my head, shielding his view of my face.

He scrunched down and took my face in his hands; searching brown eyes melted my embarrassment away. He kissed me and then got out of bed, tossing me his shirt again. He stayed with me and helped me up. I stood slowly, testing my head's ability to be independent. The hammering dialed down to moderate, and I stood upright like a normal person. Thank God the medication had started doing its job.

Chapter Sixteen

Reed

THE MINUTE WE joined Val and Willow in the kitchen, my roommate pounced. "*Feeling better?*" she signed with her mouth moving, a devil's smile on her face.

"*Shut up,*" I signed, sharp, intense, and fast enough for Carli to miss.

Beside her, Willow stifled laughter. I contemplated taking Carli out of here, but she needed food. Although she may have been feeling the same unease, because she made to bolt. I put a hand on her waist and secured her against my side, realizing the only one of us with a real problem was me.

"*Her hearing aids are off,*" I signed.

Willow chewed and sat up straight. "*Same.*" She then moved her loose hair aside, showing off her empty ears.

Val continued to speak and sign, something she had grown damn good at. *"If you need your hearing aids, go right ahead and ignore Reed. But Willow and I are very good at talking loud."*

Willow nodded in her cheery chipmunk way.

Carli laughed, relaxing beside me. "...*heard* you...can *try*." Her eyes met mine, worry-filled as the unease seeped back in.

I pointed to Val. *"It's not a problem, she's an interpreter. I-N-T-E-R-P-R-E-T-E-R."*

"Student." Val scowled at me. *"I'm an interpreter student."*

I pulled out a chair and sat. *"Practice is a good thing."*

Val's Cheshire grin came out. *"I make no promises to be accurate."*

Willow whispered something in Val's ear. I paid it no mind—par for the course with the two of them. I was about to start breakfast when Carli sat down beside me and pointed to the two giggling women across from us. *"Dating?"*

I poked her in the arm. *"Yes. Problem?"*

Carli shook her head. *"No."*

Good, because I wasn't ready to let her go. I stood and picked up the bag of bagels Willow had brought over, let Carli choose one, and popped it into the toaster. When I turned around, Val was watching me.

"What a sweet boy."

"The poor girl has a hangover. You want her making her own breakfast?"

"*Of course she has a hangover; you kept handing her liquor all night.*"

Willow poked her way into the conversation. "*He was just making sure she stayed the night.*"

I picked up the butter knife to prep Carli's bagel, but couldn't let this one go. I didn't even care if someone voiced my signs. In fact, I welcomed it. "*Enough. Yes. I gave her too much alcohol. Which is why I'm making sure to take care of her now. I'm a nice guy. I will always be a nice guy. Stop waiting for me to suddenly turn into a devil. And get off both of our backs.*"

I stared at Val and waited, but her lips didn't move.

"*You interpret everything, and you're not interpreting that?*"

Val grimaced and finally opened her mouth. "*No, I'm not interpreting you yelling at me. You'll have to do that on your own.*"

I brought Carli's food over to her. "*Sorry.*"

I returned to the counter and prepped a marble bagel for myself. The brewed coffee won for potent smell of the day. I took a deep breath, savoring the bitter scent before pouring a cup. "*Want?*" I asked Carli.

She shook her head. "*OJ?*" she asked.

I smiled and kissed her forehead. "*Of course.*" I got her a glass before settling beside her.

The table vibrated, and I looked over to Willow. "*Is Carli going to join our Tuesday night dinners?*"

"*The dinner's voice off. Is that really fair?*"

Willow shook her head, her long brown hair fanning her face. "*Silly deaf boy, it's not voice off; it's ASL on.*"

"*It's not voice off?*"

Out of the corner of my eye, I caught Val's mouth moving. Thank God.

Both Willow and Val shook their heads.

I turned to Carli. "*Want to join?*"

Her eyes grew wide. "*ASL class.*"

"*Class then eat.*"

Carli looked at each of us, then back to me. A smile played at her lips. "*OK.*" She leaned in and kissed my cheek. I didn't know what I did to catch a girl like her, but I wasn't about to let go.

BY THE TIME I dropped Carli off and made it back to the apartment, the cleaning brigade had just about finished. Score. I hopped onto the couch, with my hands behind my head.

Val and Willow, both with their hair pulled back by colorful scarves or whatever girls used, propped hands on hips.

I removed one hand from my head. "*I'm ready to handle your BS.*"

"*We cleaned.*" Willow stomped the floor.

"*You also shared one of the worst parts of my past.*"

"*Again, she needed to know,*" Val signed.

"*And if she believed for one second I was capable of rape?*"

Willow pulled the fabric off her hair. "*One. We were clear it wasn't true. Two. That girl was on our side from the start.*"

I couldn't stop the smile. Well, that explained why I had my hand down her pants this morning.

"*Two-year drought over?*" Val asked.

"*Almost. Her head was in too much pain for that.*"

Willow turned to Val. "*He had a teenage make-out session.*" She sighed. "*I miss those.*"

Val collapsed on the couch. "*When I gain some energy, I'll show you.*"

"*Promise?*"

Val waved her off and then turned her attention to me. "*You look happy.*"

"*I like her.*"

"*A little obvious.*"

I sat up and turned to Willow. "*Do you hear better or worse than C-A-R-L-I?*"

She sat on the arm of the couch. "*We're similar. If anything, she hears more. Why?*"

"*Do you get headaches?*"

"*Sometimes, why?*"

"*She says she has them almost all the time. And the pain she was in this morning*"—I tried to find the words— "*was like no hangover I've ever seen before.*"

Val pushed herself up. "*You've just never stuck around to see the result of your 'here, have another' behavior. I'm going to shower.*"

Willow looked on with a hopeful glint in her eyes. "*Go.*" I didn't need to tell her twice, she ran down the hall after Val.

The image of Carli in pain ran on loop in my head. Over and over again I saw her curled up, barely able to move. It churned deep in my gut. Normal or not? I had to know. I tapped the couch for a few minutes before setting up a text to my mom.

Me: You home?

Mom: Yup, what's up?

Me: I'm calling.

I checked the hall, and the light shined from under the bathroom door. They'd be in there for a while. I set up the video call on the television.

"*You look happy,*" Mom signed when she saw me, her own cheeks perking up.

"*I am.*"

"*The new girl?*"

I couldn't stop my smile from spreading farther. "*She's special.*"

"*Now you've made me happy.*"

"*But…*"

"*Oh no.*"

"*What's normal for headaches?*"

Mom's dark eyebrows drew together. "*Explain.*"

"*C-A-R-L-I claims she has headaches most of the time. She takes an aspirin every night. And after drinking too much last night, I found her curled up in a tight ball, unable to move from pain.*"

Mom frowned. "*Every night?*"

I nodded.

"*That's not normal.*"

I scratched the back of my neck. My instinct confirmed. It didn't loosen the churning in my gut.

"*Does she know why she has the pain?*"

"*No clue. She's reluctant to talk about it.*"

"*Then you let it go until you know her better. She could be aware of this and not want to share.*"

I agreed, but deep inside something nagged. I'd never forget her curled up in pain. The only thing I could equate it to was Mom after Dad died. Only Carli's pain wasn't emotional.

"*I know you,*" Mom signed. "*Do your best to let it go. Would you want her complaining about Beth?*"

"*Val and Willow told her all about Beth.*"

Mom smiled. "*And she didn't bolt?*"

No, she didn't. If anything she let me further into her world.

"*When do I get to meet her?*"

I glared.

"*Be nice to your poor mother.*"

I laughed. "*Thanks for the talk. I love you.*"

She shook her head but smiled as she did so. "*I love you too.*"

We disconnected, and I stayed on the couch for a while, thoughts of Carli running a triathlon in my mind. I wanted to help her, in more ways than introducing her to the Deaf World.

Chapter Seventeen

Carli

TUESDAY, AFTER MY ASL class, I found Reed waiting for me outside the building. He leaned against the railing, the setting sun picking up the golden tones of his hair. When he turned to face me, a shadow blocked half his face, though it didn't diminish the way his eyes lit up upon seeing me.

I waited until I was one step up from him to stop and wave. He wrapped an arm around my waist and hauled me to him, chest to chest, thigh to thigh. I whimpered at the contact. He crushed his lips against mine, tongue swiping at the seam of my mouth until I plum forgot where we were. By the time we parted, I was breathless and wondering if we could skip dinner and just go back to my place.

"Ready?"

I nodded.

"*Class good?*" he asked as we walked. His hands moved slowly and simply for me. I'd learned ASL grammar differed from English. At this point I could focus only on recognizing the signs.

"*Yes, learn a lot.*"

"*That my girl.*"

Color me stunned on two levels: one, I understood him. Two, he called me his girl. Assuming I understood him. I grabbed his arm.

"*'My' girl?*"

He stopped and pulled me to the side of a building. Ferns climbed the red brick, blocking the harsh sunlight. My back pressed against the building, greenery cushioning my head and surrounding my peripheral. His body blocked the street, his face darkened by shadows, leaving us in a secluded green alcove in the middle of the city. With one hand he slapped his chest. "*M-I-N-E.*" Then he pulled out his phone.

Reed: I warned you about the caveman behavior; don't be so surprised. You OK with being mine?

The butterflies were back in my stomach, fluttering like they were stuck in a wind tunnel and trying to break free. I had never been claimed before; no one had gotten close enough to do so. And I had always felt unworthy. Not with Reed.

Along with those happy thoughts came dark ones I refused to acknowledge. The type of thoughts reinforcing my decision to stay single. That claiming me would only lead to pain as I couldn't return the favor. Thoughts I didn't want to ponder, not now.

I pulled him into me and locked my lips with his, licking into his mouth. He met me beat for beat before resting his forehead against mine. He took a few breaths, regulating his breathing, before pulling me along to the restaurant.

Val and Willow were already there, as well as three others I remembered seeing at the party. I was introduced to a tall guy with red hair who was in Val's interpreter program, a girl with thick black glasses in the Deaf Ed program, and a skinny I Should Have Been a Model Chick also in the Deaf Ed program.

The group signed and talked. I couldn't follow everything, not with the noise level of the restaurant and my limited ASL. But I didn't feel left out. I didn't feel alone. Even when Reed wasn't paying attention to me, the table held a sense of connection. Especially when Willow caught my eye and signed something indicative of the noise level.

It amazed me how visual the language really was. I Should Have Been a Model Chick told a story, her whole body getting into the action. If I didn't know better, I would've pegged her for a drama major. Her face all but glowed with expression. She turned in different directions, hands moving large and small. I had no clue what she talked about, but I got the excitement of the story. Furthermore, it was damn cool to watch.

Reed squeezed my thigh. When I turned, he had his phone in his lap and pointed to it. I grabbed mine out of my bag.

Reed: You OK? Not left out too much?

Me: Yup, I'm good.

I put my phone away and prepared to watch more of the fascinating story, but Reed grasped my chin and turned me toward him. His eyes roamed over my face, studying me. I had no idea what he was looking for, but he nodded and let me go.

Me: What was that?

Reed: Wanted to see if you were lying.

Me: Why would I lie?

He looked at me, thumb tapping against his phone, as if wrestling with himself.

Reed: Why do you have headaches?

I stared at my screen. A prickle traveled up my spine, a prickle that said there was a reason for his question. There was a real answer to his question. Did he see something I didn't?

Me: I don't know. I've had them for as long as I can remember.

Reed: Like Sunday morning?

Me: Sometimes, yes.

When I dared to raise my eyes I found him staring at me again. He reached out and brushed a thumb over my temple.

Reed: Not normal. Worries me.

Me: Don't make me regret telling you this. No one else knows this. Not D, not my family.

That awarded me a look of shock.

Reed: Why not?

Me: We don't talk about things in my family. The headaches are my burden. I handle it.

Reed: What does your doctor say?

Me: Nothing.

Reed: You haven't told your doctor?

Me: Why would I tell her? She asks about changes, not the status quo.

Reed: How often do you have headaches?

I had one right now threatening to break through my skull and strangle him.

Me: Drop it.

Reed: After you answer the question. How often?

Me: You going to break up with me over this?

What a stupid girly thing to type. Though I saw through my own words to the depressing truth. Sooner or later I'd damage our relationship. I wasn't destined to be loved. This text was a subtle yet premature push to remain detached. He blinked at the message then reached over and intertwined his hands with mine. He shook his head no several times before pulling me in for a kiss. This kiss wasn't hot, and it wasn't sweet. Rather, this kiss said he wasn't going anywhere.

How did things get so serious so quickly? I had two choices. Either I held him off, kept him at bay, and continued to depend on only myself. Or I could risk my heart and let him in. No, risking my heart was out of the question. I wasn't sure I had one to risk. Could I be honest? Did I want to be honest with Reed?

Me: Almost all the time.

Reed: Now?

Me: What do you think?

Reed: How bad?

Me: Was mild, but all this poking and prodding from you has it up a few levels.

He let out a breath and ran a hand down his thigh.

Reed: I'm sorry.

Me: Not your fault.

He leaned forward and pressed his lips to my temple. My eyes closed on reflex, and my head quieted down.

Me: Keep that up. You have a way of removing the pain. Or making me forget about it.

He flashed me a smile.

Reed: Anytime.

Chapter Eighteen

Reed

STUDYING NEXT TO Carli was not an easy task. The closeness was enough to drive me crazy, especially as her intoxicating body wash or perfume or whatever made me extra aware of her. But that wasn't what got the best of me. She fidgeted more than an ADHD kid.

Or at least, more than the one in my class, whom I'd never seen still for longer than two minutes.

If it wasn't brushing her hair out of her face, turning a page, or writing a note, then it was the subject change. If her hands were still, then her feet were in motion, flicking her pillow. She had all her classes stacked up beside her bed as I graded a spelling lesson from my students.

I stared at one word, clueless as to how my student came to this spelling, when Carli closed yet another book. She flipped to her back, no books in hand. She rubbed her eyes, blocking off her view of me. I took in her long eye-lashes sticking out from under her palms, down to her pink lips. Her slender neck exposed and called for my touch. Unable to stop myself, I visually traced the dips and curves of her body.

Yeah, my focus wasn't much better than hers. At least not right now.

I checked my watch, noting her last subject attempt lasted seven minutes. And right about now, I enjoyed her frequent changes. I shifted closer to her. "*Pain?*" Please, no pain. After eyeing her body up and down, I had no will to continue grading.

She shook her head. "*No, C-O-N-C-E-N-T-R-A-T-I-O-N.*"

I leaned over her, close enough that the heat of her body revved my engine, and looked at her books. I could never switch subjects as easily as she did, and she had the issues?

I looked back at her, struggling to keep some space between us. Maybe a little less homework would be a good thing. "*Break?*"

Her lips curved into a smile I wanted to taste. "*Please.*"

I let my body dip closer to her. She squirmed under me, and just like that, our bodies were flush. Good to know we were on the same page. I leaned in, aiming for those tempting pink lips. As my fingers brushed her hair back, she closed one eye and flinched.

Damn, I must've hit her hearing aid.

"*Come on, give me your hearing aid.*"

She stared and the blacks in her eyes shrunk.

If she didn't trust me with her hearing aids, what was she doing about to at least make out with me on her bed? "*Trust me. T-R-U-S-T me.*"

I needed her response to this, in more ways than one. Because if she didn't trust me, we weren't having sex, and my hard-on was going to be pissed.

She studied my eyes, and I waited. Then she pulled her aids out. They were warm from her body heat as she deposited them in my hands. I reached over her, placing them on top of her book pile. Then I settled my body against hers, brushing the top of her ears.

Hearing aids or not, it didn't make one difference to me. But I liked Carli like this, natural. As she was made. I pressed my lips against her temple, kissing a path to her ear. I followed around her earlobe, nibbling on her small silver hoop earring.

Not done, not even close, I worked my way to her jawline. Only my path got cut short when she shifted and her lips met mine.

I sunk into this little piece of heaven she offered me, her soft lips moving against my own. I needed to touch. I needed to feel. I needed her. I ran my hand up her flat stomach, over the mound of her breast, stopping at the peak. She hardened in my hands. I had the sudden urge to speed things up and just take her already but forced myself to remain in check.

I wasn't the only one wanting more. She tugged at my green shirt. I left her lips and yanked the shirt over my head and threw it on her floor. The woman below me smiled, eyes heavy with desire as they trailed a path to my chest and stomach.

I wanted a view of my own. I pulled her long-sleeved tee shirt off her. Her mouth moved, and she squirmed, as if she hadn't expected just that. I wanted to make her squirm again, for me. I yanked her bra cup down and sucked her tight peak into my mouth.

Her skin tasted smooth and sweet, and her nails dug into my back. I helped myself to a second tasting, just as delectable as the first. Her body rose to meet mine, making the cramped quarters in my jeans downright suffocating.

I needed to make sure we were on the same page here. I reared up on my elbows, and as soon as I did, she rolled out from under me. Before I could blink, she tossed a condom on the bed. I couldn't stop the smile if I wanted to. Then I remembered what she had written the last time we were alone together. I pulled my phone out of my back pocket.

Me: Not that I'm complaining, but why did you point out birth control last time?

I handed her the phone, or started to. I got distracted by her head on her pillow, her bare breasts full and perky.

Carli: You seem to have that effect on me. I am on birth control, but I always use condoms as well. I learn from my parents' mistakes.

My father would love this girl. And that was the wrong thought to have right about now. Then the rest of her words filtered in. *Mistakes?* I raised my eyebrows.

Carli: My parents never wanted kids, used the pull-and-pray method. I'm unwanted daughter #4.

The pain in her eyes was something I could relate to. I shoved the phone back into my pocket and pulled her to me. "*I want you.*"

Her eyes drifted to the part of me making the extent of my statement obvious.

I laughed. "*No, not*"—I put my hands on her breasts, doing my best not to squeeze or rub or lose myself in them—"*I want* you." I indicated this by touching her head and then her heart.

This was more than just sex. But I had never been a just-sex guy.

I kept my hand on her chest, nestled between two mounds I really wanted to explore some more. My eyes remained on hers, waiting for her to register what I signed. Before an answer appeared on her face, she gripped my shoulders until our bodies met, kissing me. In her lips and her tongue, I tasted her emotions. Something I signed definitely clicked.

I settled against her and let our tongues swap all those crazy sentiments. My hands wandered, taking in smooth skin inch by inch. When I reached her pants, she angled her hips and bit my lip. I laughed against her mouth as I slid my hand into her panties and inside.

My heart rate doubled; she was more than ready, and so was I. Her eyes were closed, and I kept my hand busy while I pulled off the rest of her clothes and mine. If I didn't do something soon, I was going to last exactly two seconds.

She still had her eyes closed, a very happy smile on her gorgeous face. I prepped the condom, my hands shaking. Too damn long. I positioned myself between her legs as her eyes opened. She took in my entire body, then propped up on her elbows.

"*Your T-U-R-N.*"

I dropped my head down, doing my best not to make this moment an epic failure. I searched for something to communicate with, but my pants were on the floor, and I had no idea where her phone was. I grabbed a notebook and pen from her nightstand.

Val told you about Beth. If you touch me, it might be game over. I'd like to make a better impression than that.

And I was an idiot for sharing that much, but I had no blood flow left in my brain.

You've got nothing to worry about.

I threw the paper on the floor. *Thank God.* She wrapped her legs around me, shifting her hips, the invitation clear in every inch of her. I kissed her, hard, in a mad attempt to gain some footing, before sliding inside.

She felt good. So good I could probably have come with little effort from either of us. I laid my head on her neck, struggling to keep my breathing out of hyperventilation zone. She shifted, sinking me in farther, then stopped, allowing our bodies to be joined in a way that felt meant to be.

I pulled back, just enough to sign, "*You feel good.*"

The answer was clear in her eyes, and I almost thanked her right then and there. "*You two.*"

I smiled at her incorrect sign, grateful for the small amount of laughter taking me off the cliff's edge. I reared back and pushed back in. One push and her eyes rolled back. I knew I still wouldn't last long, but at least she was already there with me.

I continued moving against her, inside her, each push blowing a brain cell I had no desire to reclaim. Just when a small window of prolonged stamina grew from my desire to keep this going, she clenched around me. Her mouth opened, the pleasure on her face apparent. I was a lost man. As her body continued to quake, I pushed in one last time before collapsing in her arms.

Instead of pushing my weight off her, she wrapped arms and legs tight, not giving me an inch to move in.

I kissed her neck and created enough space to sign, *"You're beautiful."*

She smiled and pulled me back down for a kiss. I reached over for the paper and pen.

Think you can concentrate now?

Carli laughed and pushed at my shoulder. I got off her, even though I didn't want to. She began to collect her clothes, scratching her head as she tried to figure out which angle I'd tossed the articles in. I had no clue, so I stayed on her bed, watching her creamy skin disappear under fabric. She finger-combed her hair and put her hearing aids back on. Then she caught me staring, still naked. Heck, I hadn't even gotten rid of the condom yet.

"What?" she asked, her cheeks blushing.

I didn't know what to say. I wanted to bask in the moment before karma caught up with me and fucked up my life again. If I had pissed off any gods by having sex, I knew nothing was coming right now. Maybe later it'd kick me in the ass. But for now all remained peaceful.

I kissed her and got dressed myself. We tried to get more work done. Only now the room had that sweat-and-sex-tinged smell to it. Carli lay beside me, and I knew exactly how she felt, how she squirmed. What she tasted like.

Hmm, I hadn't done that yet.

I leaned over her and kissed her neck, wondering what the hell had gotten into me. Oh, that's right—her. She angled her head, giving me greater access. In no time our books were forgotten, and I proved I did possess better stamina.

I also let her touch me, but only because her eyes begged.

BY THE TIME I made it home, the stars had come out. I couldn't catch them in Boston, but in Somerville a few managed to poke out from the buildings and streetlights. I took a deep breath of the cooling air as my jacket fluttered against my back. The dark leaves of the thinning trees rustled in the wind.

The light was on in the kitchen, and I steadied myself, readying for the third degree Val was so good at. I checked the street and spotted Willow's Beetle. Shit. She was worse than Val.

I took the steps two at a time and opened the door. Val and Willow shared an overloaded bowl of ice cream. Multiple mounds, hot fudge, and so many toppings I couldn't figure out the flavor of ice cream. I grabbed a spoon and straddled a chair. With my spoon raised high, I asked the question with my brows.

Val sighed. Willow pushed the bowl to accommodate me, and I dug in. Flavor: mocha chip.

"*I don't think he needs the ice cream,*" Val signed to Willow.

I'd let them pick on me for too many years. "*I don't. It looks good.*"

Willow leaned back and slow clapped, hearing-style.

"*Finally?*" Val asked, more than a little shocked.

I stole a cookie from the ice cream toppings. "*I'm not dead, just cautious.*"

Willow squirmed in her seat. Val leaned back and looked at the ceiling. "*About time. Wow.*"

I reached for the bowl, but Willow held it out of reach. "*Details first.*"

"*I don't kiss and tell.*"

"Shit," she mouthed as she put the bowl down, and I felt the table groan as she slid the ice cream back my way.

Val smirked. "*How about fuck and tell?*"

"*You have your own girlfriend.*"

Val puffed out one cheek and stared at the ice cream. Right. Sweets and chocolates and two moody females. I went two years; they could handle a week.

"*What a pity,*" I signed.

"*And look: the sky hasn't fallen; the world hasn't ended. No awful tragedy has befallen us all,*" Val signed.

I shoveled another spoonful of ice cream. This one had a gummy bear in it and something minty. "*Wait until morning.*" On that thought I pulled out my phone. One text awaited me.

Carli: You left one of your students' papers here.

I grinned.

Me: Guess I'll have to come back tomorrow and get it.

Carli: Guess so.

Willow, nosy as ever, read over my shoulder. "*Looks like tomorrow will be a good day as well.*"

I took another bite of their ice cream before tossing my spoon in the sink. "*Good night.*" In my room I tugged on my shirt, ready to pull it over my head. Instead I sniffed. It had that light floral scent of Carli. I pulled it back on. I'd shower in the morning.

I pulled out my wallet and my keys, dropping them on the bureau. I palmed my phone and turned it around and around in my hand. But I couldn't do the one thing I wanted.

I wanted to call Dad.

I sat on the edge of the bed, thumb tapping the phone. I wanted to tell him all about Carli. I wanted to watch his cheeks turn pink as he warned me about safe sex and all that bullshit.

I wanted to see him.

With a deep breath, I scrolled through my text messages. I passed conversations I'd had for the past two years to the one still bolded. Untouched. For two years my phone had been yelling at me about an unread text message. With one tap, the reminder would vanish.

I clicked open my father's last text and scrolled up until I found the last one I sent.

Me: OK

Very profound, this last text I sent to my father. I looked at the ceiling. At the picture on my wall of the three of us at my high school graduation. To the window covered by a flimsy curtain.

It was time. I was done being haunted by my past. Carli had helped, even if she didn't realize it. Even if I couldn't bring myself to tell her a damn thing about him.

Dad: In life, different things hold different importance. Wealth, health, shiny new cars. Love is most important. Hold it close. Treat it well. Wealth, health, shiny new cars can be replaced. Love can't.

I stopped there, ignoring the other messages for now. A tear rolled down my cheek. I turned my head toward the ceiling.

"Sure, love is important. That's why we don't hurt the ones we love by driving into a tree at midnight." I stared straight ahead, forcing air through my constricting lungs. Tears fell down my cheeks. I looked back up. *"And yes, I'm crying. Because I love you, and I miss you, and you aren't here to celebrate the good or the bad. What were you thinking? What the fuck were you thinking?"*

I kicked off my shoes and my pants and climbed into bed. I missed the good feelings I had when I was wrapped around Carli. Much better than the aching hole in my chest.

Me: Maybe I should get my paper now?

Carli: LOL. Miss me?

Me: Yes. You would not believe how big my bed is compared to yours.

Carli: You'll have to show me sometime.

I wiped the last of the moisture from my eyes. The ache in my chest morphed into an ache in my groin.

Me: Tmr?

Carli: Can't. 8:00 a.m. class on Monday. I'll never make it back to campus.

I was in my classroom by eight, but I let her stay in her little undergrad bubble.

Me: What are you doing next Saturday?

Carli: Sleeping in your bed? ;-)

I laughed.

Me: Bed. Yes. Sleeping optional.

Carli: Good night, Reed. Until tmr.

Me: Good night.

I plugged my phone into its charger and fell onto my bed, not bothering to get under the covers. I fell asleep with a smile on my face.

Chapter Nineteen

Carli

THE MURKY GRAY sky refused to shed any warm sunlight down below as I waited outside my dorm building. I zipped my jacket up past my chin in an attempt to ward off the chill. A skinny tree stood nearby, an iron fence surrounding the narrow trunk. Trapped. Much like I felt, waiting to head home for Thanksgiving break.

Matti's beat-up Honda pulled up to the building.

"Hey, sis. Ready for another week in hell?" Matti, my emo-goth psycho sister. We were close, due to the technicality of being Irish twins. Though we weren't much alike, especially as Matti had purple hair, a couple of tats, and a couple more piercings.

"Bring it." I dumped my bag into her backseat.

"How's the boy toy?"

Leave it to my sister to completely halt my entry to her car, to the point where I still had one foot on the curb. "Boy toy?"

Matti gave me her wolf smile. "Don't tell me you haven't?"

I ignored her as I climbed in. Matti flipped her blinker on to merge back into traffic. Then she turned her blinker off to stare at me and my utter silence. "You have?"

I rolled my eyes. It had been a month since we started having sex. If Mom wasn't expecting me, I would've stayed at my dorm or gone to spend time with Reed. The latter was the most tempting.

Matti put the car into Park. "You have; you've had sex."

"I lost my virginity years ago."

"Yes, but you've had sex with the deaf guy." Matti's voice suggested inquiry into a winning scratch ticket.

"His name is Reed."

"Fine, you've had sex with Reed."

I couldn't help it. I grinned like a Cheshire Cat.

"Scale?"

My grin grew wider. "He's broken the scale. I can't come up with a number high enough."

"Damn. Does he have a brother?"

I shrugged. "He's adopted, so possibly. But he grew up an only."

Matti leaned back and sighed. "You ever think about that? Not having three annoying sisters?"

"I'll take you annoying sisters over Dad any day."

Matti wagged a finger. "Smart baby sister. Ready for hell?"

"Bring it."

A half hour later, Matti dropped me off at Mom and Dad's house. "I'll be back tomorrow. Mom roped me into being here at the ass crack of dawn to help with the pies." Matti shuddered.

"Good, you can wake me when you get here."

She stuck out her tongue as I grabbed my bag and headed up the cracked path to the front door. I took out my key and let myself in, waving Matti off.

Inside the house was dim, only the outside light shining through the white wood blinds. "Mom? I'm home," I called out.

"Kitchen," came my mother's voice.

I dropped my bag by the stairs and passed through the living room into the kitchen. I found Mom elbow deep in Thanksgiving prep, the small box television airing some soap opera.

"Hi, baby girl," Mom said, not stopping what she was doing. "How's college?"

"Good."

"Studies going okay?"

"Don't they always?" There was no room for stupidity in my household. Dad was smart. Mom was smart, so all four of us had to be smart. If we weren't, Dad lectured us, and Mom retreated further into her fantasy world.

"Good girl. Hand me the eggs, would you, dear?" She still hadn't looked my way and already gave me orders. In her mind I was probably the pretty, perfect daughter of one of her soap characters.

I opened the fridge, always bursting at the seams with food, and pulled out the carton of eggs. It was like a game of Tetris as the bread on top shifted and settled into the open space. "Good, now go on upstairs. I'm sure you have tons of homework to do." Mom grabbed the eggs, eyes glued to her recipe.

Reason number 550 why I don't cook: Mom never taught me. In order to obtain perfection, my studies took longer. My sisters could achieve the same level in half the time, which put more pressure on me to rise up to the Reynolds standard. I'd sit at the dining room table with my book while she taught my sisters. Or I'd be upstairs with multiple books while the family enjoyed their time below. Matti insisted it wasn't happy times, but tell that to the girl forced to study even when her brain needed to quit.

I grabbed my bag and brought it up to my bedroom. A burst of cold air greeted me when I opened the door, courtesy of the one window cracked open. I rubbed my hands together and closed the window, pulling my sweater closer around my body for warmth. Thanksgiving was still too early for the heat to be on at home. I had little chance of the room warming out of frostbite zone.

I blew warm air on my fingers before pulling out my phone.

Me: My bedroom is freezing. I need your warmth.

I glanced around the room, still half ghost town from Matti moving out and sparse even on my side from all the stuff I took to college. It didn't feel like home. My dorm felt like home. This felt like a boardinghouse.

Reed: What's the address? I'll come warm you up.

Already feeling warmer.

Me: Won't work. Only Andi brings men home. The rest of us keep the penis carriers far away.

Reed: Am I only a penis to you?

For the first time ever, my room began to feel warm.

Me: Much more than that. Though I do enjoy the penis-related activities.

Reed: Seriously, tell me the address.

Me: LOL, down boy. I'll be back in Boston before you know it.

I unpacked my bag and took out my books. In my dresser I found my fingerless gloves, a must-have for surviving a night in the Reynolds abode. With nothing else to do, I wrapped myself in a blanket and got started on my homework.

THANKSGIVING WAS…THANKSGIVING. Dad planted his butt in his chair and watched the game. Mom and my sisters cooked a feast. My nephews ran around while Andi's latest tried to keep them in line.

And me? I sat at the dining room table huddled into myself for warmth against the frosty interior that may have been colder than the outside. In fact, I would have preferred to be outside. At least then I could put on a coat rather than claiming my scarf a fashion statement. In front of me, I had a single book set up. I wasn't allowed to study in my chaotic way around my parents. My methods were too abnormal, too messed up. It didn't make sense to my father and therefore was forbidden. So I took the one with the most reading and gave myself breaks by trying to follow the conversation or text Reed at his mom's.

"Carli!" My dad's barking shook me out of staring blankly at the page. "You're almost graduated. Enough milking this studying crap. Get your ass in the kitchen and help out."

I slammed my book closed. "Yes, Dad."

My sisters froze in the kitchen. Mom, being Mom, continued on without even acknowledging Dad had spoken. Andi gave me a backrub as I wedged in at the cramped kitchen counter. Matti shot me a sympathetic look from the opposite counter. They set me up with tasks they knew I could handle with my limited cooking skills.

At least I was finally warm.

When dinner was ready, we all settled down at the table. With the exception of Dad, who had a plate prepared for him and set up on the snack tray in front of the television. The conversation stayed soft, so as not to disturb Dad and the game, and thus hard for me to hear. I picked at the turkey on my plate.

Not for the first time, I wondered what Thanksgiving would be like if I could hear. If my ears weren't impaired, I wouldn't be bored out of my mind and desperate to not overeat. I could talk softly to my sisters. I could feel connected.

Or, on the other hand, if they signed we wouldn't need to talk soft. We could be loud with our hands, and I wouldn't have any trouble understanding.

While I couldn't pick up the conversation, I could pick up on other details no one realized I knew. Like how Matti, with her purple hair covered in a crocheted cap much like newborns wore, kept her head down and herself quiet, in contrast to her usual loud personality. Lesli, my second-oldest sister, sat stiffly on the hard wooden bench, one hand dug into the small of her back. She wouldn't say anything about the pain, just as I wouldn't with my head. Whatever she used for coping, she'd do it when she returned home.

I spent the rest of the meal daydreaming about a very different Thanksgiving celebration with a certain male whose texts kept me entertained.

Chapter Twenty

Reed

MY AUNT'S BLUE Prius sat in Dad's spot. Two damn years and his missing car still hit me like a brick to the head. I shoved thoughts of Thanksgiving past down into a deep box, then shut it tight. Outside I took in a breath of the cool fall air before grabbing the paper bag filled with squash and potatoes.

The smell of turkey and stuffing greeted me at the door. I took a moment to let the scent fill my system. I shifted the bag to my other hand and made my way into the kitchen. Mom's and Aunt Toni's backs were to me. From the bopping of their heads, music must have drowned out my sounds. I reached for the light switch and flicked.

Mom spun around, a wide smile on her face. Her curls were held back by two clips, and she wore a flowered apron over dark pants and a teal shirt. She came over, wrapped her arms around me, and kissed my cheek.

Aunt Toni washed her hands and then greeted me as well. Her blond hair fell to her jawline. She had my father's hair, my father's eyes. Like each time I saw her, the empty part of my heart tugged. She patted my cheek as I finally set the bag down on the table. "*Your mom says new girlfriend?*" Her hands moved slowly and awkwardly, hesitating as they switched from one sign to another.

I turned to Mom and raised my eyebrows. Mom smiled and went back to cooking, angling herself to see any signs. She was a worse gossip than my friends.

Aunt Toni waited with the patience of a saint. She started signing the same time my parents did, but since she wasn't around me all the time and had a demanding schedule, she still signed like a lower-level ASL student. Her heart was in the right place though.

I cleared my throat, but before I found out if I remembered how to work my vocal cords she placed a hand on my shoulder and shook her head.

"*What? Is my speaking that bad?*" I teased. And realized I signed slower around her than I did around Carli.

Aunt Toni smiled. "*Terrible.*"

I shrugged and picked up the oversized squash. After I grabbed the cutting board and thick knife, I found my aunt staring at me. "*What?*"

"*Girlfriend?*"

I laughed and put down the knife. In as simple language as possible I explained about Carli. When I finished, both women exchanged a glance. A spoken conversation passed between them, but due to the angle of their faces, I couldn't pinpoint a word.

I stomped on the floor.

Mom turned to me, grinning widely. "*We agree. You're falling in love.*"

I rolled my eyes and picked up my knife, only to turn back to them. "*We recently started dating. It's way too soon for that.*"

Mom shook her head once she stopped voicing for me. "*Not with that look in your eyes.*"

I got enough of this shit from Val and Willow. "*Your point?*"

Mom kissed my cheek. "*It's been a long two years. Nice to see you happy again.*"

I sunk the knife into the center of the squash, working the ends to get it through the thick flesh. I couldn't deny Carli made me happy. A part of me desperate for healing had begun the process. That thought launched an idea in my head. It rolled, a pinball batted back and forth and lighting up the board. By the time the squash shared space with the turkey in the oven, I let the ball drop.

I washed my hands and eyed the two women in front of me. The closest family I had left. "*I had a few texts from Dad the night he died.*"

Aunt Toni's hand flew to her mouth.

"*Same as the video message?*" Mom asked. The hidden implication: I hadn't looked at them.

I nodded. "*I read the first one a month ago.*"

Mom's eyes filled with tears. "*Carli really is good for you.*"

I held back a laugh; if she only knew.

"*When do I get to meet her?*" Mom signed.

"*Never.*" I grinned, fully into teasing mode. "*Your grandchildren will be a mystery to you.*" I paused as I reached for the peeler. What. The. Hell? Where did that come from? They joke I'm falling for Carli, and I supply the whole children concept?

I looked at my mother, at an absolute loss for words or anything. I needed to toss out a joke or peel the potatoes. But my own words now tumbled in my head, playing the pinball game, hitting the bumpers to remain in action without a single flipper moving.

Mom smiled, her brown eyes warm and full of emotions. She walked over, caressed one cheek, and kissed the other. I had dug my hole deep with this one.

"*After that, 'soon' is the right answer.*"

"*After that, 'never' is the right answer.*" I turned, but Aunt Toni stomped her foot.

"*The right* answer," she mouthed with her signs, which was good, because she didn't sign "answer." She stumbled with her hands and turned to Mom before speaking the rest.

Mom interpreted. "*The right answer is when you become comfortable with those words.*"

I shook my head and picked up a potato. Nosy bitches. Yet I loved them anyways. As I peeled and chopped, I wondered how that conversation would've gone if Dad were still with us. He'd be peeling with me, probably questioning the ETA of said grandchildren. Mom would've slapped his arm, pointing out the shocked look or whatever was on my face proof of no immediate plans to procreate. Then Dad would have gotten sappy, he would've…

No clue. I'd never been serious about someone before. I'd never been an adult and dating someone with him around, and Beth certainly didn't count.

Aunt Toni bopped her head as she chopped vegetables. She wasn't married, but she was the younger sibling. Maybe she'd know.

"*What would Dad say?*" I asked.

"*Related to what?*" Mom asked.

I rolled my head. And dug my hole even deeper. "*What I said earlier.*"

Mom smiled, a sad laugh in her eyes. "*It's possible he would've cut himself, thinking that was your way of telling us you already got Carli pregnant.*" Her shoulders laughed. "*After the blood was cleaned up, and your constant reassurance you weren't becoming a father, he'd think about it. By the time the turkey was cut*"—her eyes traveled to the ceiling—"*he'd want to meet her. Once you promised, on the life of that fictional first child, he'd explain how wonderful love can be. To take your time, but be sure to follow your heart and not let go.*"

Aunt Toni wrapped an arm around Mom, the moisture in her eyes agreement enough.

My own eyes felt a little wet. "*Thank you,*" I signed to Mom.

Several hours later, I waved good-bye to our last guest and closed the front door. Mom had retreated to the kitchen, and I went to help her clean. I found her sitting at the table, two cups of coffee in front of her. I took the opposite seat.

Worry lines creased her forehead. "*Related to Dad*"—she turned her mug until the handle faced her—"*did you read the letter?*"

Wasn't expecting that. "*Val?*"

Mom nodded. "*I'm your mother. You get a letter from the adoption agency. I'm allowed to be curious.*"

"Not yet."

"*Do you plan to read it?*"

I shrugged. "*Why would I read a letter from a family who gave me up twenty years ago?*"

Mom sipped her coffee. "*You don't know why.*"

"*Dad had a lot of theories.*"

"*Yes, he did. None of them true. He was scared. We heard stories of biological parents stealing back adopted children. And he'd seen situations where genetics trumps how a child is raised. We love you. All we ever wanted was the best for you. If anything, we had a bad taste in our mouths, finding a language-starved three-year-old and wondering how they could have ignored your needs.*"

I reached across the table and squeezed her hand. "*Thank you for adopting me.*"

She grasped me when I tried to pull back and kissed my knuckles. "*I'd pick you again a million times and never regret it. Same as Dad.*"

I stared at the steam rising from my mug and took a sip.

"*You might get some answers if you read the letter.*"

"*You say the same thing about the video message Dad left.*"

"*Both are true. You don't have to do anything with the letter, only read it.*"

I took another sip of the too-hot coffee for distraction. "*I don't want to read something I don't want to know.*"

Mom sighed. "*Knowledge is power. Don't live in fear of the unknown.*"

"*I'll think about it.*"

I did think about it. I thought about all the deep shit of the day as I drove back to my apartment. Carli, Dad, and the letter, a fucking weight on my shoulders. In the darkness of my room, I stretched my neck in much-needed solitude. Val and Willow were spending the night at Willow's parents'. I had the place to myself, perfect for brooding without prying eyes.

By ten I was fed up with thinking and scrolling through my Facebook feed in the dark of my bedroom. My eyelids grew heavy. One minute I was watching a video in ASL and the next my phone vibrated in my hands, jerking me to attention. A text from Carli scrolled across the top of the black screen.

Carli: You still awake?

Me: I am now. You OK?

Carli: Getting better. I'm outside.

Me: Locked yourself out of your parents' house? ;-)

Carli: Nope. I'm outside your place.

I blinked as her words registered through my sleepy haze. Carli was here? I flipped on the lights as I made my way to the kitchen door. Outside, a car sat next to the tiny patch of grass. Carli made her way to me, and all the troubling thoughts faded away.

"*Why not—*" and I pointed to the doorbell as she climbed the last few steps.

She paused midstep, in pajama bottoms dotted with penguins and her bulky winter coat. She pointed to me, her ear, and shook her head.

I grinned, doing my best not to laugh at how hearing she remained after all this time. I gestured her in and pressed the button. Inside the kitchen, the receivers flashed.

Carli's jaw dropped open in awe, and she said something. She turned to face me, pointing to the light, eyes filled with wonder.

"*Yes.*" I closed the door and walked over to her. "*Why here?*"

She stepped into me, touched her cold fingers to my lips and then to a spot on her head. I didn't understand how I managed to help her, but it felt damn good that I could. I closed the distance between us and laid my lips to her head. My heart struggled against the confines of my chest, and the smell of her shampoo flooded my nostrils. I kissed different spots on her head and face until finally, finally catching her lips with mine. Everything I felt inside tumbled out, a pure passion ready to consume us both.

She felt it too, had to, when she climbed up me. I wrapped one hand under her rear, the other on her back. She clung to my neck and sunk in deeper to an already scorching kiss.

Something in the events of the day had created an urgency I rarely unleashed. I backed her to the wall as all sense of restraint burned to ashes. I wedged one leg between hers. The minute I did, she squirmed. I needed her closer. Yesterday.

I disposed of her jacket and collected the ends of her university sweatshirt in order to pull it over her head. And blinked at what I found.

"*Two?*" I asked, taking in the blue sweatshirt she still wore. She was always cold, but two?

Carli glanced around, clearly looking for something to help us communicate. "*Home cold.*"

I suspected that was an understatement of colossal proportions. "*Pity*," I signed. Then I crashed my lips back to hers, fully intending to warm her up the best way I knew how.

Under her blue sweater I found a thermal shirt that matched her pants. She wasn't kidding about being cold. More determined than ever to warm her to boiling point, I snaked my hand under her shirt. I expected more clothing but found none, not even a bra.

She was going to be the death of me. Especially as she squirmed closer, her breast jiggling in my hand. She pulled my shirt over my head. I wasn't ready to let go of her just yet and allowed the shirt to dangle on my arm. I rubbed her smooth skin, and she stopped kissing me. She looked at the wall and then back at me, her eyebrows raised in question.

I hadn't contemplated that far, but now that she had...I smiled at her. Yes, the wall in the kitchen would be just fine. Take advantage of having the apartment all to ourselves.

Only I wasn't prepared. I could either carry her to my room or set her down and grab a condom. I looked at her. I looked at the wall. I held up a finger as I removed my leg wedged between hers. "*Stay.*" If I tried anything more complex, I'd be a blubbering idiot. Didn't matter if she had full ASL comprehension.

I jogged down the hall and into my bedroom, nearly fumbling with the condom in my haste to get back to Carli as quickly as possible.

Once I returned I wasted no time wrapping her back into my arms and crashing my mouth to hers. An urgency took over me, and I stripped her of her pants and underwear. Once the fabric left her feet, she slipped out of her shoes and wrapped her legs around me.

This woman always threatened to make me last a nanosecond.

She rubbed against my leg, the same urgency I felt displayed in each little shift of her body. She let go of my lips and pulled her final top over her head. My eyes ate up her body, every inch of her pale skin glistening in the kitchen light. I was rock hard and straining against my bottoms, and I needed the last barrier gone. I pushed and squirmed until my pants were around my ankles, then kicked them off. My entire body felt on fire, and I knew I was rushing.

I had passed cool ten minutes ago.

I bit the wrapper open and rolled on the condom. All the while, Carli remained pinned between my body and the wall, squirming enough to drive me crazy. I angled her and thrust inside, nearly setting off rockets at the sensation of her surrounding me.

Her head fell back against the wall. The expression on her face matched everything I felt. I pulled out and thrust back in. She dug her nails into my back. I pulled out again and pushed a little deeper. As I continued to move, time slowed to a halt. My heart thumped to the pace we set, our bodies slick against one another, my heart as connected to Carli as our bodies.

My body reared up, head and mind in sync. The tingling started, the warning bell flashing in the corner of my mind. But Carli hadn't come yet. In fact, she still writhed. I took her earlobe into my mouth, tongue flicking the lobe around her silver hoop. Her body arched into me before finally letting loose.

She drank me into her with her climax. I tried to fuel her, but two thrusts later I lost my own battle and let her body suck me dry.

That was... Wow.

I lowered us both to the floor, ending up flat on my back with her on my chest. Never had I experienced anything quite that mind-blowing. Something Dad had told me came to mind with sudden clarity: "*Sex is better when it's with someone you love.*"

My heart rate refused to slow. Dammit. Mom and Aunt Toni were right. I looked to Carli, still breathing heavily herself with her head on my chest, a beautiful smile planted on her face. "*I'm falling in love with you.*"

Dude, stop signing. I shook my head, hoping like hell that sign hadn't been taught to her yet and wouldn't be anytime soon. I kissed her, needing to taste her after a revelation like that.

She pulled back and crawled away from me, and I wondered if she knew. She returned with her phone, trembling at my side, skin breaking out in goose bumps. I grabbed the phone from her, part avoidance if she had understood.

Me: Why don't we get under my blankets?

Then if we needed to talk, we could. God I hoped we didn't need to talk.

Carli: I have to get back to my parents' house. They aren't too keen on missing children. So now I feel like a prick: Thanks for the sex, have to run!

I laughed at her note. Thank God! I hauled her up my body and kissed her.

Me: Stop by for sex anytime.

Carli: If I have a massive headache again tomorrow, you'll be seeing me.

My smile faded. Her headaches bothered me. Not just because I didn't want her to be in pain, but the nagging feeling that it was something else returned. I rubbed a hand over her forehead.

"*I'm fine,*" she signed.

I barely resisted shaking my head. "*You're always fine.*"

She disentangled herself from my arms and got dressed. I ran to the bathroom, disposed of the condom, and then grabbed my pants on my way back. I had just pulled them over my hips when she pointed to my pants with questions in her eyes.

My father raised a better gentleman than that, certain activities in the kitchen ignored. I picked up my phone.

Me: It's late; I'll follow you home.

Carli: It's Black Friday. The drunks are home on turkey hangovers, and the shoppers are making sure they get to the mall in one piece to fight over some item that's an additional 10 percent off.

Me: Where did Bitter Carli come from?

Carli: Welcome to Holiday Carli. I'm sorry. I normally keep this all inside. You're getting the nitty-gritty part of me.

What did it mean if her words only made me want her more? She pulled on her second sweater, and as soon as her head popped free, I held her face in my hands. I pressed my lips to hers, my heart pumping emotions I could no longer deny.

"*I like you. A-L-L of you. I'm falling in love with you.*" I rubbed my thumbs over her cheeks, letting the sign hang in the air, letting the scary emotions find purchase.

"*I like you too.*"

Her words hit a tender spot in my heart. It wasn't equal footing. I didn't think for one second she was where I was. But I wasn't ready to go there any further. Better this way. I kissed her some more, needing it to soothe the ache in my chest. Then I let her go, alone, after she promised to text me once she arrived.

I watched until her taillights disappeared down the street. I'd just handed over my heart to an unsuspecting recipient. And I had no idea what to do about it.

Chapter Twenty-One

Carli

WITH THREE WEEKS of the semester left, the pressure was on. In January I'd be full-time student teaching. A scary thought: my journey of being a full-fledged student ended in three more weeks. All too soon I would be on the other side of the classroom.

I couldn't focus on that at the moment. No, at the moment I needed to focus on my notes from Dr. Ashen's class. They were strewn all over Reed's queen-size bed as I tried to make sense out of what I'd jotted down when my head ached up to killjoy level.

Reed answered my frequent questions from his position on the floor. He leaned against his dresser, his own notes on his lap. The notebook passed between us like a hot potato, fragments of our entire relationship concealed between the pages.

He wrote and turned the paper around for me to read.

You really were half-asleep in class.

I nodded as I reached for the notebook. Killjoy level meant I fell asleep during break. Not my shining moment.

Yup. All I could think of was, how am I going to handle being a teacher if I can't handle a three-hour class?

Reed frowned at my note and moved up to the bed with me. I rested my chin on his shoulder, reading as he wrote.

You are amazing. You never let on that you're in pain, yet it's constant. Look at your work all over the bed. Insane, to me, but you found ways to make it work for you. Just think of a struggling student—how you'll be able to help them by being you, by being unconventional, by knowing there isn't a right and wrong way to learn.

My heart swelled at his words, at his support. At his utter acceptance of me. He didn't need Perfect Carli. He saw my flaws and for some reason wanted more. I pulled him to me, kissing him with everything I felt. Something inside multiplied, and divided, and yielded in a square root. The result? Confirmation that Reed had broken my ranking system. My heart had latched on and refused to let go.

He pulled back. "*No. Study.*"

I licked my lips in invitation, and he got off the bed like I was lava. I laughed and picked my work back up.

A few hours later, Reed had left to pick up dinner and I relaxed at the kitchen table with Val and Willow. Or rather, Willow, as Val was watching Reed leave.

"Okay, he's gone." She scurried over to the table. "Now, spill. You two look happy together."

I laughed. "I guess so. What's there to spill?"

Val tapped her fingers together before speaking and signing. "Let's see, Reed's more relaxed than he's been in years and has that perma-smile on his face." Val looked at me pointedly. "Which matches yours."

I felt my cheeks. Damn, she was right. "He makes me happy. He's unlike anyone else in my life."

Willow turned to Val and signed something voice off, something that included the same sign I'd seen from Reed Thanksgiving night.

"Wait, what was that?" I asked, and noticed my hands had moved with my voice.

"What was what?" Willow asked.

"That sign." I did my best to copy it. "I've seen that sign before. What does it mean?"

Willow and Val exchanged a look. "Where did you see that sign?" Val asked, caution in her voice.

I was missing something here. "Reed."

Both of them squealed and were back to voice off signing.

I banged on the table. "Hello, asking a question here. What does that mean?"

"Does Reed normally sign and not explain to you?" Willow asked.

"No."

"Did he explain this one?"

"No." And all the dictionaries were set up to search from English. I had no means of searching from ASL as I could with the Spanish I took in high school.

"Then we really shouldn't." Val grabbed Willow's hands and gave her a look that clearly said to keep quiet. Willow pouted but didn't come to my rescue.

"Come on. If the two of you are flipping out over this, shouldn't I have the same information? I've obviously shared something big. So now you two know something private, and I'm left clueless." I threw my hands in the air in frustration.

Val sighed and let go of Willow's hands.

Willow sat up straight. "Was this the sign?" She did what I had seen from Reed, her pointer finger moving from chin down and out to her hand.

I nodded.

Her effervescence faded and her face took on a serious tone. "What are your feelings for him?"

I rolled my head back and groaned. "How the hell does that relate?"

"It relates," Val said. "Have you two talked about your feelings for each other?"

"I don't see how…" The night in question came to mind, the look in his eyes, the shaking of his head after he signed the first time. "This"—I copied the sign—"has to do with feelings?"

They both nodded.

"Tell me," I pleaded.

"Answer my question first," Willow said. "What are your feelings for him?"

I took a deep breath. My emotions were classified information, even from myself. Sealed in a manila envelope and hidden in a vault. I needed something for Willow and Val and found the only explanation I had. "He's broken my ranking system."

"Close enough." Val got up, and checked out the window. "It means 'falling in love.'"

My mouth dropped open and my heart tried to climb out of my chest and hug Val.

Willow held up her hands. "Now, did he sign anything else with that? This might not be the full story here."

I tried to think, but my brain was suddenly scrambled and fighting over the combination of the vault. "There was something else. I can't remember what. Could he really be falling for me?"

"Don't sound so surprised."

"I am. I'm not the girl who guys like."

"Why, because of your ears?" Willow smirked. "Think about it. You're not disabled to him, or to us."

"I don't feel disabled around him. Or you two." The words came out before I fully contemplated them. I didn't feel disabled. My entire life I'd been forced to hide my hearing loss, felt less than because of it. Reed had changed more than my ranking system.

Val smiled. "Good. Now it's up to you if you want to show him you know what that sign means or not. Just remember, he thinks you don't."

I wasn't about to embarrass him. Not when I had no idea what my own feelings were. It was better that he didn't share the meaning of the sign. Saved me from being put on the spot.

My own feelings didn't matter. They were foreign to me and would prevent me from ever giving 100 percent of myself to someone else. Perfection issue aside, I plain didn't know how.

Chapter Twenty-Two

Reed

CHRISTMAS MORNING, I woke up in my childhood bed, under the green-and-blue-striped comforter I'd had since my teen years, once I convinced my parents I'd outgrown the trains theme they bought when they adopted me. The early light cast a half shadow across the room, changing the green walls into a pine shade. As a kid I thought it changed purposely for Christmas. I laughed at my younger self as I threw the blankets on the bed, called it good enough, and made my way downstairs. My nose carried me to the kitchen, where Mom stood flipping pancakes.

For nineteen years it had been Dad flipping pancakes. The man must have skipped sleep on Christmas Eve, because he always beat me. Or maybe I made a lot of noise, because as my sleeping habits changed so did his flipping ones.

The last two years we didn't have pancakes; Dad's passing was too fresh. I guessed time did heal most wounds.

Mom turned. Her mouth opened as her body jumped, and her free hand flew to her chest. I glanced behind me. "*I'm quiet today?*"

She laughed. "*Don't know. Music's playing.*" A smile crossed her lips.

"*Dad used to play music?*"

Mom's grin grew wider. "*Yes. Loud. Very bad music.*" Then the smile morphed into that sad smile one had when a happy memory of a lost loved one both warmed and tugged at the heart.

I crossed the room and pulled her into me for a hug. "*Merry Christmas.*"

She touched my cheek. "*Same to you. I thought it was time to get back to normal. If you can move on, so can I.*"

I shook my head and collected plates for the table.

After breakfast was eaten and gifts were exchanged, Mom got a faraway look in her eyes.

"*Something wrong?*" I asked.

She shook her head, watery eyes catching mine. "*I used to wonder what Christmas would look like when you were all grown up. Would you still come home? When you got married would you go to your wife's parents' house or here? And—*" She cut herself off and laughed. "*And this is inspired by your new girl. I'm sorry, but I see the look in your eyes, on your face. I know this isn't something light. And I can't help but wonder. Before I always kept my thoughts off you, talked with your father instead. But he's not here to tell me no.*"

I squeezed my eyebrows together. *"I'm confused."*

Mom sighed. *"What do adopted children do as they get older? Do they want biological children, the way most of us do? Or do they have the urge to adopt, to save another child like they were saved?"*

"Who says I want children?"

She threw a pillow my way. *"You teach third grade."*

"And send them home to their parents after I feed them lots of sugar."

Mom laughed with me. *"Humor me. Paint the future."*

I leaned back and sighed. *"I haven't been dating Carli that long."*

*"I know. I'm not asking what will happen. I'm saying"—*she gestured around the room—*"what do you see in five years? If you could paint your own future, what would it look like?"*

I pinched my nose, refusing to let any images form. *"I'm trying to imagine something too soon."*

"Five minutes. It stays here. If you beg, I'll slip something in your drink to make you forget."

I wanted to protest, but then I got a good look at her. The pancakes brought us both back to the past, reminded us of the missing member of our small tribe. She needed the hope of the future.

I'd be lying if I didn't agree.

I leaned back and looked around the room. Imagined extra stockings hanging, extra presents under the tree. And the image formed. Three extra stockings. Two children running around, playing with toys and creating that Christmas ADHD rush of excitement. I'd sit on the couch, coffee mug in hand. Next to me would be my wife, just as enthralled with the scene.

The image crystallized. My wife had light skin, brown hair, brown eyes. Carli. The kids…I couldn't see them, couldn't begin to imagine how genetics worked on a personal level. But in my head, in my heart, I knew they were blood.

Was this really five years in the future? Couldn't be. The kids were much too old. And Carli had a big family. With three older sisters, I couldn't fathom a quiet Christmas with my mom.

With a shake of my head, I brought myself back to the present, and registered on Mom instead. "*I always thought adoption or natural didn't really matter. Though if I did adopt I'd want to adopt a deaf kid. But…*" Did I dare share what I'd just imagined? "*I think I'd like to try for children I'd have a genetic connection with.*"

Mom nodded, a smile on her face. "*And the wife?*"

I sighed. "*Too soon for your crap.*"

She laughed. "*I knew I wanted to marry your father after two months. Took him a little longer. It's hard, being the one with your heart on the table. You either get the high of having the feelings returned. Or chopped into tiny pieces. But one of you has to be the first to put it out there.*" She shook her head. "*Sorry, I'm thinking of my life, not yours. You're twenty-three. She's twenty-one. Don't listen to me.*"

I scooted over to her side of the couch and wrapped an arm around her. "*I love you.*"

She patted my cheek. "*And the girl?*" I moved away as she laughed. "*Sorry, couldn't help myself. I'll be good. I promise.*"

"*I don't believe you.*"

"*Of course you do. If I don't start behaving, I'll never meet her.*" Mom rubbed her hands together, the teasing fading. "*But if you want a genetic connection, all you have to do is read that letter.*"

I rolled my shoulders back. "*You don't know who he is or what he wants.*"

"*Neither do you.*" She sighed at my unmoving hands. "*You've already lost a father, maybe—*"

"*No. No maybe. I have one father. The man who raised me. Not the one who gave me up.*"

"*Did you throw out the letter?*"

No. I hadn't. "*Why are you pushing this?*"

"*Because I know you. You keep all this pain stuffed up inside. You shut yourself off, keep others at bay. Does Carli know about you father? Either one? You can't get that future until you let others in.*"

"*I let her in.*"

Mom gave me that look, the one clearly telegraphing *stop the bullshit.*

I let my eyes drift to the beige carpet. "*I'm enjoying my time with her. No agenda. No restrictions.*"

Mom nodded. She got my meaning. Dad had a million rules for everything. Even dating. A small smile formed against my will. "*What would Dad say about Carli?*"

Mom laughed and pulled a knee to her chest. "*Oh my. Well, for starters, he'd be convinced you were going to end up with those children by next year, probably twins. Which means Carli wouldn't finish school, or find a job, or some-thing. And both of you would be stuck living here, with the kids, who would be rambunctious little devils. And your work would suffer. Forget about the masters."* Mom shook her head. *"Such a drama queen."*

She was right. Dad would have gone off on a tangent like that, running with a little hint of a concept and leading into a personal apocalypse. Each time he did, I would label him foolish, then alter my behavior.

Mom signed the same words Dad would've. Yet nothing changed. For the first time, the apocalypse didn't sound so bad.

Chapter Twenty-Three

Carli

CHRISTMAS WAS LOUD and overwhelming. We exchanged gifts and ate. Dad yelled. A lot. We were too loud. The boys were too rambunctious. Dad's gift from Mom sucked.

We all got quiet at that outburst. Mom just got up, grabbed the gift—a very nice sweater, the kind he wore all the time—and threw it in the trash.

Merry Christmas?

Needless to say, no one wanted me to stay at home. So when I mentioned I had a friend who lived closer to the middle school I would be student teaching at, they were fine with cutting my winter break short. And no, I didn't mention I was staying with Reed. Heck, they still didn't know I had a boyfriend. Mom could go back to pretending the characters on TV were her real family, and Dad wouldn't be bothered by the reminder of his imperfect daughter.

Therefore, at 2:00 p.m. on January 2, I pulled up to Reed's home and let out a breath of relief. My car was now in my possession for the semester since I would be commuting to a classroom full time.

God. Could I handle this? Could I really handle this?

I had always dreamed of being a teacher. But dream + reality didn't always yield a successful outcome. The closer reality came, the more I freaked. Bottom line, I had no clue if I could actually do this. My heart screamed "yes, teaching will be great!" Meanwhile my brain made a word problem out of coconuts and bananas and had me on hold to loud elevator music while she worked out a problem that made absolutely no sense.

All those coconuts and bananas went flying when a knock on my window had me jumping in my seat, still restrained by the seat belt in a this-could-have-been-a-crash movement. It was no crash, just Reed standing outside my door. *"You OK?"*

I nodded, shook the scattered fruit away, and got out of the car. I expected Reed to go for my lips; instead he went for my head, lips to the spot that always hurt the most.

"How know?" I signed.

"Your eyes."

I stared at him. Logically, it made no sense. Emotionally, it made perfect sense. How could he see what others couldn't?

He wrapped me in his arms, and I relaxed into him. Then a silly grin broke out on my face. For the next three weeks I got to live with him. I pulled back and kissed him while doing a little happy dance.

This might be the best break ever.

MY SEVENTH-GRADE CLASSROOM was on the small side, with twenty-five desks set up into five rows. Whiteboard, wall of windows, and a large imposing teacher's desk completed the room.

I wasn't convinced I wouldn't throw up.

"Good morning, Carli."

I turned around and found Heidi, my middle school cooperating teacher. It was her algebra class I was taking over.

"Good morning," I managed without my voice breaking. Good start.

"Are you nervous?"

I let out a shaky laugh and held up an unsteady hand. "A bit."

She gave me a reassuring smile. "It's going to be okay. The students are really excited to work with you."

Why didn't that make me feel any better?

My first week was observation. I worked on matching faces to names as I took in Heidi's teaching style. The students' energy carried me through the day. Until the last class, when halfway through my introduction my right hearing aid battery decided to die.

Shit. At least I kept the swear in my head. No time to panic, and no time to hide. Day one and the cloak was coming off.

"How about a fun fact about your new teacher?" I asked as I moved over to the drawer where my purse sat. "I'm hard of hearing and wear not one but two hearing aids." I popped out my right hearing aid and held it up for show as I found the battery packet. "And one of them needs a new battery."

I made a big production of changing my hearing aid battery, the first time I had ever done so. A thought for another time: this didn't feel awkward at all.

With the hearing aid back in my ear, and my purse back in the drawer, I addressed the class. "Any questions about my hearing?"

"Are you deaf without them?" came a boy in the back. Shaved head, dark skin. Xander.

"My left ear, pretty much. My right ear isn't that bad. I listen to music with my hearing aids off all the time."

Once upon a time I worried about how to handle my hearing loss in a classroom, the dreaded hearing aid battery dying being the top of my list. Now it didn't bother me. Sure, I knew my students would test my hearing, and I planned on talking with Heidi for survival skills. But I felt comfortable.

Comfortable. To have a hearing loss. Amazing.

What would my father say about that?

I found Reed at the kitchen table when I got back to his place, already doing work. He looked up and a huge grin crossed his face. "*How you?*"

I dropped my bag by the door, let my coat fall behind me, and curled up in his lap. Rather than sign anything, I brushed my lips to his, giving all my excitement another outlet.

"*That good?*" he asked.

I nodded. "*Not bad.*" I then tore off a blank page from his notebook and began writing about my day, not leaving the comfort of his lap.

crushed my lips to his, giving off my excitement another
outlet.

"That good?" he asked.

I nodded. "No, sad." I then froze on a blank page from
the notebook and began writing about my days not having the same.

Chapter Twenty-Four

Reed

THREE WEEKS MAY seem like a long time, but it was over
in a blink of an eye. Just as I grew accustomed to my bed
partner—one who always shivered, complete with ice-
cold toes and nose—she was gone. Campus sprang back
to life, and Carli returned to her dorm. Her student teaching demanded more of her time than her classes had, but I
was used to that kind of schedule. She surprised me when
she continued with ASL. Point in my column, I supposed.
Though she could've been taking it for herself as well.

Before I knew it, February had arrived. I thumbed
through my phone, bringing up my father's video message. I didn't play it, even though I wanted to see his face.
Happy birthday, Dad. Why'd you kill yourself? Only I
doubted his message would match the question.

Mom and I felt it wrong to continue celebrating his birthday, so we let it go unacknowledged. Though I knew damn well she was having a bad day. In fact, Val mentioned our mothers were out together, blowing off steam on their credit cards.

I did that last year. This year I didn't feel up to it. If only Dad had left a note, anything to answer the questions.

I thumbed my phone again. Maybe I had the answers after all. Instead of opening his text or video message, I put the phone down and stared out the window. *Hey, Dad. Was it worth it?*

I SAT AT the Laundromat, a.k.a. Mom's basement. In exchange for wasting time and quarters, Mom let me continue the typical college student behavior. To thank her, I did anything around the house she couldn't. Fair trade.

Today I fixed a squeaking door in the upstairs bathroom. I tried to explain it didn't bother me, but Mom still had me tweak and adjust it until she considered it quiet.

As I waited for a load to be done, I took out my phone.

Me: Surviving?

Carli was home with her family, celebrating her father's birthday. She was less than thrilled to go. She stayed with me, in my bed, longer than she should've, and then she had to race around getting ready to go.

Carli: If by "surviving" you mean bored out of my mind and contemplating long division just for the hell of it? Yes.

I leaned against the rumbling machine, smiling like an idiot at my phone.

Me: But you love long division. Need some numbers? ;-)

Carli: Not yet, but soon.

Me: I can tell you a story. My students came up with a great one I need to translate into English anyways.

Of course, I didn't have my notes with me. The story was memorable enough. Any English I managed to get on my phone would only help me put it all together.

I waited as the dryer rolled behind me, the motions vibrating my back. Not a bad massage, all things considered.

I brought the story to mind, forming the signs I remembered. A story about a stray dog, a protective tree, and a fairy godmother. The godmother was evil, the dog had superpowers, and the tree was the mother-like creature. My students had taken over the classroom as they imagined their story, complete with standing on their desks to show the tree's height, and one dramatic fall to the floor from the godmother, saved by the superhero dog, that almost resulted in a visit to the nurse.

And my phone was silent.

Me: Silence. Are you waiting for the story or telling me to keep it to myself?

I tapped the dryer as it rumbled to a halt.

Me: Busy with family?

She must've been. I pulled my warm clothes out of the dryer, folding before I placed them back in the basket to transfer home. My phone sat on the ledge. The screen didn't light up, the phone didn't vibrate. Nothing.

An uneasy twinge plucked at my gut. I never had a good feeling about her family. Guess, like Dad, I had heard too many horror stories.

I brought the laundry upstairs. Mom put down her book when she saw me. We chatted as I tried to ignore the unease. I didn't say a word to her. This was me, being paranoid. My girlfriend wasn't responding to my messages. What an idiot. Yet the unease lingered as I headed out to my car. My phone burned in my pocket, but I resisted checking it during the drive home. The feeling refused to dissipate. I needed Carli to find a few seconds to tease me; then everything would right itself.

Once I parked, I checked my phone. No messages.

Me: OK, now I'm worried.

I shoved the phone into the back pocket of my jeans and looked around. Everything was normal in my neighborhood. I laughed to myself. I watched too many scary movies. Carli would have me stuck on chick flicks if I wasn't careful.

If only that thought succeeded at evaporating my nerves.

Chapter Twenty-Five

Carli

A QUICK COUNT of the cars told me I was the last to arrive. I pulled up along the grass in front of the house. Oh well. At least I could blame the Boston traffic.

I grabbed the blue gift bag out of my backseat and walked up the steps to my childhood home. My feet dragged along the bumpy asphalt, but I pushed forward. I wanted to be anywhere but here. Namely back in bed with my boyfriend.

Ungrateful daughter much?

Inside was the same old scene: my nephews ran around, sisters talked in the living room, Mom camped in the kitchen cooking, and Dad sat in his chair in front of the television.

Fun times.

I made my way around the room, greeting everyone, before ending up in the kitchen, the quietest spot on the first floor.

A while later the noise level grew, in part due to Dad raising the volume of the television. I was so bored I almost started counting the kitchen tiles, even though I already knew the answer = 356. I turned my attention to my phone, grateful for the small amount of entertainment Reed provided.

"Carli," my father yelled, and I nearly leaped out of my skin. "Goddammit, how many times do I need to call your name before you hear me?"

I put a hand on my chest to try to contain my racing heart. "Sorry, Dad. I don't hear well."

Dad stood, small potbelly protruding as he did so. "Then you need to try harder."

My hands shook, but I was tired of hiding what I was. "There is no trying harder with hearing loss. I don't hear well. End of story."

He puffed out air. If he had a gold nose ring he'd look like a bull. "You have hearing aids to fix it."

"I have hearing aids to amplify sounds. That's it. I hear your television and everyone talking, but I can't decipher words." Of course, I could now hear a pin drop because everyone had gone stark still around me and someone had muted the television. Didn't stop Dad from yelling.

"You should be able to decipher your own name rather than have your head in your phone."

I don't know what came over me, but I answered him honestly. "I was texting Reed."

"Who's Reed?"

Crap. Too late to back down now. "My boyfriend."

Dad pushed up his sleeves and took two steps toward me. I was twenty-one, almost twenty-two. What difference did it make if I had a boyfriend?

"Why doesn't he call on the phone and be polite?"

I took a step back, not liking the crazed look in my father's eye.

"Everyone texts nowadays, Dad," Matti piped up.

Dad stopped, leered her way, and then turned back to me. This was my own father, but I no longer felt safe. I refused to quit and squared my shoulders.

"Reed's deaf. Texting is his way of calling."

Dad's face turned beet red. Out of the corner of my eye, I saw Matti with a hand over her mouth, shaking her head. Then I realized I had signed when I spoke.

"What's that nonsense with your hands?"

My nerves were replaced with anger. "Nonsense? ASL is not nonsense. It's a language I can understand. Even in loud places like this. There are so many resources out there for hearing loss—all I got was hearing aids and being yelled at to try hard—"

I was looking toward my sisters, my ashen-faced sisters, for some form of support as I finally stood up to the man who verbally terrorized us our entire lives. I wasn't facing my father when his arm reared back. I wasn't facing my father when he swung it forward. I wasn't facing my father when his fist collided with the side of my skull. The next words were beaten out of me. Literally.

I stumbled backward as a second fist clocked me on the other side of my head. My feet slid out from under me, and I crashed to the ground. My head hit with such force the room went dark. Pain worse than any headache I'd ever had brought me out of the darkness. I still couldn't see, could barely breathe. Huddled in a fetal position, I withstood more blows.

Then the world went dark once again, and I felt nothing.

When I came to, the blows had stopped. My eyes were open, and I wondered if they ever had closed. My ears rang, but I started to focus on the chaos of commotion that was our living room. Matti was by my side, encouraging me to stand. Tears drenched her face. "Come on, Carli. Come on. We're leaving. Let's go, baby sister. Let's go." She repeated her words like a mantra, almost in a blind haze. The words were soft and loud at the same time.

Andi and…dammit, what was her latest fling's name? Whoever he was had helped pull Dad off me. I wasn't sure, but it looked like What's-His-Name had taken a swing himself. Or someone did, because blood gushed from Dad's nose. Lesli had the boys held close to her as she ushered them out of the house.

Mom stood in the kitchen, back to us, washing dishes.

I tried to stand, but my head felt like it was splitting in two. Matti supported one side, Andi the other. And then I was outside and sitting in Matti's car.

"Keys, Carli. We need your keys," Lesli said as she squatted down outside my open door. She spoke loud, almost as if she had to repeat herself. But I'd heard her speak only once.

I nodded, then wished I hadn't as my head yearned to fall off. My purse landed in my lap. I pulled out my keys and handed them to Lesli.

She walked over to my sisters, all convening outside. Andi kissed her boys, then What's-His-Name, and took my keys in her hand, before making her way over to me. "You okay?" she asked, alert eyes taking in every visible part of me.

I didn't dare nod, but I could barely speak. "Yeah," I mumbled. Or slurred. I really wasn't doing well.

Andi pulled a still-blubbering Matti into a hug. "We need to get her home. You okay to drive?"

Matti nodded. "It's the same thing all over again."

"No, it's not. We stopped it. We stopped it." Andi pulled Matti in again, then squatted in front of me.

"How many fingers?" she asked, holding up her three middle ones.

"You have three, but that's the sign for six. Which answer do you want?"

She choked out a laugh. "Good answer." Then she kissed my head and closed the door.

Matti got in beside me. "We're going back to your dorm."

My head leaned against the headrest, but it still felt like it was moving. "Shouldn't I go to the hospital?"

Matti backed out of the driveway and started down the road. "Reynolds girls don't go to the hospital."

What? I lifted my head and the world darkened along the edges and got fuzzy. Matti's hand pushed my head back.

"Rest, Carli. I'll explain later. I promise. I'm so sorry. I'm so sorry."

I relaxed into the seat and resisted wrapping my arms around my head. Instead I focused on my breathing, trying to work through the pain.

That wasn't working as a distraction, so I pulled out my phone and saw the multiple messages from Reed.

Me: Sorry, bad family day. Very bad. Matti bringing me home now.

My thumbs moved in a sluggish manner over my keys. This wasn't good.

Reed: I thought you had your car?

Me: I do. Andi's driving it.

Reed: You OK?

Me: No.

Reed: I'll meet you at home.

I thought about typing *OK*, but I never quite managed the message. Instead I let the vibrations of the car lull my heavy eyelids closed. And jerked them open when Matti practically screamed and shook my shoulder.

"NO, Carli! Don't go to sleep!"

The way she shook me had my head playing tilt-a-whirl with razors.

"I'm awake. Don't do that."

Andi and Lesli arrived the same time we did. I took my keys back and let us into the building. I wanted my bottle of aspirin in the worst way.

In my dorm, D took one look at me and jumped up from the couch. "Holy shit, Carli, what the hell happened?" She was on me in a second, holding my face in her hands. I guess I looked as bad as I felt.

I shook my head. The contents jiggled and threatened to rip and break off. Both my hands shot to my head, desperate to keep the damn thing from rolling away. I blinked back tears as I struggled through the pain. "Meds," I mumbled and when I stumbled forward Matti and Lesli had me flanked.

"Do you know what meds she's talking about?" Lesli asked.

D, eyes wide, nodded, and ran into my bedroom. She appeared a moment later with my aspirin, and I took it into the kitchen to find a drink. My movements were akin to a drunken sailor, and I had to grab onto furniture for support. Andi was two steps ahead of me and had a drink waiting. I popped two pills into my mouth and chased it down with the water.

I wanted answers. I wanted to know why my sisters didn't seem as confused by this as I did. But I just couldn't formulate the words.

My phone vibrated again, a text from Reed saying he was there. I showed the text to D, and she ran over to the door.

A minute or an hour later—time wasn't really settling in—Reed entered the dorm. He took in my sisters. Then his face dropped when he saw me. He ran over to me and took my face in his hands, eyes scanning over each part of my face.

"What happened?"

I couldn't say it. I could barely hold my aching, throbbing, falling-apart self together. The concern on his face caused my own tears to swell and slide down my cheeks.

Reed let out a breath and pulled my head into his chest. He held me close, resting his hand gently on the part that normally hurt the most, though right now every part hurt the most. I snuggled in, desperate to have him work his usual magic, to touch the spot that took all the pain away. But nothing worked, not this time. His body vibrated with tension. There wasn't a doubt in my mind he would have retaliated for me. But his touch was gentle, comforting, as I sobbed into his chest.

He pulled one hand off me, and there was movement all around. My right ear pressed into his chest, my hearing aid muffled by his jacket. But my left ear received…nothing.

I picked my head up, finding myself on the couch. I didn't even remember sitting, never mind moving here. With one hand I grasped onto my hearing aid and pulled it out of my ear. The aid looked fine, small beige shell attached by clear tubing to a clear mold shaped to my ear canal. I opened the battery door, closed it, and cupped my hand around the shell to create feedback. I held it up to my right ear, and it made a high-pitched noise, letting me know it worked. I put the aid back in my left ear.

Silence.

I pulled the aid out again and rechecked. The battery still worked. I took off my right aid, put it in Reed's hand since he was watching my every move, and held my left aid up to my right ear.

More feedback. Crap. I tossed the left hearing aid on the coffee table and put my right aid back on.

"What's wrong, Carli?" Andi asked, worrying her bottom lip.

I looked at them all. They had information I didn't. "Why are you not surprised?"

My sisters each looked at their shoes.

A sickening realization overtook me. "This isn't the first time he's done this."

Reed moved to the kitchen table, where D had her laptop set up. I wasn't sure when that happened, but I was grateful he wasn't left out. Without his comfort, I scrunched down on the couch, pushing my head into the cushion. All I wanted to do was close my eyes and breathe out the pain, but I needed them open to see my sisters and hear their answers.

Lesli sat down across from me and moved a pillow behind her back. "I wasn't a klutz. I was pushed down the stairs."

Matti squatted in front of me, eyes filled with tears. "You were born hearing, Carli. You had single-minded attention and determination. Once you got into a project it was hard to get you out of it. One day you didn't respond to Dad. The rest of us were upstairs. Dad got pissed, yelled at you for not paying attention and…" She choked up.

My mind spun, and I reached up and held it in place. "I was born hearing?" And without concentration issues?

She sniffled and nodded. "We used to whisper to each other at night, back and forth, quiet enough so that we didn't get into trouble. Then after this incident…You never heard me again. You were four years old. I knew you couldn't hear well, but I was too afraid. I didn't say anything."

"Who else has he done this to?"

Andi stepped over. "All of us. You avoided Dad like the plague after your hearing loss. And since he waited until we were one-on-one, you never heard any of the other incidents."

"So you kept this from me?"

"You had a good childhood, Carli. We couldn't ruin that," Matti said.

"Good? Good?" I exclaimed, then groaned and settled back down. The noise was too loud even for my right ear. "I lived in the same hell you all did."

"You lived in a hell where your father didn't beat you for disobeying."

I opened my mouth but clamped it closed. I looked in each of my sisters' eyes. They'd protected me. And my head was really killing me. I rubbed the heel of my palm over the worst spot and curled farther into myself.

"Um," D began, "Reed's writing in all capitals that she needs to go to the hospital, and I agree."

I looked up and caught his eyes. "*Hospital, now,*" he signed, jaw tight.

My sisters shifted awkwardly. "She'll be all right," one of them said. I couldn't register the voice and didn't catch the mouth movements.

Reed pounded on the keyboard. "No, she's not all right," D read. "She's in worse pain than I've ever seen, and I've seen her flat on her back and rolling in pain. What happens when the shock wears off? And what about the fact she's been hit in the head?"

He stopped typing and caught my eyes. "*Head pain not normal*," he signed while D finished reading, her spoken words overlapping his signing.

I held his stare. He was right. It wasn't normal. And the room swayed a bit. I tried to stand, and my head attempted to change shape.

My sisters were closer, but Reed was faster. He grabbed onto me and pressed my head against him, kissing the top of my hairline. Only it wasn't going to be enough, not this time. I shook my head, and he stopped kissing me. Since I didn't move, he didn't let go.

I heard voices, but I couldn't make them out. When I shifted, I found D's laptop propped nearby so Reed could see it and hold me. Andi stood by my side again.

"He's right; she needs a hospital. We've never gone to the hospital. Not one of us. Not right away, at least. But Dad's never hit one of us as an adult. It's up to Carli what she wants to do."

What I wanted to do? I wanted my head to stop hurting. I wanted to never have been hit in the first place. Then I wouldn't have constant headaches. Then I wouldn't have trouble concentrating. Then I wouldn't have a hearing loss. I could accept myself if this was the way I'd always been, but now I knew that was a lie.

And I needed a diagnosis. I backed away from Reed. "*Hospital*," I signed.

His shoulders sagged forward in relief.

"Hospital," I said again with my voice. My sisters didn't appear nearly as supportive as Reed and D were, but they didn't stop me.

Chapter Twenty-Six

Reed

MY KNUCKLES TURNED white as I gripped the wheel. All my energy forced into my hands to keep my lead foot inactive. I needed to drive slowly, cautiously. Keep Carli safe. Keep Matti behind us. Anger, speed, none of that helped her right now.

Beside me Carli pulled down the visor, examining herself in the small mirror. I had no idea if she'd seen her face since the attack. My guess, no. Not in the way her jaw fell open. Not in the way she took in every discoloration.

She caught me checking on her. The devastation on her face nearly broke me the rest of the way.

"*I look bad,*" she signed.

If I lied, it would be obvious. "*Yes. Still beautiful.*" It was the truth. The bruises couldn't make her any less attractive to me.

I merged around traffic, careful to keep an eye behind me and confirm Matti followed. I was sure she knew where to go, but I needed her ears and mouth once we got to the hospital.

If I used my lead foot, we'd be there already.

I glanced at Carli, to find her eyes closed. A shock of fear slammed into my system. *Don't go to sleep.* Hand shaking, I reached over and shook her shoulder. She didn't move. Panic turned sharp and lung-crushing. Cars surrounded me on all sides, too many to pull over and no place safe enough to do so. But if Carli didn't move soon, I would, and get Matti to help me. If I had to, we'd call an ambulance and fuck up city traffic. With my eyes darting back and forth between her and traffic, I shook her again and made as loud a sound with my vocal cords as I knew how.

Her eyes fluttered open as if nothing big had occurred. As if she hadn't cut off a year of my life in those few short minutes.

"I'm fine," she signed.

No. She wasn't fine. Not even close. I kept one hand on her shoulder, afraid if I stopped she'd slide away from me.

Her hand covered mine. Cold. Clammy. Why weren't we at the fucking hospital already? I should have checked to see if Mom was on duty. If so, we could have taken a longer drive and got her to take care of Carli. I could've…

No. Closest hospital. End of story.

I pulled into the emergency room parking lot, and Matti parked beside me. We helped a disoriented Carli out of the car. I didn't know Matti, she didn't know me, and we couldn't really communicate. But she sent me a look I understood 100 percent. This wasn't good. We were both worried, and in that moment we didn't need words to know the same troublesome thoughts ran through our minds.

Matti won me over at the check-in desk. We stood there, all but ignored. She banged on the counter, mouth flapping, hands waving. The check-in staff looked up and followed Matti's gesture to Carli, propped against my side. Once Carli's face registered, the game changed.

They brought us to a half cubicle and started talking to Carli. Only Carli scared all of us by not answering. She'd open her mouth, but even I could tell she wasn't saying anything. Matti took over, talking while she filled out the paperwork. She gestured for Carli's wallet, and I got it out of her purse before Carli could turn around for it.

Next to the computer monitor, I focused on the white sign with multiple different languages all saying the same thing: interpreter. They even had the ASL symbol. I wanted to request one, but this wasn't for me; it was for Carli. It sucked that I couldn't communicate. But I wasn't the patient.

The paperwork took too damn long. Yet I knew Mom would yell at me for thinking such thoughts. Carli rubbed her forehead, laying her head against my shoulder. I could no longer see her face. Matti looked over, concern and anger on hers. From her gesturing and her lips, I guessed Carli's eyes were closed again.

Before I could react, a wheelchair appeared next to us. I got Carli into it, and her eyelids fluttered open, only to close again.

We moved to a small room. The nurse spoke to Matti and placed a pressure cuff on Carli's arm. Perk of having a nurse for a mother. I knew the reading wasn't good. No way was she being sent back to the waiting room.

They moved Carli to a bed in the ER. The white curtain pulled to give her some privacy. She stared at the ceiling, not moving when a nurse in blue scrubs entered. She spoke, presumably asking questions, and Matti did most of the answering.

After the nurse left, Carli caught my eyes. *"I'm sorry."*

I squeezed her hand. *"You have nothing to be sorry for. OK?"*

She didn't respond. She eased down to the pillow. I didn't know if she understood I had signed to her.

This was the most terrifying moment of my life. I glanced to Matti. I'd guessed her skin was the same shade as Carli's normally was, but right now it paled. And I hadn't witnessed the attack like she had.

Carli continued to stare and I placed my hand on her shoulder, needing to touch her, to comfort in some small way. Matti paced back and forth. I pulled out my phone.

Me: Are you OK? Should you be seen yourself?

I handed the phone to Matti, forcing her to stop pacing. She read the screen and shook her head.

Matti: I'm fine.

A small smile crossed my lips.

Me: I'm dating your sister. I know that trick.

Matti's eyes warmed when they met mine.

Matti: I don't like being here. I don't like knowing this happened. Again. I don't like anything about this situation. But physically I'm fine.

Me: And emotionally?

She lowered the phone and looked at Carli. I followed her gaze. Carli's eyes weren't right, as if she barely registered on anything.

Matti: Don't ask questions you wouldn't want to answer yourself.

Touché.

The nurse came back in and said something to Matti and me. Matti grabbed my phone as we were both ushered into the hall.

Matti: They need to speak with her alone.

Outside we sat down on the floor, our backs against the wall. I drummed my fingers against my raised knees. A few feet away, the nurse's station bustled with activity.

My phone vibrated, and I pulled it out.

Val: Willow and I are going to grab a pizza. You gonna be home? Is Carli coming over?

I banged my head against the wall and took a deep breath.

Me: I have no idea when I'm going to be home. I'm at the hospital. With Carli. Her father beat her up.

Carli was going to hate me for that. But I wasn't about to let her out of my sight. So either I would be staying with her at her dorm, which Val would need to know, or she was coming home with me, and Val could see for herself something wasn't right. Not at all.

Val: OMG! Is Carli OK?

I tapped my finger to the screen.

Me: Don't know. Don't think so.

Val: Do you need me to interpret?

Me: Carli can hear.

Well, maybe less, but spoken English remained her primary mode of communication.

Val: I wasn't talking about Carli.

Me: I'm not the patient.

Val: No, just the overbearing boyfriend who won't be able to communicate. I can leave here in five minutes.

Me: No. Matti's here, Carli's sister. I'll be OK.

Val: If you change your mind, or need anything, let me know. Willow and I will stay by our phones.

Me: Thanks.

A man in a white doctor's coat walked past and into Carli's room. My foot tapped against the harsh white tiles. I didn't like sitting outside. But it had to be done.

Matti barely moved beside me. She rubbed a spot on the inside of her wrist. Over and over again. Black ink marked the area, but wasn't smudged by her movement. I gestured to her wrist. She let go and held it out to me. In beautiful cursive the tattoo read: *The nightmare never ends.*

I wanted to say I was sorry, but that seemed too trivial and inconsiderate given the situation. Certainly not worth typing it out on a screen in the middle of a sterile hospital floor.

She gestured for my phone, then took out hers before sending me a text from her own number.

Matti: Not many people understand.

Me: I bet you have your own horror stories.

She pulled the purple crocheted cap off her head, fluffing up her purple hair.

Matti: Dad never liked an audience. Until today. But the sounds... Well, for those of us who can hear, they traveled through the house. I couldn't imagine how Carli missed it, but she did. Those sounds, and what I saw today, were just about worse than anything that man could do. Physically, at least.

She didn't meet my eyes after I read.

Me: Why are you sharing this with me?

A small ghost of a smile crossed her face.

Matti: Well, who you gonna tell?

I laughed. I reached out and put my arm around her, pulling her into my side. She placed her head on my shoulder, allowing me to give her some small comfort. Sure, we didn't know each other. But we both loved the woman in the room behind us.

The doctor came out of the room and stood in front of us. We both rose to our feet, mine still twitching. He began speaking, talking to both of us. I tried to catch a word or two, but I couldn't focus. Matti listened, talking back and forth with the doctor. He walked away, only to return a moment later with a yellow legal pad in hand, writing. He turned it to me when finished.

Carli has a concussion. We're going to do a CAT scan to rule out any bleeding in the brain.

He waited until I finished reading. I nodded, and he walked off. I reached for my phone, and when I finished typing, I handed it to Matti.

Me: Thank you.

THE GOOD NEWS: the CAT scan showed no bleeding or any other extenuating injuries. The bad news: it diagnosed Carli as having a mild traumatic brain injury. Since she was four. First time I'd ever been right and wished like hell I wasn't. Her headaches weren't normal—they were due to her brain injury.

Her concentration issues were also related. I hadn't pegged that one.

She curled up in the passenger seat, and I let her rest. One of my hands clutched the wheel; the other held Carli's. She agreed to let me take care of her. In fact, she almost seemed relieved. The day had faded away while we were in the hospital. Now the sky was dark and the streetlights shined. I didn't turn on the light in the car in order to communicate. Carli had been forced to stay awake and alert all day. I'd give her this small window to rest. Especially since I had to wake her every two hours.

I pulled up to my apartment and parked the car. In the dim light, I realized Carli wasn't resting; she was crying. Each time I thought my heart couldn't break further, it did, for her. I undid our seat belts and wrapped my arms around her, pulling her into my chest. I brushed her hair back, then rubbed my thumb against her damp cheek.

She looked at me, and I didn't know what to say, what to do. What could I possibly do to make up for what she'd been through? I kissed her, soft and sweet, doing my damnedest to let her know she was loved, cared for.

I wasn't one to rush, certainly not in matters of the heart. I'd been burned in that department before I could shit in a toilet. Times of trauma, of strife, made or broke a person. They removed whatever lens a person viewed the world with and forced the individual to look without any filter.

I was looking at Carli, bruises and all. She held my heart.

No longer temporary, if temporary was ever really an option. She had me. Forever. There was one match for my heart, and she was it. End of story.

I brushed her cheek again when I ended the kiss. At least her cheeks were now dry.

The kitchen light shone from the apartment. I hadn't even shut the door before Willow pulled Carli into a hug.

Val studied Carli's mangled face. "*You look awful,*" she said in both languages.

Carli turned to me. "*What did you tell them?*"

I shrugged. There was no way around the truth. Either I told them, or they'd be asking a hell of a lot of questions right now.

Carli turned to Willow. She pointed to her left ear. "*Can't hear…hearing aid.*"

I touched her shoulder. "*Same.*" I couldn't help but find some humor in the situation.

Carli stared at me and then began to laugh. Only her laughter soon faded and she held her head.

I hated seeing her in pain. At least this time I had an appropriate medication for her. I pulled out her OxyContin bottle we'd filled at the hospital. Then I grabbed a cup of water before handing both to Carli. She took out one pill and swallowed it down with water.

"*Do you need anything?*" Val asked.

Carli's large eyes met mine. Her mouth moved, and she pointed to me. A small piece of my torn heart mended. Foolish, really. Carli's own mending remained a long ways off.

In my room she changed into one of my tee shirts and climbed into bed. Her eyes met my clock and the time blaring proudly there: 11:00 p.m.

"*Wow, long day,*" she signed.

I placed a hand on her face. "*Yes.*"

Her eyes filled with tears. "*I'm sorry I'm broken.*"

Air brushed my eyeballs with how wide my lids had opened. "*What? No. You're not broken.*" I kissed her, soft and sweet, willing her to believe me. "*You're perfect.*" She was. Perfect for me.

Carli managed to find her phone.

Carli: Brain injury. Not perfect.

I stared at the words running across the screen.

Me: Perfect. Look at how far you've come with a brain injury. You are amazing.

How could she not see this? She was a college senior with an undiagnosed brain injury. Her crazy study habits were her way of coping. She'd come so far on her own where another person would have suffered without help.

I took in her face and the doubt clearly spelled out in her eyes. Then I took in the bruises, growing darker and stronger since I first saw her. To think, I had been doing my laundry when my girlfriend could've died. That long space between texts, coupled with the uneasy feeling, could've become permanent. Holding back, being cautious, and I almost had to say good-bye before saying I love you.

I ran my hands through my hair, the overwhelming reality of the day hitting like a punch to my own head. How close had Carli been to death? If her sisters hadn't interfered when they did, would one more punch have taken her from me? Was a difference that close?

Me: When I first saw your face...I could have lost you. This could be much worse.

Carli: I don't know if I can work. Ever.

Me: Sleep. Rest. Don't jump to conclusions before you have time to recover.

She nodded, and I collected our phones before placing them on the nightstand. I climbed into bed with her, pulling her close. Carli normally squirmed a bit before settling down. This time she was asleep before a single squirm.

I lay there, arms wrapped around her, staring at the light glow of electronics on my ceiling. I shifted my head, placing it gently on top of hers, to the point where we barely touched. *I almost lost her today.* My heart sped up. I wasn't sure I could survive losing Carli.

Chapter Twenty-Seven

Carli

As instructed, Reed woke me every few hours. I moaned, grumbled, and batted him away each time. I just wanted to stay asleep. He forced me to answer a question or two, then let me go back to slumber land.

The light shined through the shades by the time I woke on my own. I rolled over to see the clock: eleven thirty. I had slept, on and off, for twelve hours. For a full minute—I checked—I lay there, staring at the bumps on his ceiling. I did nothing, not a thought in my head, not a desire to do anything. Then the sticky surreal sense of reality floated back to me. Normal wasn't normal anymore. I wasn't normal anymore, if I ever had been. With any luck I had survived the absolute worst day of my life. Time to retire that list.

My hands glided over my throbbing head. I didn't dare apply more than a whisper of pressure. I felt broken and battered. Even with the soft touch I found the swelling from my father's blows. At least my neck still connected it to the rest of my body. But my thoughts…jumbled together. Like I climbed up and down at the same time, moved forward yet walked backward, ran yet lay down. Stuck in an Escher painting. I tried to focus on something, anything, but the thoughts kept floating past, sometimes at warp speed.

My left ear felt blocked. I snapped my fingers by my right ear and heard the sound. Then I snapped them by my left ear. Silence. I put my finger in my ear and wiggled it around. No difference.

If my left ear didn't work, if my brain didn't work, how was I supposed to be a productive member of society? How could I teach without a clear brain? How could I teach without two working ears?

Congratulations, Carli. You've made it to your senior year of college. Thanks to your father, you are now destined for a life on welfare. Lucky me.

The sudden urge to run away, from everything and everyone, overwhelmed me. I lifted my head, only to have a freight train of pain start at the back and rocket to the front. Pain traveled everywhere, so intense I tasted the bitter metal of it. With slow movements, I put my head back on the pillow and curled up into a tight ball to protect myself from the outside world.

Protect myself. When the pain got bad, I always curled up, I always protected myself. Not from the pain, I now realized, but from experience.

My father deserved his own beating until his head hurt like mine did. Until his back hurt like Lesli's did. Until he knew fear like all his unwanted daughters did.

Tears spilled down my cheeks when two hands joined mine on my head and warm lips pressed into my hair. Reed took me into his arms and held me close as I soaked his tee shirt. I grasped onto his shirt, wanting to climb into him, anything to take away this pain. This reality. When I calmed down and let go of his shirt—leaving wrinkles in my hands' wake—he fetched my meds. I didn't fight him. I just took them.

"How...feel...today?"

I rubbed my hands over my eyes. Processing the signs was like squeezing my brain into a vise.

"Awful."

"Want..."

I knew this sign. I'd seen it before. I'd used it before. But I had no clue what it meant. Tears slid down my cheeks again. I reached toward my phone, and Reed retrieved it for me.

Me: Can't focus, can't concentrate. Sign hard. I'm sorry, so sorry.

He leaned on the bed and kissed my forehead, lips pressing with determination. Then he pulled back and looked at me, speaking without words. Only I could no longer follow the words. He picked up his phone.

Reed: Second day always worse. Rest up.

He tucked the covers back around me and left me to rest. I stared at his dark wood furniture and let my mind drift to a happy, desolate place. Sleep didn't claim me, but neither did boredom.

I, Carli Reynolds, was as good as a vegetable.

Later—again, I had no clue how much time had passed—I heard something I couldn't quite place. The door opened a crack and a hand reached in, flicking the lights on and off. Willow stuck her head in. "Want…?" she said in both languages. I understood the *want* only because of her signs. My right ear tried to process the rest and failed.

I shifted myself upright and was thrilled to find my pain down to a normal level.

Normal meant I still had pain. Lucky me.

I pointed to my hearing aid. Willow—who stood patiently waiting for me to get my head into some sort of functioning order—grabbed it and handed it over, before joining me on the edge of the bed.

"I can't look good."

She laughed, her voice now discernible. "Oh, you don't. If you ever want someone to think Reed's mean to you, now's the time."

"I don't know what's going to happen from here. I can't hear. I can't focus. Reed tried signing to me, and I couldn't process the words."

"You were just beat up. Let your body heal first. This all might be temporary. Even the headaches usually last only three to six months."

I glared at her. "I've had mine for almost…almost…" $22 - 4 = ???$ "Since I was four." Why couldn't I do the math? My breathing hitched, and my brain stuttered and refused to work.

Willow grabbed my arm. "Calm down; it's okay. Breathe. We did some research. For starters, don't try to work your brain this week. Take it easy. Let your brain heal. Give yourself time. Don't worry yet. Promise me."

I nodded. "But work, school..."

"You're on break this week, no school. I'll give your father this much credit, at least he has good timing."

The door opened and Reed stuck his head in. "*You hungry?*"

Was I? Had I even eaten yesterday? "I should be," I said and signed without even thinking about it.

"*What do you want?*"

I shrugged.

He came into the room and brushed a thumb over my lips. "*Pain less?*"

"*Yes.*"

"*Good.*"

He gave me a kiss and left.

"He's worried about me," I said to Willow.

"He's pacing like a 1950s father in the maternity ward."

My eyes flew to the closed door. He'd been as affected by this as I had. I didn't need to wallow in self-pity. Willow was right; I had to let myself heal. I could try to behave normally.

"Help me up."

Willow did as I asked. My feet touched carpet, supporting my weight in spite of her assistance. I made my way into the kitchen, where Reed pulled together something for me to eat. He paused when he saw me. I walked right into his arms and put my head on his chest.

Whatever he held clanged to the counter as his arms went around me and held tight. Protective. Here I was safe. He let out a breath, like he'd been holding it for a day. He probably had.

I looked into his eyes. *"Food later. Help shower."*

He signed something to Willow, but I didn't pay any attention. Then he helped me into the bathroom. I took my hearing aid off and placed it on a high shelf to stay dry. The fullness of my bladder finally registered, and I forced Reed to turn around. He gave me an amused smile, but obeyed. He prepped the shower while keeping his back to me, then disrobed and climbed in after me.

First time I had a man in my shower, and I wasn't allowed to do anything. The hospital had put me back in the "no pounding" scenario.

I did need his warmth, his touch, and I pressed my naked body into his. The water rained down on my back. Steam filled up the room. Reed held me close, muscles bunching from restraint. Between us, one part of him didn't give a damn about the hospital restrictions.

I raised my head to his, lifted onto my tiptoes, and kissed his scruffy jaw. He held still, but I kept kissing until he relaxed and kissed me back. The warmth flooded from every direction, and a feeling of belonging blossomed. I hadn't been wanted by my father, and I had the scars to prove it. My mother did nothing to protect me. My sisters were just as damaged as I was. But this man gave me all of him.

As the kiss heated up, he pulled back.

"No, we can't."

"*Sorry. You, me, feel good.*" Dammit. Not quite what I wanted to say. "*You M-A-K-E me feel good.*"

He cupped my face, and brown eyes so full of emotion met mine. "*I love you.*"

My heart squeezed. And froze. No. No. This wasn't what I wanted. Wasn't what I needed. Didn't he understand? Couldn't he understand? He had eyes. He had to see.

I pulled back, out of his grasp. "*I broke, damage. You no*"—I tried to make the sign for love, but couldn't—"*want.*"

He stepped back to me, placed one hand on my cheek. "*Yes. I want you. Yes. I love you.*"

I closed my eyes to try to keep the moisture inside, but a tear broke free. And since the water hit my back, I couldn't use it as an excuse. "*I broken, so broken.*" I was. Reynoldses weren't made to love. Proof was in my father's hands.

Reed placed his forehead against mine, then pulled back to sign. "*Not broken. Not to me.*"

I shook my head as more tears streamed down my cheeks. I had always suspected I wasn't wired for love. Now I knew it to be true. Reed was best to get away from me. Find someone who could love him back. Find someone who wasn't a fucking mess.

More tears fell. I may not be capable of love, but I still wanted this man. Right now he was the only good thing in my tilt-a-whirl-from-hell life. I rose onto my toes again and wrapped myself around him, kissing him with everything I had. I could only hope he knew he was special to me.

The first real smile in twenty-four hours crossed his face, possibly the most beautiful thing I'd ever seen. *"No sex."*

I laughed and dropped my head to his shoulder. He grabbed the small shampoo I kept at his place and gently, so gently, massaged my hair, cautious of my scalp. He must have found the lumps, as his demeanor grew somber.

Soap came next, though he didn't offer to let me take over. When he got to my breasts, my whole body wanted to liquefy. No pain, no ringing in my ears, no lack of concentration plagued me at that moment. When he moved on, I grabbed his hand and moved it back.

He shot me a sexy-as-hell grin. I expected him to pull away. Instead he stepped into me, hands slipping over my erect nipples, and found my mouth. Hot and sweet, his hands and mouth were my own piece of heaven.

His breaths were fast when he pulled back. Eyes locked with mine, he moved one hand south, and I quivered when he reached my belly button. And kept going. My body was more than ready to accept any part of him, but I grabbed his arm to stop him.

"Not me only, not again."

That awarded me a laugh. *"Yes. You anytime. You alive, in my hands."* He signed something else, something about me being enough for him and not needing his own release if he could take care of me.

I whimpered when his hand touched my stomach again and spread my legs in invitation. He wrapped one arm around my back for support. His other hand rubbed against my entrance before slipping inside. Everything in my body concentrated on the one spot that felt oh so good. I clutched onto his shoulders for purchase in a world I felt completely lost in.

He moved slowly—no fast movement for my poor head—yet I still climbed, fast. As I got close he moved his hand from my back to my head and crushed his mouth into mine. It sent me flying, but also kept my head safe as my body unraveled from his ministrations.

When I came back to earth, I pulled back enough to sign. "*I thought you said no?*"

He laughed and kissed my temple. "*Oops.*"

Chapter Twenty-Eight

Reed

I LEANED AGAINST the counter and breathed in the bitter scent of ground coffee beans. In the living room, Carli and Willow watched *Penelope*—again—and Val buried her head in a textbook.

Me? I needed coffee and planned to mainline it for the rest of the day. I had managed about three hours of sleep, all interrupted. Or less. I needed my alarm only once to wake Carli. The rest of the time I waited in the dark as the red LED lights of the clock slowly inched through the night.

Even now I struggled to keep my eyes off her. The angry red and purple bruises cut me deep at each glance. The dazed look in her eyes cut me worse. The research Willow had done all pointed in the same direction: Carli needed time. But like Carli, I was anxious to get her back to normal.

As the coffee dripped and the movie played, I checked my phone. Again. Everything on repeat. I had sent Mom a text, asking her to call when she got home from work. She hadn't responded. Payback for the night Dad died when I didn't answer my phone for hours.

Mom wouldn't do it on purpose, but in my head I considered us even.

I held my mug of black coffee, steam billowing, by the time she texted me back. I had her call my cell and slipped into the bedroom, knowing Val and Willow could take care of Carli.

I propped my phone on my dresser and sat down on the bed once I answered the call.

Mom greeted me with a, "*You look like hell.*"

"*I didn't sleep well.*" Well, hardly at all, same deal. "*I'm sending you a picture. Put on your nurse's hat and give it to me straight.*" I fumbled with my phone and sent Mom a picture of Carli's discharge papers.

Mom's face fell as she read, then popped up to mine. "*Who? What happened?*"

"*Carli. Her father beat her.*"

Mom's hand flew to her chest. "*She OK?*"

I nearly laughed. "*You're looking at her discharge papers.*"

"*That's only half the story.*" But she picked up her phone again and squinted at the screen. "*How is she now?*"

"*Watching a movie with Willow. She's not herself.*"

"*She's allowed. Her body's been through a lot of trauma.*"

I plowed a hand through my hair. There needed to be a magic phrase, something I could do to get her back. To heal her. To rid that haunted, distant look in her eyes. I stared at the floor, trying to process everything, when Mom waved and caught my attention.

"*It's hardest being the healthy one watching.*"

I nodded, and she explained what she knew of brain injuries and concussions for the next twenty minutes. No bull, just the facts. One message repeated over and over: Carli needed time to heal. Mentally. Just like her face needed time to recover from the bruises, her brain needed time as well. And may need much longer than the bruises.

"*Text if you need me. I'd rather meet Carli on better terms, but if you need a nurse, I'm here.*"

"Thanks, Mom."

She eyed me up and down. "*You're a good man.*"

I raised an eyebrow. "*Why? Because I forced an abuse victim to go to the hospital?*"

She shook her head. "*No. Because you take care of the woman you love.*"

I nodded and ended the call. She'd already pegged my feelings. No use denying it.

LESS THAN A week later, I helped Carli put away her belongings in her dorm. She stood in the middle of her small bedroom with a face that screamed "*lost child.*" She rubbed her temples and a deep-seated worry settled into my chest.

"*You OK? Want me to stay?*" I asked. Only her eyes remained distant, not looking my way. I waved until her eyes met mine. "*Want me to stay?*"

She shook her head, a stubborn streak crossing her brow. "*Thank you for the help. But I need myself.*"

I forced a smile I didn't feel. "*OK.*" If I stayed any longer, I'd bring her back home with me. In order to respect her wishes, I had to leave. I kissed her once and then walked out of her dorm.

Once I closed the door, I let my head connect with the wood and let out a breath. I felt…off. Unsettled. I couldn't explain the roaring emotional roller coaster I was on, couldn't pinpoint why I felt this way. Regardless of internal emotional turmoil, Carli wanted time alone. End of story.

Back home the place felt open and empty. I pulled out a chair and sat at the kitchen table. The unsettled feeling wouldn't dissipate, and my nerves ran raw. The smart thing to do would've been to go out for a run, but even my legs rejected that idea.

I thumbed through my phone past all the different threads of text messages, until I landed on the oldest. Dad's. His temper was a slow coil he held in check. His hands would slow down, and the force would show on his face. I couldn't imagine him lashing out.

I couldn't imagine what had actually happened to Carli.

My father would never have hurt me. I wasn't his blood, but he never treated me as anything less. Carli's father had four biological daughters and beat them all.

I scrolled through his messages until I found the next unread one.

Dad: Love is unconditional. Love can be slow to realize or a quick onset. Mom was slow, cautious, step by step.

You were instantaneous. I saw your eyes, and I didn't care what problems you had. You were mine.

I put the phone on the table and looked up at the ceiling and the ugly rectangle fluorescent light. Two years and he managed to have the right words for the situation.

I played the last two sentences in my mind: *I didn't care what problems you had. You were mine.* Two years ago, I wouldn't have gotten those words. Now I felt them. I knew them. Carli wasn't instantaneous, but she wasn't slow and cautious either. She was fire, burning through my resolve. Whatever setbacks the attack gave her didn't matter. I wanted to be there for her, to help.

The door opened, and Val came in. She looked around the empty kitchen. "*Carli back home?*"

I nodded.

"*You OK?*"

I scratched at my cheek, hairy after a week of not shaving. "*Worried.*"

Val cocked her head to the side. "*You love her.*"

"*You just recently figured that out?*"

She smiled. "*No.*" The smile faded. "*Her recovery will be hard.*"

"*I know.*"

I fiddled with my phone, still with Dad's message on screen. The table vibrated, a bang, not from the phone. I looked up to Val's large eyes. "*You finally read your father's texts?*"

"*I read one a few months ago.*"

"*When?*"

I kept my smile in check. *"When I wanted to tell him about Carli."*

Val squeezed my wrist, then read the screen. I didn't try to stop her. *"Wow."* Her eyes shot up to mine. *"He really did kill himself."*

"I should title these 'Life Messages to My Son, Sent through Text.'"

"What about the video?"

"Not yet." I wasn't ready. It would be the last time I'd see my father.

"He proves blood isn't everything. Your dad was a good man. Carli's father should rot in hell." Val's brown eyes turned cold and harsh. *"She should stab him in the heart."*

I laughed. Weight lifted off my shoulder, even as my hands clenched with the desire to do as Val suggested. *"Want to help me?"*

"In theory? Yes. In reality? It's her decision."

"I don't like that."

Val stood and placed a hand on my shoulder. *"You have to."*

Chapter Twenty-Nine

Carli

REED HADN'T SHAVED since the attack. The length of his beard gave me a sense of time lapse in a period of my life when everything blended together. When I felt as though I had lived in hell for hours on loop, those prickly strands insisted I survived longer. But break was over, and tomorrow he'd shave. I wanted to ask him not to. I needed that sense of stability when my world had none. Instead I let him get back to normal, when I knew I never could.

My sheets chilled my bare feet as I climbed into bed that night. I huddled into myself for warmth, shivering with the covers pulled up to my chin. Each little twitch of my body sent a stab of pain to my head. Twitch. Stab. Twitch. Stab. I curled up farther, pressing my head into the cushion of my pillow. I had taken my OxyContin, but the damn meds weren't doing their trick. Which I suspected was more to make me forget about the pain than mask it.

I tossed and turned, more uncomfortable with myself than my position. Eventually sleep did claim me, only for the rude awakening of my alarm clock going off before dawn.

In a daze I went through my routine and headed to my car. I hadn't checked on it since I'd parked it at my parents' house. Andi obviously had her own head on straight, because I found my car safe and sound in student parking.

I got behind the wheel and took a deep breath. I could do this. I could be normal. Today was no different from two weeks ago. The only difference was a diagnosis I was now aware of.

And no hearing in my left ear.

I shook those thoughts aside and got into traffic. Radio off, I kept my attention on the road. I hadn't driven since the day of the attack. I clutched the wheel, focused on the car in front of me, not willing to give my brain a chance to wander. Halfway through my trip, I relaxed. Stupid. I knew how to drive. I knew where I was going. I could do this.

Once I parked, I pulled down the visor to check my makeup. Much more than I was used to, but it covered the ugly purple splotches. I smiled at my paler-than-normal reflection, the smile fake and half-assed. At least my injuries weren't visible.

In the classroom, I breathed a sigh of relief when I found Heidi waiting for me. We'd e-mailed a few times over break and on Reed's encouragement, I had shared the truth. Better to have support as I dealt with my injuries.

"How are you feeling, Carli?" she asked as she made her way over to me.

"Nervous." I laughed. "Here are the papers I wanted you to double-check for me." I had managed to get a little work done during my week from hell. It took less than ten minutes to prove my confidence had been shot. *Thank you, Dad.*

"Anything you need." She'd said as much in the e-mail, the truth of her words clear in the concern in her voice.

By the last class, I was ready to curl up in bed for a week. My head throbbed, but not outside of typical bounds. Small victory. I shook a mental pom-pom twice, lackluster cheerleader for the win, and began packing up my bag when my phone vibrated.

Reed: How did it go?

Me: Survived.

Reed: Want to grab some dinner?

My head throbbed at the suggestion.

Me: I would love to, but my head needs to rest. I'm going to go home as soon as I can and sleep until tomorrow.

Reed: Need me to make sure you eat?

I read the words twice. As they sunk in, a goofy grin worked its way onto my face.

Me: Probably not a bad idea.

The long day caught up with me on the drive home. Stuck in traffic, I willed tears to stay in my head. When did I turn into Crying Girl? Heidi had said I did okay, but I felt like a failure. I wasn't on my A-game; I wasn't able to give my students the best of me. And so many times, I needed a student to repeat what he or she said.

My own thought processes were still slow. At the board I needed extra time to generate my own answers. Heidi didn't catch me on any mistakes, but I didn't have any confidence in myself anymore.

By the time I parked my car, I was ready to crumple. I blinked tears away as I started the walk back to my dorm. The cold February weather nipped at my cheeks and tried to sneak under my jacket. I shivered as people passed on all sides. Tiny specks of snowflakes fluttered in the air, disintegrating the moment they touched the pavement.

When my legs were ready to collapse, I arrived at my dorm—and sobbed at the bottom of the stairs, the kind of sob spurred on by pure exhaustion. One deep breath, then another, and I dragged my feet up each step until I made it to my floor.

Inside I was alone. I made it to my bedroom, dropped my bag and coat, and collapsed onto my bed, crying myself to sleep.

I was woken up sometime later by Reed shaking my shoulders. I rubbed my eyes and blinked him into focus. D stood beside him.

"*You scared us,*" Reed signed.

He helped me to a sitting position. "Sorry, I fell asleep," I said and signed.

"The poor guy had to wait for me to get here. You didn't answer your phone or the buzzer," D said.

"What?" I got up and grabbed my phone from my coat pocket. Sure enough, I had missed a dozen texts from

Reed. *"I'm sorry."* I elongated the sign and walked right into his arms.

"You need a light doorbell."

"What's he saying?" D asked.

"That I need a light doorbell."

"What's that?"

Reed walked over to my door, knocked, and then flipped my light switch several times.

"That could work," D said.

They both turned to me.

I blew out a breath, and the hair stuck to my cheek stayed. Ugh, couldn't have been a pretty sight. "How do I get one?"

Reed grinned and kissed my forehead. *"I'll help. Have pizza, maybe cold."*

I frowned and went to sign *sorry* again, but he stopped me and shook his head. The word was becoming a bit over-used in my vocabulary. I could make up a new list: overused words. Already on the list: *sorry, normal, tears.* Sucky list.

I washed my face as the pizza heated up. When I came out, Reed rubbed a thumb over the exposed bruises. *"Better."* I'd stopped looking at myself barefaced, so had to take his word.

After dinner he made sure I took my OxyContin and curled up with me in bed. Unlike the previous night, I settled right down in his embrace. Reed had become my personal teddy bear and security blanket. I knew it wasn't a good place to be, but I allowed myself this small win-dow of dependency.

Chapter Thirty

Reed

THANKS TO A bastard of an internal alarm clock, I woke before my phone vibrated. The glimpse of the outside world between Carli's blinds hinted at the winter wonderland the forecast had predicted. Snow meant bad roads and snow days. I'd complain come June, but right about now, I banked on the snow day. Only my phone held no notification of my school closing or delayed. Damn. Fueled by responsibility, battling reluctance, I slipped out of bed and away from Carli. I checked the news with one last hope that perhaps I missed an e-mail. Many schools were closed in the area, including hers.

Mine was open.

The streets outside her window had me blinking to adjust to the overabundance of white. Thick snow covered the sidewalk, dwarfed cars. The roads had been plowed and still took on a thin white coat. School was open?

I could play dumbfounded later. Right now I had to get my ass moving to arrive at work on time. I grabbed my clothes and was buttoning my shirt when Carli lifted her head and blinked at the outside scene. "*Snow?*"

I nodded. "*Yes. My school's open. Yours is closed.*"

She sat up as I grabbed my shoes. "*You knew, snow?*"

"*I tend to check the weather report. I hoped closed today.*" I pulled on my second shoe.

"*But, snow, car?*"

I was never getting out of here. I grabbed the notebook by her bed.

I knew it was supposed to snow. I took the T in last night, hoping there would be no school today. No such luck.

Carli picked up her phone as I continued gathering my belongings. Before I could finish she stopped me. "*Need a ride?*"

A ride would be a lifesaver. And a wonderful idea popped to mind. I gave her a kiss. "*Why don't you join me?*"

"*Are you sure?*"

"*Why not?*" As a teaching student with a hearing loss, this was a great opportunity for her.

Her eyes traveled around some distant realm before she nodded.

With her help, and her car, I headed home first and grabbed clean clothes before driving us both to my school. For all the white covering the land, the roads were surprisingly easy to manage. I fishtailed only once, on my street—a.k.a., the last place sanded in any storm, ever.

I parked my car to the side of the tiny white school I worked at. Carli didn't move. Seat belt still pressed against her bulky jacket, her jaw all but hung open as she gaped at the building. "*Small*," she signed.

I worked at a Deaf school, with only students who had a hearing loss. What did she expect? I raised one eyebrow. "*How many Deaf kids do you think I have?*"

That stopped her gaping mouth. I headed through halls filled with student artwork, into the main office to sign Carli in and get a visitor's pass. Paulina, the secretary, was already busy, and judging by her expression, handling multitudes of calls in different languages. She raised a single eyebrow at me while I had Carli sign in.

"*My friend. She's visiting me today.*"

Paulina's second eyebrow joined the raised stance. I grinned. She relaxed and shook her head.

"*You have one kid out so far—Kenny.*"

He lived the farthest away, so I wasn't surprised.

I brought Carli down the hall and into my classroom. I hit the lights and settled in at my desk. Only Carli stood by the door, taking in my room. "*What?*" I asked.

"*Six?*" She pointed to the semicircle of student desks.

She never had a peer with a hearing loss prior to me, and she was surprised? "*Yes. Six students.*"

"*My classes range from twenty-one to twenty-five.*"

"*How many of those students have a hearing loss?*"

Comprehension settled in. "*One.*"

Carli continued to take in my room. I looked around, trying to imagine how it looked from her perspective. High up on the walls I had the alphabet in English and

ASL. Student artwork crowded the small wall space, along with some posters by ASL artists. The room was colorful, visual, tapping into my students' needs.

I moved to my desk as she checked out my students' work. At one point, she caught my attention. "*You like your job?*"

I smiled. "*Yes.*" I was about to say more, when the black hands of the clock ticked into view. "*I have to go pick up my students. Wait here. Feel free to use my desk or anything else.*"

I headed to the front of the building and collected my students as buses and parents dropped them off. Once all five arrived, I made my way through the hall. I walked backward, signing with them about the snow as they tried to convince me we needed to make a snowman instead of have class.

I flicked the lights as I backed in, notifying Carli of our arrival. My students took off their coats and brought their bags over to their desks. They all noticed Carli and looked back and forth between the two of us.

I stood by the whiteboard and waited for all five to give me their attention. "*My friend. Her name C-A-R-L-I.*"

Amanda raised her hand, her red hair pulled back in sloppy braids. She waited until I caught her eyes before signing. "*What's her sign name?*"

I leaned against the board and rubbed my chin. Two or more Deaf people were usually needed for sign name creations. A situation I currently had with my students. "*She doesn't have a sign name yet. She only started learning ASL five months ago.*"

Brad raised his hand. *"Deaf or hearing?"*

I shot Carli a look before answering, happy to have a little play on words to show her and the students. I signed *deaf* and *hard of hearing* simultaneously, matching up the beats of the signs. Both were two-beat words, and one-handed, allowing me to blend them together perfectly. An ideal way of representing Carli, one smooth movement to identify both her ears.

It had the added benefit of winning over my students. They all turned to her, accepting her as a peer, as someone they could look up to.

Jack waved. *"Is she your girlfriend?"*

"Nosy students. Men and women can be friends without dating." Now I just had to not act like a man in love, and no one would call my little lecture bull.

Amanda raised her hand. *"Then she really needs a sign name."*

Oh well. I eyed Carli. *"You're right. Want to help me?"*

The excitement level of the room bumped up a few notches. Sign names commonly used the first letter of the first name positioned over different parts of the upper body. Sometimes the first letter of the last name became incorporated. Most of the students began throwing out ideas with *C* in the movement. Since they didn't know her last name no one opted to use it. As they were convinced we were an item, they almost matched her sign name to mine, an *R* to the side of the forehead, but that didn't feel right.

Amanda came up with the winner, the *C* to the heart. A sign name I felt matched the person. And I'd finally be able to stop using a generic one for her.

I got my students back on track and resumed the scheduled lesson plan. When I glanced at Carli, I found her watching me, just as interested as my students were. I wondered how much she followed. I signed differently in class than with her. My students were native users, or if they weren't, needed to see native language. I signed full ASL grammar with them, when I sometimes switched into more English grammar with Carli or my friends. I definitely wasn't slowing down. It was a side of me I hadn't shown her.

Well, one of many.

After all my students were picked up, I made my way back to my classroom and Carli. I didn't bother flashing the light. She sat at my desk, head bowed over her work, long brown strands covering the sides of her face. The world behind her was white and sunny, casting an angelic glow.

I walked over and grasped the edge of my desk. She jumped, and I couldn't help laughing.

"*You scared me,*" she signed.

"*Sorry.*" Though I really wasn't.

"*You're an amazing teacher.*"

My smile grew wider. I grabbed a clean piece of paper and fished a pen out of my cup holder.

I enjoy giving them a good day. Not all of them have ASL at home. Some of them have parents like yours, not understanding their hearing loss. I was lucky that my mom signs and that she helped me get a good education. I want to give a little of that to my students if I can.

Once again, I mentioned only Mom. Dad was the one who taught me English, who taught me…everything. And yet I hid him like I hid the dirty secret of his death.

She pointed to my words. *"See? Amazing."*

She continued to look like she fit in my world. And with her ears, her experiences, and her desire to teach…I tapped the paper and began writing.

You could do this, you know. Teach Deaf students.

Her eyes shuttered, and she shook her head.

I don't know enough ASL.

I turned the paper so I could write.

You can learn. Maybe get your masters in Deaf Ed.

Her eyes cleared into an emotionless void.

Learning anything new is questionable at this point.

I shook my head. How could she not see?

You keep picking up more signs, and that's since the attack.

Her hands shook as she raked them through her hair.

I need to see if I can graduate first.

I squatted in front of her.

You can. You will. I believe in you. The Carli I met is still there. She's a little slower, a little more cautious, but she's still there.

I felt her, I saw her. Couldn't she see herself? Her father hadn't taken the woman I knew, the woman I loved.

But her eyes were not the same as they had been. She ran a hand across my cheek before signing, *"Thank you."*

We made it back to campus so Carli could attend her ASL class. A little over a week since her attack and she was getting back to normal. How could she not see how much she was recovering?

I hit the library and got some studying in while Carli was in class. I caught up with her after, and we joined the Tuesday night dinner.

"*Looking good, sweetie,*" Willow said when we arrived, before pulling Carli into a hug.

"*Reed dragged you into his classroom, huh?*" Val teased.

"*Good experience for her.*" I leaned on the table, all but begging Val to bring it.

Willow waved, interrupting the stare Val and I had started. She turned to Carli. "*How's classes with the left ear?*"

Carli's hair fluttered by her face. She pulled it back into some complicated twisted thing at the nape of her neck. "*A struggle. My brain's not…right…*"

Willow frowned. "*What are you going to do? I mean, in my own class I turned off one hearing aid today and only lasted ten minutes. Then again, my kids speak fast, and half of them have accents.*"

Carli shrugged. "*I don't know…not yet.*"

Val's eyes bored into me, a silent question brewing in them. In her defense, she'd seen me do this before. The whole reason Willow was in the Deaf Ed program? Me. I'd had a hunch it would be a good match, and I was right.

I wasn't wrong with Carli.

"*No,*" Val signed.

I tried, and failed, at hiding the smirk. "*Too late.*"

"*Leave the poor girl alone.*"

Amazing she could sign such a phrase with a straight mouth. I draped an arm over Carli's shoulder. *"Never."*

At the end of the meal, I caught Carli rubbing her temples. Her eyebrows pulled tight across her forehead. Dammit. I pressed my lips to her head, doing what little I could to make her feel better.

I made sure to walk her home. Once she was safe, I kissed her good-bye, even though I wanted to stay. After she was inside, I jogged back to the restaurant, where Val waited to drive us home.

"You can't convert everyone, you know," she said in greeting.

"Nothing wrong with planting an idea." I tried to keep walking, but Val grabbed my arm.

"She was just beat up. She's struggling. She doesn't need your pressure."

"She looked happy in my classroom. Plus, with her deaf ear, this might be a better match."

Val shoved her hands into her hair and started walking. Then she stopped abruptly and turned. *"I don't want you getting hurt."*

I took a step back. *"What are you talking about?"*

She took a moment to gather herself. *"Your heart is on the table. I see it clear in everything you do. But hers is not. She's holding back. Until she recovers, there is no moving forward."*

I looked up at the inky-dark sky. *"I love her. I'm not going anywhere."*

Val nodded. *"What happens if she doesn't love you back?"*

Chapter Thirty-One

Carli

I WOKE UP to what could only be described as shards of glass rocketing around my skull. The shards rocked back and forth, scraping and dragging along the way. If I moved, the scraping would shoot up to turbo. Odds were a few synapses would break in the process. I'd lost enough cranial functions. I couldn't risk losing any more. My eyes refused to open. My body refused to uncurl from the fetal position. Hands on my head, I tried to keep it from falling off.

Through my tears, I reached to my nightstand, knocked over a notebook and a box of tissues, fumbled past my cell, before connecting with my OxyContin bottle. I managed to get the top off and a pill in my hand, then swallowed the pill.

Shit. Wrong move. Mistake.

Now I couldn't drive. I knew there were a few other student teachers at my school, but I wasn't friends with them and had no idea if they were even on campus. Besides, I still couldn't move out of bed.

Way to go, Carli.

Tears raced down my cheeks, and I did nothing to stop them. I stayed in bed, curled into a pathetic lump, willing my head to fall off already.

The intense pain had me shivering. How could pain be cold? I rocked back and forth, a pathetic excuse for a human being. A hand shook my shoulder. I forced one eye open and found D, mouth flapping. With my right ear pressed into the pillow, I couldn't register a single sound.

"Can't hear, can't move head," I said.

D looked around, hands in her sleep-tousled hair, and grabbed the notebook by my bed.

What can I do?

"Nothing. I already took OxyContin. Now can't go to work."

Need me to contact your school?

Yup, I did. Badly. I was able to direct D, and she handled notifying the school I was sick. By then the medication had started working, just enough so I could move my head. D grabbed my hearing aid, and I put it in.

"I've never seen you like this," D said, rubbing my leg.

"Getting more common now."

D frowned. "Need anything?"

A lobotomy. "Not yet. Check on me before you leave? I think I'm bedridden today."

"Sure thing." Another long look and she left me alone. I pulled out my phone.

Me: Bad day. Life sucks.

Reed: :-(

Me: I'm going to wallow in self-pity once I gain enough mobility to wallow.

Reed: You were doing better.

Me: Haven't you gotten the memo? I'm never getting better.

Reed: Don't give up.

Me: Talk to me when I'm not high on OxyContin and home from work.

I tossed my phone on my bed and curled back into myself, closing my eyes against the world. If only it would go away, all of it.

The sun was high in the sky when I dared open them again. My head still killed me, but I couldn't figure out if it was time for more pain meds. I hadn't had a day this bad since the attack. Which proved I pushed myself way too much the day before. And all I did was watch Reed teach, a little prep work, ASL class, and dinner with friends. Okay, so maybe that was too much. At least for me.

I turned and eyed my medication. A hopeful thought floated around my banged-up, messed-up, fucked-up brain: a way out. The amber bottle was half full. Perky little pills grinned at me, called out to me. They promised to take my pain away, my lack of concentration away, my dependence on society. One handful would solve all my troubles.

I stared at the bottle for minutes or hours, I wasn't sure. Time stopped when my brain got bad. My hands didn't move toward the bottle. No, they stayed at my side. In my head, I imagined reaching out, depositing the pills into my hand. Maybe one pill, maybe ten. Perhaps the whole bottle. The smooth edges would feel good against my palm, good inside my throat. It wouldn't be hard to swallow. One at a time or all at once. I could do it.

If my hand would move.

Coward.

I rolled away from the medication and closed my eyes to the world, to the pain, to the utter disappointment in myself.

What parent could do this to a child? Didn't parents want their children to have bright and full futures? Mine was dark and empty. And as I lay on my right ear, silent.

I was still in bed, having gotten up only to go to the bathroom, when my phone buzzed. Or rather, when I finally paid attention to my phone.

Reed: Want some company?

I picked up my head. Bad idea, freight train. Instead I gained a small notion of smarts and checked the time on my phone: 5:00 p.m. Holy shit. When did that happen?

Me: You downstairs?

Please don't be. I hadn't even brushed my teeth yet and wanted to stay in my own hell.

Reed: Yes.

Dammit.

Me: Give me a few minutes, head bad. I'll text you before I buzz.

As slowly as I could, I lifted my head and got myself standing. The room spun with the pain, but I gritted my teeth and made it to the front door. I texted Reed and pressed the buzzer. Head against the wall, I knew I wasn't going to last long on my feet. I cracked open the door and grasped furniture for support as I made my way back to bed.

One of these days, he wouldn't find me curled up in a ball of pain.

I felt him before I saw him, strong arms wrapped around me. He pressed his head against my own, cushioning me between the pillow and himself. He didn't sign hello, he didn't move me—he just held me. And I cracked. The sobs came fast, tearing out of my soul. His arms tightened around me, and he scattered kisses over my head.

I really didn't deserve this sweet man. Especially when I had nothing to give him. Not my mind, not my heart, nothing.

When I calmed down, he reached for my pills, those teasing tempting pills, and placed one in my hand before getting me some water. I took them both and watched him as he put the pills back on the nightstand. If I took more, he wouldn't be burdened by me anymore. He could find someone with a functioning brain to be with rather than my messed-up self.

He took my face in his hands, thumbs brushing my damp cheeks. One hand moved, caressing my fading bruises. His somber face, so full of pain, caused me to crack further.

I definitely didn't deserve him.

He wrapped me in his arms and pressed my head against his chest. My right ear picked up his fast heartbeat.

I breathed him in, his warm masculine scent almost like an aromatherapy treatment. I shifted into him, wanting to climb inside.

I wanted a do-over on life. A get-out-of-jail-free card. Though if my ears worked, I might not have met Reed. So maybe I wanted a do-over on my brain, not my ears. At least not my ears from before the second attack.

Reed shifted, checked his phone, then looked deep into my eyes. "*I guess this isn't a good birthday?*"

What? I grabbed my phone and searched for the calendar. Holy shit. It was my birthday. And I had spent the day in bed, curled up in pain.

Dad gave me one last birthday gift after all.

I turned to my pillow and curled up on my bed again. Only this time Reed wouldn't let me.

"*Come on. Shower. Get dressed. You'll feel better.*"

I didn't want to shower. Or get dressed. I wanted to stay in bed and will the remaining hours of my birthday away. But his determined face required some action from me to wipe away the look.

Once my head calmed down, I gathered up my clothes and made my way into the bathroom. The warm water soothed my body, even calmed my head further. In the foggy bathroom mirror, I studied my face as I combed my hair. The purple marks were fading. Pretty soon the only marks remaining from the attack would be internal.

Lucky me.

Back in my living room, I skidded to a halt. The place was packed. Reed and D were there, but so were my sisters, Willow, and Val. They all made a loud noise, which I couldn't decipher, but I could follow those who signed.

"*Happy birthday!*"

I blinked back the tears as Reed pulled me into his side and handed me my hearing aid. I fitted the mold to my canal and flipped the shell behind my ear.

"*What's this?*" I asked.

"*A party.*"

Yeah, Reed, I figured that part out. I turned to my sisters. "We're celebrating this weekend, my birthday and Matti's."

"You deserve your own party this year. And fortunately for me, that means I get my own too." Matti's words teased, but her face still held the same haunted look, ever since Dad turned on me.

I held out my arms, and she crossed the room and hugged me close.

"*When, how, plan party?*" I asked Reed, and realized I needed to seriously thank Val as she slipped into interpreter mode.

"*After your text this morning.*"

"Nothing like a message at the ass crack of dawn instructing you to not wish your own sister a happy birthday," Andi lamented.

Reed watched Val then turned and winked at Andi.

"How are you feeling, Carli?" Lesli asked as she sat with a hand on her back.

"Better question, how are *you* feeling?"

She smiled, but it didn't reach her eyes. "Pain is normal, right?"

I nodded my aching head. "Right."

My sisters talked around me. Unlike during parties at home, they made sure I could hear and partake. Dad wasn't there to tiptoe around. Or wield his fists. And the saddest part was, I didn't miss Mom. These three were my family. My mother let my father be king, fueling her own fantasy world. She never showed us love. She never supported us, not even when Dad wasn't around. And not one of us had heard from her since the attack.

After we ate, and they made me blow out twenty-two candles that threatened to set off the alarms, Reed dropped a box in my lap. The white wrapping paper was covered with math equations in children's handwriting.

He grinned when I looked up at him. "*Your students?*"

"*Yes, my students. Your brain…works.*"

I ignored him and looked over the paper, once again forced to blink back tears. More careful than ever before, I picked at the tape and removed the wrapping without a single tear. Then I folded it up and placed it aside.

Who cared what was in the box? His students had already given me the best present.

I opened the lid and pulled out a light doorbell.

"*So you can hear the door.*"

There were two doorbells and an adaptor. Along with a clock like he had. I was still looking at the boxes when Val spoke for him.

"I wasn't sure if you were able to hear your alarm or not. You don't have to use it if you don't need it. The doorbell I know you need, so don't fight me."

I looked up at his worried face. Had I mentioned I didn't deserve him? I stood up, stepped over the box, and laid a kiss on his lips that had my sisters hooting.

"*There's more.*"

I held his gaze as I reached for the box and felt around the bottom. I pulled out a square jewelry box. Not a ring, thank God—much too big for that.

Inside I found a necklace with a heart, lined with what looked like diamonds. I locked eyes with him again as D let out a whistle.

This was too much, all too much. Didn't he know I was a dead end? I wasn't a long-term bet. Heck, I probably wouldn't last a year. And yet he'd given me something that spoke of longevity. His actions through this entire ordeal had been nothing short of amazing.

And I still had nothing to offer him.

"*I love you,*" he signed. In front of our friends, in front of my sisters, knowing Val was interpreting.

A tear rolled down my cheek. I needed to tell him to stop signing those words, to stop feeling things for me I couldn't feel in response. But, for some reason, I crossed to him and flung my arms around his neck. He held me close, breath tickling the crook of my neck. I wanted to break down and sob again. Instead I managed, "*Thank you.*"

I untangled my arms and held up my hair so Reed could clasp the necklace on. I felt like a traitor, even as my fingers played with the heart.

"Well," Andi began, "gonna be hard to top lover-boy over there, but we'll try. We know your left hearing aid isn't powerful enough for you anymore. We weren't sure if a new one would help and know the aids are expensive."

Lesli groaned and rolled her head back into the couch. "How could we not? Every time you needed a new pair it was a war between Mom and Dad."

"What are you talking about?"

Matti gave me a look. "I thought for sure you'd have heard them?"

I shook my head.

"Mom had to go to bat to get you new aids. Dad felt it wasn't worth it."

"Mom stood up for me?"

Lesli answered. "I think she was more concerned about the state coming knocking if you didn't have adequate hearing aids."

"Anyways," Andi said, giving Lesli a look, "we looked up exactly how much they cost and…damn. So, here you go." She handed me an envelope. "Use them for a hearing aid or anything else you may need to get started on your own two feet."

I opened the envelope to find a check for $3,000. My hands shook. The feather-light paper weighed the same as a boulder in my hands. I couldn't…They couldn't…"No, uh-uh. I can't accept your money."

"It's the least we can do."

"The least you can do is being here, right now. Which means the world to me. I don't need your money." I shoved the piece of paper out, ready to shift the weight to a sister. Andi crossed her arms. Lesli put her hands behind her back. Matti stuck hers under her butt. They held eye contact, part challenge to fight, part refusal to partake.

"Take it. If you don't need a new hearing aid, you can splurge on a girls' trip to Florida," Matti said.

I shook my head, eyes glued to the green paper in my hands.

"Please," Andi said. "We know you're concerned about the future. Let us help."

I swallowed the lump in my throat and put the check in my back pocket. There was no way I could ever truly thank them or repay them. In turn I pulled each sister into a bone-crushing hug, which they returned with equal fervor.

A few hours later, my sisters had gone home, and Reed had set up the doorbell and alarm clock for me. Willow and Val left, and D went to her room, giving me a few minutes alone with Reed.

"*Birthday improve?*" he asked, charming me with his smile alone.

"*Yes.*" Best birthday to date. And it started off the worst.

"*Good.*" He proceeded to kiss me until my legs turned to jelly. Then he headed home himself. Alone in my room, I tried to process everything, but it was too much for my poor brain to handle. I changed into my pj's, took another OxyContin, and climbed into bed.

I didn't bother doing the math to figure out if it was time to take the pills. Heck, my head wasn't hurting outside of normal. I took the pills because that's what I did every night. It was part of my bedtime routine. Take off hearing aid; swallow pills.

In the dark my eyes flipped open. On my fingers I counted the hours between my last pill and now. Not enough time had passed. Only I wasn't worried. Not really. Should the worst happen, my sisters would get back their money and no longer have to worry about their messed-up baby sister.

I fell asleep with a smile on my face. First time that happened without Reed beside me.

Chapter Thirty-Two

Carli

THE SUN BEAT down on my back as I swam for shore. I was close and yet land kept moving farther and farther away. My arms and legs screamed at me. A bright light flashed three times; then clouds covered the sun. The world grew darker, the water turbulent, as I continued to try to get to shore. The light flashed again. My legs gave out. I slipped under the water and—

The light flashed three times.

I sat up in bed, taking deep breaths that failed to get enough oxygen in. The lamp by my bed flashed three times. Care of my new alarm clock. I reached over and flipped the switch before falling to my back. If my heart ever stopped ramming against my rib cage, I'd text Reed to yell at him.

The annoying *beep beep beep* of my old alarm clock moved up in points, even if I did run the risk of sleeping through it. And considering how deep of a dream I was in, I ran the risk.

I gave my new clock the evil eye as I got out of bed. Feet on the carpeted floor, I felt my head. Normal. Huh. The amber pill bottle called out to me, a Cheshire cat grinning. I wagged my finger at it and got ready for the day.

The students in my first class were tired from who knew what. My second class I already knew was a handful. Today proved no different.

At the board, I wrote out a few equations. As I finished with the isosceles triangle, a paper airplane zoomed past my head.

I froze, marker in hand, and turned on my heel. Two of the boys stood in the back, laughing as they made the airplanes. "Let's see if she can hear..." Zachary's voice trailed off as he noticed me watching him. He flipped his too-long hair off his face and threw the airplane anyway. It dived and landed by my feet.

"Fifty points," shouted Max and high-fived Zachary.

"Zachary, Max, since you two are already standing, why don't you come up and see if you can fill in the blanks on the board?" I held out my marker.

"Nope," said Max, before he jumped into his seat.

Zachary remained standing. "Why don't you get some ears that work. We've been calling out the right answers the entire time."

A quick survey of my class and I had no clue what I had truly missed with my back to them. Not good. Control slipped through my fingers, and I needed to rope it back in, fast.

"In that case you can put the answers on the board, since you obviously all know what they are." I gestured to the board.

He strode to the front, clutching his baggy pants to prevent them from pooling around his ankles. He was tall for his age, with an unhealthy dose of anger. At the board he picked up a red marker, shimmied his pants on his hips, and wrote "fuck you" in large letters. My entire class laughed, though half of them sounded more like gasps.

"Clean that up," I said, and dammit, my voice quavered.

Zachary cupped his ear. "I'm sorry, what?" His voice dripped with mocking, letting me know that I'd used that phrase far too often.

I swallowed. "I said," raising my voice, "clean that up."

"Right away, teacher." He said *teacher* with a heavy dose of loathing.

A shiver raced down my spine, and my head scrambled to stay one step ahead of him and not succumb to the sudden massive headache I had. Zachary picked up the eraser and erased everything but the swear.

I froze. All my training went out the window. What was I supposed to do? How was I supposed to gain control?

The students caught on to their teacher being worth, well, fuck. They started talking to each other. I couldn't pinpoint a single conversation. Zachary threw the eraser at the board, leaving a mark of blue dust. I was close enough to the board that I flinched, hard, and took a step back. Bad move. Any chance I had of gaining control was long gone.

Where was a wormhole when needed? I bent to pick up the eraser, but another student, Tanya, was already there, erasing the prints left on the tile. She said something to me, but I couldn't hear it over the ruckus of the room. I stood there like a lump, struggling to come up with the right answer.

Tanya erased the board a minute before Heidi arrived. Another student must have slipped out of the room because she stood behind Heidi.

"Hey," Heidi yelled, and all twenty-five students quieted down. "What is going on here?"

"Our teacher can't hear. We called out the answers, and she just ignored us."

"Is that true?" she asked and made eye contact with each student.

"No, they were making fun of Miss Reynolds," Tanya said.

"Little brownnoser bitch," Zachary yelled.

Tanya leered at him, but Heidi was faster. "Go to the principal's office, Zachary. None of this behavior is acceptable. Do you understand me?"

Zachary stood up, gave both Tanya and me a hate-filled look, then held his pants as he half walked, half limped to the door. He banged both palms into it, creating a loud enough noise that my left ear got happy, before leaving.

"Anyone else have a problem?" Heidi asked, eyes trained on Max, who was now quiet as a mouse. "Good." She turned to me and moved over to the desk. Using my notes, she took over the class.

Way to go, Carli.

At the end of the day, all I wanted was to curl up with my OxyContin bottle. I needed to go home, recharge, and figure out how to do it all again tomorrow.

"Don't leave yet, Carli," Heidi said before doing just that and leaving the room.

Fifteen and a half years of schooling, and my future was over before I could graduate. I collapsed on my desk chair and put my head on the desk. This couldn't be happening. How could things go so wrong so quickly?

I couldn't stop the tears and had my face hidden in the crook of my arm by the time Heidi came back. I wiped my cheeks, careful to avoid revealing my bruises, and lifted my head.

"I'll understand if you don't want me back."

"You don't get off the hook so easy," Heidi said. "Let's work through the problem, see if we can't help you regain control."

I shook my head, a fresh tear sliding down my cheek. "Between my hearing and the brain injury, I just don't think I have a future anymore."

Heidi leaned back. "A future in teaching, or a future in general?"

Well, crap. "See, my brain doesn't work the way it should. How am I supposed to teach?"

"You've only had two days back since your attack, and it hasn't been that long. Let's not jump to any conclusions. Instead, we're going to brainstorm how you can regain control. You start. Take a few moments, and let me know what you can do differently."

She looked at me with support and encouragement. I closed my eyes and took a deep breath through my nose, counting to five. Then I begged my throbbing head to not fail me before I answered.

That night, at bedtime, I spilled two pills into my palm. They rolled around, such happy little pills. I popped one in my mouth. The other I held up to the light, studying the shape and the angle. Eventually I grabbed my water and swallowed.

HEIDI SHADOWED ME all day on Friday. My head continued a very accurate portrayal of synapses misfiring. My heart wasn't into the teaching. All I wanted to do was go home and go to bed.

The students yawned and stared out the window. I tried to engage them, but I didn't really care enough myself, so how was I supposed to get them to care? I didn't do anywhere near my best. I did the bare minimum.

Worse? I was okay with bare minimum.

Heidi sent me home with instructions to rest up over the weekend. Her facial expression said I needed to get my shit together. On my drive home, I gave some serious contemplation to withdrawing from the course, and college, until my head worked again. Which more than likely was never.

Back at my dorm, I collapsed on the couch and stared at D's television. There wasn't any captioning in here, and I couldn't pick out a word being said. I didn't care. Made it easier to turn away when my phone vibrated.

Reed: How did school go today?

Me: Still sucky.

Reed: Want some company?

Me: I just want to take it easy. I plan to go to bed soon.

Reed: OK, get some rest. Tomorrow?

My heart ached. I wanted to wallow tomorrow as well. I wanted to stop pretending. My whole life I'd been pretending. Now I knew better. I couldn't hear, my brain was injured, and I was most definitely, without a doubt, not normal. Couldn't I spend one goddamn day not pretending and just be the useless lump that I was? The useless lump I would never rise above.

But I knew he wouldn't let me.

I glanced toward my room, where my pills awaited me. I needed a feel-good moment. Badly. A handful or two would do the trick, take me far away from myself. Free me.

Me: OK

I couldn't. Could I? I held the phone to my chest. Something felt off. Me. I was off. I was losing myself. Slowly but surely.

The door opened and D entered. "Hey, how goes it?"

I thumbed toward the floor.

D shooed me over and joined me on the couch. "What you need is a night out. You've been cooped up inside for two weeks. Let's go out and get drunk and stupid."

"I don't need to get drunk to get stupid. My father took care of that for me."

D grabbed my chin and forced me to look at her. I nearly broke at the underlying fear in her eyes. It connected to something deep inside, something that said maybe she had reason to be afraid. "Don't go there, Carli. Or I'll be forced to psychoanalyze you." Odds were the psychoanalysis had already begun. She clasped hands with mine and yanked me to my feet. "You need to be twenty-two for a change."

"I've only been twenty-two for two days."

"Exactly. Stop acting like an old lady."

Didn't anyone get what I was going through? No. And I had no idea how to explain it, how to make them see just how messed up I was.

Instead of fighting her, I changed into skinny jeans and a sweater and fixed up my makeup. D came out in a short skirt and skimpy top.

"No, you still look like a teacher." She reached into the back of my closet—skimpy-clothes territory—and pulled out a short black skirt and maroon halter top. I didn't want to be slutty. I didn't want to run the risk of some asshole putting his hands up my skirt. But I still had no fight in me. I changed into a skirt barely long enough to cover my ass and top that gave me way more cleavage than normal. At least D let me put back on my sweater to handle the chill of the night air.

Before we left, I ran back into my bedroom. I didn't know what the night would hold and needed my security blanket. Namely: a pill.

We hopped onto the T and when we got off, I realized we were closer to Reed's place than ours. A pang of guilt hit me. I told him not to come over so I could go to sleep, and now I waltzed around the streets of Cambridge, wearing clothes that barely covered my ass.

The list for the day included Bad Teacher Carli and Bad Girlfriend Carli.

Cold air embraced my bare legs and blew up my skirt as we hurried toward our destination. At least the fast pace controlled my shivering.

We got to the party, and it was already in full swing. The bass rang out through the apartment. My left ear bopped to the beat, all jittery with a noise level she could hear.

I followed D into the slightly quieter kitchen. The place was standing-room only. We stood shoulder to shoulder in the small space, where we mixed up some drinks and toasted being in our twenties. I couldn't latch on to a conversation. Before Attack, I could. After Attack, I couldn't.

I finished my cup and poured another.

Every cologne and perfume known to man filtered through the air, toned down only by the alcohol and one dude retching into a trash can. The music was loud as sin, but people still talked over it. They laughed, flirted, and had fun.

Out in the living room, D acted her full twenty-two years. She danced with some stranger who already had his hands on her ass.

I leaned against a wall, absorbing the atmosphere. They were all my age, college students like me. They were all drinking and laughing and having a good time. Yet I didn't feel part of this crowd.

I tilted my cup to my lips, letting the tangy drink wash away the tears threatening to well in my eyes. Parties like these were more enjoyable when I was slightly smashed.

Or absolutely fucked.

Something was said and everyone laughed. I threw in a fake laugh, invisibility cloak firmly in place. Loneliness seeped in, not giving a damn I was surrounded by people. My now-empty cup provided me with an excuse to leave the crowd, still laughing and talking over the noise.

In the kitchen I poured a pity drink into a red plastic cup. I lost count of how many I'd had but knew the equation bordered on: one too many + pity drink = way-too-drunk Carli.

A tall blond guy joined me at the drink table and said something, but I couldn't make out a word. Instead of faking it like I used to, I pointed to my left ear and shook my head. He said something else and took a step back. Only he bumped into another party member. Awkwardness ensued as he mouthed to the person and walked off without another glance in my direction.

I had just identified myself as deaf. And for all intents and purposes, I was. Especially at a party like this. I could be miserable at home; I didn't need to be miserable surrounded by people.

Me: Sorry, D, I'm done. This isn't my scene anymore. You gonna be OK if I scram?

D: No, wait a minute. I'll toss this loser, and we'll dance.

Me: No, stay if you want. I can't hear, my head hurts, and I'm not normal anymore.

D: :-(I'm not letting you leave alone.

Me: I'll text Reed. But only if you're OK alone.

D: I'm always OK. I see a few of my buddies.

Me: Good. Have fun.

I moved to grab my coat and swayed more than I expected. I hadn't had that many drinks. I'd had…No clue. Damn. I pulled on my sweater and coat, grabbed my bag, and headed out into the night.

When I got to the street, I sat down on the building steps. I squeezed my legs closed to give myself some sort of dignity and tried not to think of my skirt rising up above the cold concrete. The cool air soothed my head as I breathed in the city fumes.

It wasn't that late. I could walk to the T and head back to my dorm. Only when I moved to stand the world tilted a little too much.

Bad girlfriend of the year coming in three, two, one…

Me: You still up?

I rubbed my hands on my goose-bumped legs as I waited. Why hadn't I worn gloves?

Reed: Yeah, trouble sleeping.

Deep breath. Own up to your mistakes.

Me: This is bad. D dragged me out to a party. Only due to my left ear I can't hear a thing. And my head doesn't work like I'm 22. It works like I'm 42 or 52. Or not quite living at all. I bailed on D, but I'm closer to you and may have drank a little more than I thought. Or at least more than I can now handle. How can a brain injury affect my tolerance?

I paused, thumb poised over the send icon. I contemplated erasing it all. I could just tell him I missed him and to pick me up at the train station. Or I could send it and let the world crumble where it may.

I hit Send and shivered while I waited for a response.

Reed: When did you last take your meds? You're not supposed to drink with them. And where are you? I'll get you.

Me: Last night.

I hit Send before realizing the lie. I'd had one before I left. Maybe that was why I felt loopy?

I gave him the address and huddled farther into myself while I waited. The frigid air nipped at my bare legs, and up my skirt. My cheeks were numb from the chill. I was trying to see through the curtains in the apartment across the street when Reed pulled up. My stomach flipped, not sure whether he'd be upset or not. I stood, smoothed down my skirt, and walked to his car. I may have swayed a bit, but the fuck-me heels would do that to a person.

When I got in, Reed reached over and held my face still, studying me with eyes that always saw far too much. One hand left my face to flip on the inside light. I pulled back and put on my seat belt.

"*Why?*" he asked.

"*Why what?*" Did he know? Could he tell I lied?

The tension in the car threatened to leak out onto the street.

"*Why did you drink? Why did you go to the party? Why did you tell me you were sleeping?*" And the unasked question: Why did I brush him off?

At least he didn't ask about the pills.

My throat clogged, each swallow pushing tears up and down as they threatened to overflow. This handsome man waited for me to answer. He'd given me everything he had. And I ditched him to go to a party.

I couldn't look at him anymore, couldn't see the pain in his eyes, pain I had caused. I leaned forward and put my head in my hands. No longer could I keep the tears inside. I sobbed into them as Reed hugged me from over the center console.

When my tears subsided I sat up and had to look at his even more pain-filled face. "*I'm taking you home with me,*" he signed.

"*I need my medication.*"

He looked at me good and long, and I braced myself for the fight. In the end he nodded and drove me home first. I packed a bag, grabbed my meds, and then we went back to his place.

The car ride had been blessedly warm, but I was still to-the-bone cold and didn't dare take my long jacket off. Reed told me to wait. He ran a hand through his hair, shoulders tight with tension. He checked the time, then did something on his phone. A minute later he checked it again and moved into the living room.

From the doorway, he set up something on the screen that looked like a Skype call, but it was on his television. The bottom corner held a box with a live image of himself.

A woman with black hair sprinkled with gray, and tight curls, appeared on the screen. Her skin was a rich brown, and her nose indicated an African heritage. Her eyes warmed into a smile when she saw Reed.

She signed back and forth to Reed for a few minutes, her smile fading as they went along. At the end of the call they each signed *"I love you"* one-handed before disconnecting.

"Who was that?" I asked as soon as he turned around.

"My mother. She's a nurse." He moved past me and unzipped my bag lying on the kitchen floor. He pulled out my OxyContin and placed it on top of the kitchen cabinet where I couldn't reach.

What the hell?

He turned to face me, ignoring the fire burning in my eyes. *"No medication with alcohol."*

"I can't sleep without meds."

"Then you shouldn't have drank."

Why did I text him? *"Give me my medication."*

"In the morning."

In the morning, I would be unable to move from pain. I shook my head, hands balled in fury.

"Do you want to die?"

I let go of my balled fists. Unfortunately for me I didn't respond, not right away. And the expression on his face shifted 180 degrees to something close to terror.

"You want to die?" he asked again, softer, taking a step forward.

I took a step back. No. Yes. I waved to myself. *"This not life."*

He took another step, and another, until I was backed into the wall. A wall I happened to be very familiar with. One hand weaved through my hair and held my head. He leaned forward and kissed me. Not light. Not easy. This was full of passion. The ever-present tears spilled over my cheeks as I wrapped my arms around him, unable to resist.

He pulled back. "*You feel that?*"

I nodded.

"*That's life.*"

He claimed my mouth again as his free hand undid the buttons and removed my coat. I let go of him and allowed my coat to puddle by my feet. He broke the kiss and got a good look at what I was wearing. He let out a breath that caressed my cheek.

"*You look alive to me.*" He pulled me back into him, one hand running up my bare thigh and under my skirt to cup my behind. A very different kind of goose bumps broke out on my skin. I arched into him, needing more.

"*You feel alive to me,*" he signed, removing the hand from my head to do so. He grabbed my hand and pressed it to his chest. Beneath my palm his heart beat fast. "*You feel me?*"

I nodded and angled my head for his kiss, which he gave me. He lifted me up, and I wrapped my legs around him. Inside I wasn't damaged, not when I was in his arms.

"*I feel alive with you.*" It was the truth. For the first time in two days my world wasn't falling apart.

He wrapped my arms around his neck and carried me into his bedroom. When he set me down, I pulled my sweater off. He took me in from head to toe. "*You're definitely alive.*" Still roaming over me, he stopped at my neck, where I wore his necklace. A smile so full of love broke out. How was it my own heart shattered?

"*Make me forget I'm broken.*"

The smile remained, but it no longer reached his eyes. "*You're not broken.*" Then he didn't allow either one of us to say anything else. He pushed me down onto the bed, hands teasing my nipples through the clothing until my nerve endings were doing complicated math equations. When I writhed, he removed one hand and slipped it back under my skirt. He swiped my undies to the side, teasing my center with smooth strokes.

"*You feel that, right? That's living.*"

And here is where I was glad I wasn't learning ASL only in class. "*No, this is fucking.*"

A laugh choked out of him, and his hand stilled in me. I'd have to thank Willow for showing me that sign.

Here was everything I needed. Reed got off me and stripped out of his clothes in gloriously smooth movements, revealing that mouthwatering body to me. Then he removed my panties and nothing else. And damn if that didn't turn me on further. Condom prepped, he shifted up my skirt the inch farther it needed to go and entered me.

My brain got a little delirious with pleasure at that point, able to concentrate only on him moving inside me, on his scent, his touch, his taste as I licked his shoulder. Oh, I'd miss this if I left. Miss this feeling of euphoria. Miss this feeling of love. Miss this feeling of Reed.

He stilled his pace, which was just warming up to perfect. I opened my eyes, and he brushed a hand over my head, a silent question. Was I bang-able? The thought alone caused me to laugh, and he groaned and thrust in, breaking off my own laugh.

"*Head fine.*" And for the moment it was.

He let his head fall forward. It had been a while. We'd had sex only twice since the attack, both times slow and sweet. I didn't want sweet. I wanted to feel alive. Damn the consequences.

I arched up into him, fast glides with my hips, begging him to let loose, toss out the control. Claim me. He took another deep breath and then joined me. Hard and fast, sending me flying in no time. Only he wasn't done. Still pumping fast, he lifted my shirt, pulled down my cups, and sucked me into his mouth.

Who knew a second orgasm could hit so fast? I hadn't even fully come down to the ground from my first before the second, more powerful one ripped through me. I wrapped my legs around him, kissing any skin I could find, meeting his thrusts as best I could.

He managed to send me flying one more time before he groaned and collapsed in my arms. His breaths teased my skin. I held tight. In his arms, I didn't have a brain injury. In his arms, my ears didn't matter. In his arms, I felt perfect.

He pulled back and leaned on one arm. "*You OK?*"

"*Yes.*" I was more than okay.

"*Good.*" Then he rolled to his back and took me with him.

Chapter Thirty-Three

Reed

I HELD CARLI for a while, until she picked up her head with curiosity brewing in her eyes. She hesitated for a moment, as if wrestling with herself over something. "*Your mother's black?*" Her cheeks pinked.

I laughed. Well, that explained the hesitation. I grabbed the blankets, wrapping us both up in them. "*Half and half.*" I guessed it was a good thing I hadn't introduced them yet. I needed to explain a few things to Carli. For starters.

I reached over and grabbed a notebook and pen.

My grandma was black, grandfather white. Quite the scandal back in the day. My dad was white as well. They used to joke that her heritage plus his created a Hispanic kid.

Her eyes took in the paper, then darted to my face, more questions swimming around. Before I could sign or write, she returned to the paper.

1. Past tense for Dad? 2. Hispanic?

"*Problem?*" I asked before holding out my arm and pointing to my bare skin. "*Not a tan.*" She rolled her eyes, and I collected the paper.

My birth mother was Brazilian, birth father Puerto Rican. We have no idea if they were born here or there. My father died two years ago. Car crash.

I needed to share more than that. Needed to explain why I got so bossy about her pills. But words in either language wouldn't come. She'd been through enough—she didn't need my sob story added on top.

"*I'm sorry,*" she signed, the sincerity of the sign on her face.

I shrugged. Anger and sorrow at my father's loss still battled for higher ground. Nothing she needed to know. Time to point this conversation back toward her.

That's life. No one can predict the future—best to make the most out of each day and what we have. Even if that's a messed-up brain and a lot of pain.

And that looked like something Dad would write. It didn't resemble the truth. Truth was, Dad made a decision. But how could I explain it all to someone who never met him?

She shook her head, bringing me back to the present and my comment about her.

"*What's wrong? You've been quiet for two days,*" I asked.

She shifted upright and grabbed the pen and paper.

On Thursday I lost control of my classroom. My co-op teacher had to step in. Good chance my career is finished before I graduate. If I graduate.

She struggled more than I had thought. On top of everything, it couldn't have been a good feeling. I put the notebook down and pulled her into me until her head rested on my chest and my arms wrapped around her. I rocked her gently as I held her, anger building inside me for the asshole who did this to her. Family had always meant a little something different to me than others, but this man—this "father"—didn't deserve her.

Made my own issues with Dad driving into a tree seem trivial at best. On that thought I let her go so I could write.

We all lose control from time to time. All you can do is pick yourself up and try again. Dad always told me he acquired his mad bluffing skills from teaching. He died before I had my own classroom, before I could ask him any specific questions.

Her eyes were glossy when they met mine. *"I'm sorry."*

"Not your fault." Don't turn into him.

She nodded and rubbed her temple, a grimace on her face not boding well for her pain level. Why did she have to hurt herself by drinking?

Why don't you take some ibuprofen? Maybe you don't need the OxyContin anymore.

I sent up a silent prayer. I needed Carli off the prescription pills yesterday.

"OK." She may have smiled, but her eyes told me she doubted if the lesser pills would work. With any luck she'd

think differently come morning. She hopped up. *"I'm cold."* She reached into my drawer, rummaging around for what I assumed was one of my university sweatshirts. She'd been getting more use out of them than I had. Her eyebrows pulled together. *"You H-I-D-E mail?"*

She pulled out the letter. Shit.

"Not really." I stared at her, not ready to deal with this other part of me I hadn't shared. On top of everything I divulged already in one night. My time was up.

She held the letter in one hand, the other propped on her hip. Head cocked to one side, she waited me out, staring me down until I broke.

It worked.

I ran a hand through my hair and grabbed the notebook.

I received the letter the first day of our linguistics class. A little birthday "gift" from the adoption agency. I haven't read it, but I'm assuming the person who wrote it is my birth father.

Carli's eyes grew wide as she read. Then she shook her head.

How is it I never knew your birthday?

I looked up to find her frowning at me, as if it was her fault. Everything added up; it wasn't fair in one night so much was dumped in her lap.

"Sorry. I'm not good at letting people in. Ask me anything."

Her lips curved. *"Later."* Then she picked up the letter, separated the split seam, and raised her eyebrows.

My heart sprinted. Did I want to know what it said? I hadn't thrown it out, but I hadn't given it much actual consideration. "*I don't know.*"

"*I'll read it. Let you know.*" She held her thumb up then down.

I swallowed, desperate to alleviate the dryness in my mouth.

"*Trust me,*" Carli signed, effectively trapping me. This wasn't just allowing her to read a letter from someone I hadn't seen in twenty years. This was trusting her with the letter. With me.

I nodded, and she pulled the letter out.

Whatever the words were, they were written on a white lined paper ripped from a notebook. Something fell into her lap, and I caught sight of pictures before Carli flipped them over. Only the backside had writing on it. The one on top? The date of my birth.

All signs pointed in one direction: Juan Suarez was, in fact, my birth father.

I stared at the back of the picture as Carli read. Did I look at it? Did I not? I had no pictures prior to the age of three. I didn't know what kind of baby I was, what I looked like. I only knew the frustrated three-year-old without language.

At birth, none of that would've mattered. Before I thought it through, I picked up the top picture and flipped it over.

The image in front of me was a generic hospital scene. Woman and man sitting on a hospital bed, holding up a small child bundled in blue-striped cloth. The baby slept and could've been any baby for all I knew. But the adults…

I looked like Juan. To the point it could've been me standing in the picture. I had no clue what I inherited from the wavy-haired brunette smiling at the camera, but Juan made it clear.

These were my biological parents. The baby in the picture was me.

They looked happy. They looked young. If I had to guess, I'd say they were younger than I was right now.

Nothing in this picture explained what happened three years later.

Carli folded the letter and returned it to her lap, covering the other pictures. I held out the one I had.

Her eyes widened. "*Wow, look like you.*"

I pointed to the letter. "*What say?*"

"*What want know? What not want know?*"

I scrubbed a hand over my chin, my skin scraping against my five o'clock shadow. Judging by the photo, something else I inherited. Up until now, everything I had was nurture, not nature. I picked up our notebook.

I want to know why. But I also don't want to know why. Which doesn't help you at all. I have no idea if I ever would have opened the letter.

She pointed to my first sentence. "*Yes.*"

So the answer I'd wanted all my memorable life was in my girlfriend's lap. "*Good? Bad?*"

She shrugged. "*H-O-N-E-S-T.*"

I tried to take a deep breath, but that wasn't happening anytime soon. "*What do you think?*"

She held my eyes for a minute, then handed over the letter. I didn't bother breathing. In fact, I'm pretty sure I held my breath.

Reed,

This letter is twenty years too late. I don't know if it will reach you. I don't know if you can even read it.

I was 20 when you were born, your mother 17. We thought we could do it all. We were wrong. Babies are expensive, and my factory job couldn't sustain us. Elania couldn't work, and we couldn't afford child care. We moved in with my mother. She was still very upset we had you at a young age. Refused to help at all, only with the roof over our head.

Elania hated living there, but we had no choice. I search for a second job, and when I did find more work, Elania grew more upset I wasn't home to help care for you.

Then you didn't speak. Spanish. English. Nothing. We tried everything we knew. Nothing worked. My mother…she said some not-nice things. Elania still wasn't happy. I was working a job I didn't like, unable to provide for my family. We started fighting.

You never reacted to the fighting. Years later I wondered if that was part of the problem. But when I was there, it was too much. Elania left. She didn't tell me; she just left. I came home from work, and Mother said you were crying. She let you cry. I had no idea how long.

I tried for a week to take care of you, but I failed. It killed me, but I couldn't care for my son. Mother said I needed to give you up. I agreed.

You were not a baby. I don't know what happened, if you were too old to find a good home. I hope you did. I wished every night I made the right choice.

It took me five more years to grow up enough to handle things on my own. I married. You have three half siblings: two boys, one girl. I did it right this time.

Every year on your birthday, and many times more, I think of you. I hope for good things for you. I know I failed. But maybe I did right in the end.

Why wait until now to send this letter? Because now you're my age when I gave you up. When I held you for the last time. When I watched you take a stranger's hand and walk away from me. You never looked back; you looked forward. As if you knew what waited for you was better than what you had. Maybe you can put yourself in my shoes. A single father with a child who needed more. Needed things I couldn't provide.

I have enclosed pictures of you, and a picture of my family today. If you want to contact me, please do. My arms are open. If not, I understand. That's the bed I made when I let you walk away from me wearing two different sneakers and a dirty Elmo shirt.

Juan

I put the letter down and leaned back against the headboard. Carli curled up beside me, resting her head on my chest but angled to see my face.

"*You OK?*" she asked.

Was I? Christ. I had no idea. "*Don't know.*"

She scooted up and pressed her lips against mine. I angled my head, taking the kiss deeper, pulling her closer to me. "*He sounds like a good man,*" she signed when she pulled back.

I raised my eyebrows. She responded by pointing to the bruises on her face, visible now that some of her makeup had rubbed off.

I grabbed my phone.

Me: We don't know that Juan didn't beat me. He just didn't admit to it.

Carli: My father would never have written that letter. He would have been the one walking away without looking back.

At a loss for what to do, what to say, heck, what to *feel*, I reached for the pictures. Four of me, mostly on my own. The last I must've been close to three. It looked so similar to the ones Mom and Dad had, yet so different. My eyes were different. How was it my eyes were different right from the start? I had no language. I couldn't communicate. Could it be, like Juan suggested, I knew I was in a better situation?

The last picture wasn't of me at all. It was of Juan, a little salt and pepper in his dark hair. A blonde, roughly his age, tucked beside him. Three children stood nearby, the oldest around thirteen, youngest around five. Even with a different mother we looked alike. The youngest, a girl, had a big smile and pigtails, and my first thought wasn't that this was my sister. My first thought was whether my own daughter would look like her.

Assuming I had children. Something churned inside. Instead of staring at a picture where I shared blood with four members, I looked at Carli. I thought of those hypothetical children I had envisioned, all the clearer thanks to Juan's pictures.

I wanted it. A family. Blood. Yet I looked at Carli. A woman who hadn't wanted to see me tonight until she ended up at that party. My phone buzzed.

Carli: What are you thinking?

I nearly laughed.

Me: Thoughts you don't want to know.

Carli: Humor me.

Me: Family. Genetics. Only I'm looking in the wrong direction.

I didn't send the message right away, just stared down at my words. The last thing she needed was my scaring her.

She took the decision out of my hands when she pried my phone away and read my unsent message. The rise and fall of her chest increased as she read, and her eyes watered. She looked at me, just looked at me, and I saw it. I saw how she felt in the intensity of her irises. I knew it was there. But like everything else, she needed to find her own path through her recovery.

I took my phone back.

Me: I can't meet them. Not yet. Maybe I'll send Juan a letter thanking him for contacting me. But face-to-face? I'm not ready.

This time I sent the text, and Carli picked up her own phone. *"OK. How feel now?"*

Regardless of anything and everything, Juan gave me answers. My birth parents were young; they were unable to care for me. They didn't realize I was deaf. My hearing loss, if genetic, wasn't present in either family to the extreme they'd be aware of it.

My birth mother left. Maybe Elania would spin a different tale. Truth was, she didn't send a letter.

I pulled out my phone and sent a text to my mother, just a simple *"I love you."* Later I'd thank her for being my mother. For adopting me. For working with me when my own blood could not.

And Dad…Christ. Dad too. Pills, texting, tree, and all. Only one problem remained: I had answers from Juan. I didn't have any from Dad.

I tossed my phone aside and pulled Carli into my arms. Maybe I'd watch the video soon. But not tonight.

Chapter Thirty-Four

Carli

ON MONDAY MY students gave me a headache before I even had a chance to sit down. If it wasn't a question on the assignment or a request to go to the bathroom, it was them acting their full thirteen-year-old selves. My tolerance hovered in the negative ranges, flashing one clear thought: I wasn't up to this teaching thing anymore. I wanted to wave the white flag and withdraw. But then what would I do? I couldn't go back to my parents' house, and I didn't have a job or money to go out on my own. I needed the degree, even if I never taught.

Never taught. The thought caused a pang in my heart. My dream remained my dream, even if no longer attainable.

By the end of the day, I was ready to curl up in a ball of pain. Therefore, on Tuesday, I brought my OxyContin with me and took one once I got to class. It took the edge off of being a bad teacher, that's for sure. Made everything a little more manageable. Point for prescription drugs.

Rinse and repeat for Wednesday and Thursday. I skipped my ASL classes. Since I audited the class anyways, it was no big deal, though Gina did encourage me to drop in when I felt better.

She didn't know, like I did, that I wasn't getting better.

On Friday, I counted down the minutes to the end of the day like my students. My control slipped in my other classes as the students realized I was loopy and they could get away with murder. All true.

In my room, I texted Reed, told him I was settling in for an early night, and promised I meant it this time. I even took a picture of myself, already in my pajamas, makeup off, last remnants of my bruises easily seen, and sent it his way.

I followed that up with a pity cry and another pill. Didn't matter I had taken one an hour prior. The pills took the pressure off of trying to be something I wasn't anymore.

SATURDAY, I GRADED papers while I waited for Reed to come over. I checked each answer with my master sheet. Twice. A tedious and slow process, but I had caught myself making mistakes. Not acceptable. I was stuck on an answer that looked right but wasn't matching up when a strobe light plugged into an outlet flashed. My buzzer had gone off. The sound was quieter than before the attack. Without the light, I would've missed it.

I scurried off my bed and pressed the buzzer. A few minutes later, a lamp by my bed flashed twice—my new doorbell. Had I let him know how much I appreciated his gift?

"*Cool doorbell,*" I signed when I opened the door.

Reed looked good. Damn good. He wore his wool jacket, in contrast to the jeans with a hole around one knee. I hadn't seen him much during the week due to my inability to do anything. Standing within touching distance of him eradicated a lot of the stress holding me down.

He moved to me, hand on my head, and kissed me like he hadn't seen me in, well, a week. I guessed I wasn't the only one feeling this way.

"*Happy you like the doorbell.*"

He removed his coat and hung it on the hook by the door, revealing a short-sleeved tee shirt underneath. No surprise there. Then again, that might be due in part to the temperature we kept the dorm at. Not short-sleeved temp—not for me, I wore a sweater—but not anything near winter degrees.

Reed followed me into my bedroom and paused at the door. He looked at the single project on my bed, then at me, then back to the project. I raised a shoulder, feigning indifference. "*I'm not the same.*" With my new, weaker brain capacity, I could handle only one small task at a time.

"*I see…*" His hand lingered in the air as he caught sight of my OxyContin bottle. And held. I'd never seen anyone else do math in their head before, but I would've bet my sisters' $3,000 check he was counting. "*Pain?*"

Shit. Was I in pain? It was background sensations for me now, constantly there, a part of who I was. "*Yes.*"

He ran two hands through his hair and walked in a small circle. "*Don't lie to me. Are you in pain enough to need those?*" He signed fast and pissed off, but I managed to follow him.

"*I'm always in pain.*"

He pushed past me and picked up the bottle, shaking the contents out in his hand. He dropped each pill back into the container; one by one they disappeared from his hand. Then he froze, eyes no longer on the pills. He bent and picked out a bottle from my trash. An empty one.

Shit.

He didn't sign anything. Storm brewing in his brown eyes, he picked up the second bottle and raised his eyebrows in question. I didn't have any answers. I held my head high and forced my chin not to quiver.

"*You. Swallow. All.*" He pointed to the empty bottle.

I snatched both bottles from him and put them back on the nightstand. He grabbed the half-full one and pocketed it. I spun around to him. "*What the fuck?*"

"*You really want to kill yourself? Or…?*"

I had no idea what the last part was, but I didn't care. Not this, not again. I wasn't thinking about killing myself, or whatever else he accused me of. I just needed the pills to cope. I just needed them to handle the fragmented pieces of my demolished life. "*No. Need pills to live.*"

"*No, no.*" He paced again, hands flapping, clearly knowing I wouldn't understand what he needed to say.

He took a deep breath and slowed down. *"Pills not good. Will hurt you. Don't...father win."*

"Too late. My father won the minute he hit me. Again."

A tear slid down his cheek, and I took a step back. I'd never seen a man cry before. The men I knew didn't shed any emotion except anger. But Reed wasn't like that. In his eyes he didn't hide the pain I caused him. I may have been broken, but I was breaking him.

I waited for this to break me. My insides remained distant, cold. I stared at his pocket, where my medication was. I needed them, and he blocked them from me.

He made a motion of cutting his wrists. *"...Not the answer."*

The words came through in a fog. I couldn't process them. Tears welled in my own eyes, and I remained where I was, not moving, not signing, not doing anything but stare at the bottle bulging in his pants pocket.

And no, right now he wasn't happy to see me.

"What happened to taking ibuprofen?"

Why would I take ibuprofen when I had OxyContin?

"Talk to me. Please."

What was I supposed to say? *"Talk? Talk how? Brain not work."* It didn't. My actions weren't my own.

He clenched his fists, knuckles turning white, and released. Then he whipped out his phone, typed a message, and held it up for me to read.

Reed: I understand you're in pain. You're not normal. But you're hiding behind the attack, behind the pills. You want to teach? Teach. You want to graduate? Graduate. No one is stopping you.

I clenched my own fists. It would be so easy to knock some sense into him. Show him what it was really like for me. Get out some of this pent-up aggression I had no escape for. A red haze threatened to overcome my vision, chanting that it would solve all my problems.

I closed my eyes and released my fists. I was not my father. I was not my father. I was not my father. How easy it would have been. How wrong. I turned to the wall as the tears slid down my cheeks, and I pulled out my phone.

Me: You don't understand. You may think you do, but you don't. Ever try to think of something, anything, and the answer isn't quite there? So you think harder, search deeper, and grasp that answer from the depths of a fog? That's my brain. Every. Damn. Day. Ask me what I ate? Fog. Have to solve a math equation? Fog. I'm not hiding behind anything. I'm in a fog. And it's not clearing. It's not getting better. It's getting worse. And you want me to swim through that fog every damn day? For the rest of my life? What life is that?

I clicked Send and rested my head on the wall.

Reed: So the answer is to give up? Have you tried thinking without the pills? Have you tried other avenues of working through the fog? Counseling? It's only 3 weeks since the attack. Is that long enough to give up? To really give up? And don't answer, because you'll just spout more bullshit.

He moved to the door, a chasm of epic proportions growing between us. He didn't understand, couldn't understand. Therefore I let the chasm grow, even as it killed me inside.

Chapter Thirty-Five

Reed

MY HEART STOPPED, plain stopped, when I saw the colored pill bottle sitting in the trash. I no longer saw her trash can. I saw Dad's drawer and the multiple bottles I found after his death. I saw the damn tree he plowed into. The casket...

Every stable thought in my head shattered in a violent death. No longer did I have any ground to stand on, any purchase. This couldn't be happening. Again. This couldn't be fucking happening!

I needed to know where this pill issue stemmed from. I released the door knob and turned to Carli. *"If you don't have your pills, what else would you use?"*

Carli's mouth dropped open in shock, and damned if that didn't help the ache in my chest some small bit. *"Use for what?"*

Slowly, painfully, I signed, *"Suicide."*

"*Nothing.*"

The answer was quick, clipped, as if she still hid something. After letting me, in she'd begun shutting me off. The irony caused me to laugh.

Carli's face screwed up tight. "*Fuck you.*" She turned on her heel, brown hair flapping over her shoulder. I grabbed her arm and held tight while my other hand secured my phone.

Me: I'd gladly fuck you, but I don't think either one of us wants that right now, except for an angry fuck. You've been abusing pills. I'm not leaving you alone.

Carli yanked her arm until it broke free. "*I'm not a kid.*"

Me: No, but you're struggling. I'm not allowing something to happen to you. I love you too much to let you allow any more pain in your life.

Carli: The pills weren't pain. Love is pain.

The first time she mentioned love to me and she coupled it with pain. This was a whole new direction I hadn't seen. I didn't think there was anything left in me to break, but she always managed to find more. Her eyes remained glued to the floor, and I took hold of her chin, forcing her head up until her eyes met mine. I saw pain there, the same pain I felt.

"*If fight love, then pain. Stop fighting.*" God, had she been fighting me all this time, keeping the wedge between us? I wanted to engulf her in my arms, kiss her until she couldn't deny either of our feelings. She turned to her phone before I could react.

Carli: Family is love, right? Family did this to me. I don't have the capacity for love or much else. Don't you see? I'm beyond damaged. You should cut your losses while you can, find someone who can love you back. Find someone who still has a heart.

Family was more than blood—family was also a choice. And regardless of the anger I still felt, at all the rips in the foundation, I still chose her for my family. She continued to decimate me, and I stuck.

Family shared. Or they ended up headfirst into a tree. It was time I stopped steering us toward the damn tree. I stomped over to her nightstand, my hand grasping the half-full pill bottle from my pocket. I placed it next to the empty one, my gut lurching at the sight. A lineup of past and present. A lineup to prevent the future.

I faced Carli. *"Pills."* I gestured to her bottles. *"Pills killed my father."* I broke into slow and full ASL, using the classifiers that set up the 3-D language. I motioned taking one pill, then another, then the whole damn bottle. Opened a car door, got inside. Made a point of not putting on my seat belt. Held my hands against the wheel. Set up the tree in the distance. Switched to far-away scale, the "three" hand shape representing the car heading closer and closer to the tree. I switched between close up and far away, mimed texting, until the car and tree collided. *"Dead."*

Carli gasped, and her hands flew to her mouth. But it wasn't enough. My language and hers, both were needed to make sure she understood the full extent of what I was telling her. I picked up the notebook and her pen.

I'm sorry I never explained enough about myself for you to understand this. My father died in a car accident, yes. After his death, Mom and I discovered he'd been abusing pills. We don't know why; we can't ask him. He was driving at midnight, texting me when he hit a tree.

She blinked, her eyes threatening to overflow. She took the notebook from me.

I'm so sorry. But I am not your father.

Her chin jutted high and everything—everything—careened off the road. I picked up her empty bottle, held it level with my shoulder before dropping it into the trash. She continued to stare, face now void of emotions.

"*Fine, I give up.*" I couldn't go through this, not again. I took the other pill bottle and handed it to her. "*Go ahead. Kill yourself.*"

She took a step back, hands raised. "*No. I don't want them.*"

I cocked an eyebrow.

Her head tilted down as she pulled her cell phone out of her back pocket.

Carli: OK, I do want them. It would stop the pain. Mine. Yours.

My insides broke to such an extent I wasn't sure the liquid dripping down my face wasn't blood.

Me: It would stop your pain, yes, assuming no afterlife. But my pain? No. HELL no. My pain began when my father died. Not while he struggled in silence. My pain intensified when I found his unfinished text. My pain turned downright suffocating when I watched his body lowered into the ground. My pain doesn't end. You can end yours. But those pills don't end mine.

We headed for the tree—only she was in the driver's seat.

Chapter Thirty-Six

Carli

MY HANDS SHOOK as I held my phone and read Reed's words. Over and over again. Each word a stab to my heart. He held nothing back in his face, all but exposing his mangled heart. And suddenly I got it. I was supposed to heal him.

I failed.

My pain became his pain. It wasn't right. It wasn't fair. But some pain couldn't be solved with a prescription bottle. His couldn't.

And with a shocking gut punch, I realized mine couldn't either.

Not the pain from my concentration, not the pain from my reality. Only the physical pain from my head. The most manageable pain I possessed.

I placed my phone nearby, blindly fumbling around until I hit a surface. Then I touched Reed's cheek, wiping the tears away. Tears I caused. Tears I didn't want to cause. He didn't deserve my pain. He didn't deserve this. He was too damn important to me to deserve this.

But my thoughts weren't my own. They weren't clear, and I didn't know how to explain all this to him. His eyes—God, his eyes. I'd never seen them so lost, so broken. I grasped his face in my hands and mashed my lips to his in a no-holds-barred, take-no-prisoners kiss. The kind that heated from zero to sixty in two seconds flat. He grasped onto my waist, yanking me into him as he angled his head, taking the kiss deeper. I clutched onto him, desperate, as tears slid down my cheeks.

I needed him inside me, and not in the way we were clearly heading as he pulled my shirt over my head. I needed him in my head, in the chaos.

In my heart.

I needed him to know things I couldn't say in either language, things I couldn't even tell myself. I wanted him to know me better than I knew myself. But words wouldn't come, not with the OxyContin in my system. Heck, maybe not without it in my system. I could only will him to know, will my heart to beat the truth into his.

He slowed the kiss, and his heart kicked up a beat. Somehow the impossible happened. I felt this thing between us, whatever Carli + Reed equaled. The pulse at the base of his neck, where my lips now clung, jumped to the rhythm, to the math, so the Xz that we created thrived in him as much as it thrived in me. I clung to him, and words bubbled up inside, wanting to be released.

Vanishing before they could form.

Reed pulled back. "*I don't want to lose you.*"

But that was always the plan. Nothing lasts forever. My head, the pills, this fight—all proof. We'd reached the point of no return. I hated it, absolutely hated it, even as I knew it had to happen. I shook my head as more tears threatened to fall. I tugged at the button on his pants, desperation settling in. Desperate because I couldn't give in to what I wanted, what I needed.

Him. I needed him. And not just for tomorrow.

A tomorrow that would never come. All we had was this last moment, and I had to tell him how I felt before I never had the chance.

My tongue wouldn't form words and couldn't form words he'd understand. So I used it to taste his body as I revealed his skin, lapping at the ridges and bumps, the smooth and the hairy. I almost had him, too, but he stopped me once I got him flat on his back.

"*What are you doing?*"

"*I need you.*" Finally, some words. Words that worked. He crashed me to him, removing my own clothes as our mouths spoke the language of lovers, the language we shared equally and fully.

For the first time ever, I almost skipped the condom. I just wanted him, needed the connection. Reed, sans brain injury and those damned pills, had his head on straight and protected himself. He lay flat on my bed, and

I straddled him, taking him inside. No longer protecting myself. Because he had me. All of me.

There would never be a happy ending; my father made sure of that. A part of me would die when this was all over. Nothing I wasn't already used to, thanks to my brain injury. One more hole in my soul, in my damaged life.

First I needed this, with him. He needed this before the rug finished being pulled from underneath us. I showed him as best I could, using our bodies as communication. Flesh against flesh, heartbeat to heartbeat, lips to lips. I showed him until we both flew over the finish line, until we lay sated in each other's arms.

I couldn't look at him, kept my head buried in his chest. I wanted to pause time, find a time machine. Anything to save this, save us. I bit back the tears as I got off him and then collapsed into a sitting position beside him. The pills stood at attention. Reed was right—they hurt him, they caused his pain.

"*I can't...*" I closed my eyes, trapping the moisture inside. I couldn't do it. I couldn't ignore the pills. I couldn't deal with the pain.

The bed shifted, and I opened my eyes. Reed mirrored my image, both of us naked. Both eyeing the pills. Minutes stretched past, and his breathing increased. He got up, but I stayed as I was. Deep inside, a part of me struggled to break free, to change the course, to hit me on my damaged head. Too deep inside, too buried by other shit.

When I took in Reed again, he was dressed and typing on his phone. I grabbed a robe and fished out mine.

Reed: Can't or won't?

Both. I stared at him, a silent plea on my face: don't make me answer that.

Reed: I can't and won't stand by as you kill yourself. Been there, done that, fucked me up for two years. And here I am, back in the same story.

I blanked my face and forced my thumb to move over my phone.

Me: That's why I can't. Won't. I'm no good for you. I'm not a long-term bet. You are. You deserve better than me.

I watched his face as he read. I braced myself for the crumble. Not the way his eyebrows furrowed. Not the way his jaw clenched. He shook his head, looking anywhere but at me. With steam all but rising from him, he picked up my pills. I stood to get them, but he held me back, managed to open the container lid, and dumped them all in the trash.

"What the fuck?" I said, not caring he couldn't hear me.

He gathered the empty pill bottles and threw them into the trash with such force that the can tipped sideways, pills sliding onto my floor. He looked at me, anger and exasperation on his face. Lost for words, as lost as I was.

No words, no texts, nothing passed between us. He stomped out. Away from me. Forever.

I really needed another pill.

I crawled on the floor, picking up each small round destroyer of my relationship. One by one I collected them back into the bottle. A sob burst out of me, then another, and another, until I could no longer see what I was doing.

I ended up in a puddle on the floor. The only way to communicate the turbulent chaos inside was to cry. I hugged my knees to myself, rocking through the tears, through the pain, through the fear.

When I checked my phone, I had a new text.

Reed: For the record, you don't see yourself. You don't see this amazing woman who's already overcome so much. You don't see the fighter spirit that continues to move forward no matter what is thrown your way. You don't see that you do have a future. It might look different than it did before, but it's still there. You can adapt and rise above.

One thought came to mind: What if I can't?

Reed: Don't give up. Don't stop fighting just because you have a diagnosis.

I started a response—"What if I fail?"—and stared at the words on the screen. Failure had never been an option. Not until now. Was he right? Was I giving up? Throwing my life away because of one bad blow. Literally.

The pills in my hand called to me. Taunted me, really. They would be my failure even as they were my lifeline.

I dumped them back onto my hand until ten nestled together. Reed's face came to mind. The total devastation. The reality that if I eased my pain by swallowing what lay in my hand, I'd hurt him.

Didn't matter what I did. I hurt him.

I sat there, I didn't know for how long, holding those pills in my hand. Until the pink color transferred to my sweaty skin. Until I felt numb, as if the medicine was absorbed rather than swallowed.

Could I really rise above? What kind of a future did I have with a brain injury?

I deposited the pills back into the container and finally got dressed. My homework taunted me, teased me with achievements now lost. I picked up my laptop and typed in *mild traumatic brain injury*.

I went straight to the personal stories. Many with injuries worse than mine. They hadn't succumbed to the lure of pills. Then again, I wasn't heading toward any success story in my current state.

One thing connected each story: they continued to live and made accommodations for their injury. The type of accommodations I made as a kid, with my study habits. The kind of accommodations I would need to make again if I wanted to teach.

I gathered my books and set them up around me. Normal. I had to get back to normal. Carli normal. I opened my first book and got to work. Only my mind wandered to my troublesome class. Time to follow my haphazard focus. I put the work aside and grabbed my notes from my meeting with Heidi. The answer was there, somewhere; I knew it.

The only question: Could I find it?

On my paper, I circled one word again and again with my red pen: *control*. I needed to show them I still had it. Even when I didn't. I drew lines all over the paper, making connections out of the suggestions. As my red pen bled over the notes, an idea slowly formed. It was almost painful, forcing my mind into gear, making sense out of things I couldn't. Somehow I weathered through.

An hour later I wasn't sure, but I had an idea and was excited to try. I also had spent an hour on one topic. Unheard of.

AT BEDTIME I stared at the amber container holding those tempting, teasing pills. Pills I wanted. The pull remained, the promise of fixing all my troubles contained in that small container.

Or I could fix my troubles my own way. Without the pills. One step at a time with my haphazard thinking skills leading the way. I pulled out the ibuprofen instead.

I collected my phone, set up a text to Reed, and froze. No. I couldn't text him. Not anymore. We were over. That thought alone made me wish I hadn't taken the ibuprofen already. I wanted to tell him what I'd done, what I'd accomplished. I wanted...

Him.

Too late.

Sleep wasn't easy. I didn't have that blissful OxyContin euphoria. I tossed and turned without my personal comfort system. The room was too cold, then too warm. I ached but couldn't get comfortable. At some point I managed to nod off.

When I opened my eyes to the morning light, I was forced to close them again. The throbbing from my temples wasn't ready for the light. This wasn't unusual. I gave myself time to wake up in darkness, then slowly introduced light. The headache was loud and proud, and tinnitus came screaming in to round out the Carli Horror Show. But I was used to this. I could manage this.

I hoped.

And thus began my challenge to put my life back together. Or rather, to see if I could. One small step at a time.

Chapter Thirty-Seven

Carli

MONDAY MORNING, I stared at my face in the bathroom mirror. My mouth had a slight frown to it, and the bags under my eyes were less than attractive. But my bruises were down to a yellow tint. No makeup necessary.

"Welcome back, Carli," I said to my expression, trying out a smile before letting it fade at the double meaning. Was I really back?

Maybe yes. Maybe no. But today I was going to be a better Carli. Even if my heart ached more than my head. An ache even the tempting pills wouldn't help. I pulled the hair back behind my left ear and fastened a clip, exposing my silent left ear. New look. New Carli.

Single Carli. I had learned my lesson. No more dating. Not now. Not ever.

"You ready?" D asked as I grabbed my coat.

"No."

She grasped my shoulders in a mini hug. "You've got this." I absorbed her support and her confidence, since I had next to none. Failure followed me like a shadow, but unlike Peter Pan, I didn't want to keep this particular shadow attached.

Heidi waited for me in the classroom, as she had since things spiraled out of control. I patted my bag and willed myself to have the confidence I once had in abundance.

"I have a plan. With any luck it will at least be a step in the right direction."

"Good." She couldn't hide the smile. Then she studied my face. "Your bruises are almost healed."

My hands flew to my face on instinct.

"I was looking for it, Carli. It wasn't noticeable. Feeling better?"

I let the cool morning air fill my lungs. "About to find out."

My first class was more awake than they had been in two weeks, which I took as the boost of confidence I needed. Once they left I had five minutes to prep for the troublesome class.

No time for any fears or worries. Only time for action.

From my bag I pulled out two sets of note cards and a spool of yellow caution tape. On each desk I placed a single card before roping off the entire area with the tape. On the whiteboard I set up the second set of cards, sporting each student's name.

Heidi entered before my students and took in the scene. "Has there been a murder?"

I laughed. "Not yet. I'm trying something new."

She investigated a card by the board, and then by the desks, the corner of her mouth tipping upward at the very ends. She moved to the back of the class, ducking under my yellow divider. My students were very confused when they arrived, but I gave nothing away until they were all crowding the front of the class.

"Your seats have been changed. In order to find your new seat you will need to solve an equation." I pointed to the row of note cards on the board. "This game is simple. Find your name, solve your problem, and find your new seat."

My students gathered the cards and set themselves up on the floor, or standing, or over by the windows. Heck, some of them took over my desk. I removed the yellow tape blocking off the desks.

Since the equations involved what we were working on, I learned who was good with the material and who wasn't. Slowly the students moved to their newly assigned seats. As each one moved, I checked my chart to ensure they did the math correctly. Most got it right. A few made mistakes, but I worked with them on correcting them.

Zachary and Max were not pleased with their new desks apart from each other, but I wouldn't allow any deviation from the plan. Either they sat in their new seats or the principal would be waiting for them. They eyed Heidi for the truth to my statement, and she backed me up.

Max mumbled something from his spot near the front, by my left ear.

"Care to repeat that?" I asked, hands on my hips.

"You can't hear nothing," he grumbled. Since I was facing him I heard him.

I leaned against my desk and crossed my ankles. "Not true. My right ear hears a decent amount. My left ear, on the other hand, can hear certain loud, deep sounds, like a motor running. How about raising your hand when you need to ask a question? My eyes work fine."

"Why don't you get a new hearing aid and fix your ear?"

"Because a hearing aid won't fix my ear. Hearing aids are not like glasses. They only magnify sound. Ever have a bad connection on a phone and making the sound louder doesn't help? That's hearing aids."

We talked about hearing loss for a little longer. I even took off my right hearing aid to show my students what it looked like.

By the end of the day, I was exhausted. My head wanted to scream but remained screwed on, one small victory. A better victory was the praise I received from Heidi. I had a lot of work ahead of me, but for the first time since the attack, I had hope.

THE DAYS WERE long and painful. Pain from my head. Pain from my heart. The head was getting better. If I kept ibuprofen in my system, I could manage. I knew this. Didn't stop my daily battle with the pills.

Ten minutes a day I looked at them. Held them, even went so far as to put one in my mouth. Each time Reed's face would come to mind. The pain from his image was caused by the pills. Could not be solved by the pills.

Therefore I continued to exist, even if I was a shell of myself.

One Tuesday I planned to head straight home after work and lock myself in my bedroom, an action D called frustrating. I called it survival. Otherwise I'd become her first counseling patient, and I needed to do this on my own. Win or lose.

Willow wanted me to join the ASL dinner. I bit my lip as my fingers hovered over my phone.

Me: I don't think that's a good idea.

Willow: You're still our friend.

Somehow I didn't think this "our" included Reed.

Me: It will be awkward.

Willow: I can tell him to stay home.

I shook my head and blinked to clear my eyes.

Me: No, don't do that. I'll come.

Because I wanted to see him.

I was the last to arrive. The group was easy to spot, several tables pushed together and full of signers. I homed in on Reed. He faced one of his friends, a tight smile on his face, bags under his eyes, and it appeared as though he hadn't shaved since I last saw him. He looked like the man I first met, only without the good humor. I wanted to reach out and touch him, feel those bristles against my skin, against my lips. I wanted what I could never have.

His back stiffened, and he looked my way. Our eyes held. He lured me more than the pills. But I could give in to neither. I swallowed my heart, and a bit of my pride, and pulled the most flippant thing I could find out of my ass.

"*See, still alive*," I signed, even as I wanted to say, "*Take me back.*"

His face hardened, and he turned away without a word. I had half a mind to go home and swallow the entire bottle, but my name rang in my ear. I scanned the table until I found Willow waving. Val, meanwhile, gave me a look I couldn't read before turning to her roommate.

I took the vacant seat across from them, at the opposite end of the table from Reed. It was weird. We'd always sat together, and now there wasn't even an empty chair anywhere near him. "Hi," I said and signed.

"You look good," Willow said, hands moving with her words.

I laughed. "I most certainly do not." I needed to start using my makeup again for my drooping eyes.

"I meant your bruises."

I shrugged. "External heals. Internal doesn't."

Willow frowned, and I shook my head. The waitress interrupted, and I ordered myself a drink. I was going to need a large one to make it through dinner.

I tried to get lost in the conversation, but Reed was right there, so close and yet so far away. I didn't know if I could make it through another dinner. Not until I managed to move on from him. If that was even an option. I snuck a glance. And found the back of his head.

Message received. *Move on, Carli. You made your bed; now lie in it.* Yet I was never good at listening to my own advice. Or any advice, it seemed.

"How's he doing?" I asked Val and Willow.

They shared a look, and that was all the answer I needed. My drink landed in front of me, and I took a healthy swallow. Tonight, this would be my vice.

Chapter Thirty-Eight

Reed

WHY'D SHE HAVE to show up? It was one thing for Willow to invite her, claiming Carli was part of the group. Ignoring the fact she was part of the group because of me, and she'd ripped my damn heart out. I didn't want to see her. Not yet. Not ever.

And here she was, drinking alcohol, probably floating the pills in her system. I tried to ignore her. After the end result of my father's self-destruction, I didn't need to watch Carli go through the same. But she'd always been a magnet. I kept checking her face, searching in vain for something, anything, to prove she wasn't heading for her own tree.

Her eyes weren't quite right. Her face pained. I didn't know how to read her, not anymore. I wondered if I ever could.

At one point she rested her elbow on the table, rubbing at her temple. The same place I had held, rubbed, and kissed countless times. And each time, she would smile. Each time would help her.

I clenched my hands and stayed where I was, fighting against every part of me that wanted to take her into my arms. Stupid, really. She had her own pain meds now.

"You finished drooling over her?" Tanner asked, pulling me away from tracking the pain crossing Carli's face.

Yes. No. Neither worked. *"Fuck off."*

Tanner shook his head and took a swig of his beer. *"Going to let your dick shrivel up and fall off again?"*

I took his beer away. *"No."*

Tanner ignored the beer. His eyebrows shot straight up. *"No? Beth I understood; she de-balled you. But Carli"*—he shook his head—*"you de-balled yourself."*

I chugged on his beer, slapping his hand away when he tried to claim it back. *"Asshole,"* he signed once I finished.

I wasn't sure when I'd start dating again. It wasn't going to be years, that was for damn sure.

Tanner tapped the table. *"What's the plan? You going to close yourself off, not accept anyone new into your world?"*

I glared at him.

"That's what you did. After Beth. Carli was the first person you accepted into your world. And that shit ended badly."

I reached for my own beer and took a healthy swallow. In truth, I had no answers. I hadn't thought beyond the pain and fear. But Carli sat apart from me. Carli chose her vice. I had no choice but to move on.

A FEW WEEKS later, I shifted my beer as the woman across the table signed. Long brown hair, bright blue eyes, and a coloring more similar to mine. Jill was the first Deaf person I had dated in a long, long time.

If only I felt something for her. Instead of nothing.

I took a sip of my beer, laughing at the right parts of the story. Jill was good-looking, funny, and easy to talk to. So why the hell did I want to be anywhere but here?

The answer was the deaf/hard of hearing woman I couldn't get out of my mind. She was stuck on loop. Even when I envisioned her with those damn pills, it didn't diminish my desire for her.

But she wanted the pills more. And that was the final straw. The end. It had been over a month. Shouldn't that make a difference by now?

I let my gaze drop down to Jill's cleavage. A nice view, the way her shirt gapped and gave a hint of something lacy underneath. Only I felt like a cheating creep rather than an interested partner.

I took another swig of my beer as something purple caught my attention. Over at the bar, a woman with purple hair glared at me. Matti.

I stiffened and dragged my eyes back to my date. *"I'm sorry, I see someone I haven't seen in a while. Do you mind if I say hi?"*

Jill glanced in the direction I'd been staring. *"Purple hair?"*

"*Yes.*" Then I gave in and opted for the truth. "*My ex's sister.*"

"*Oh.*" Jill glanced back and forth. "*Go ahead.*" Then she flipped her phone over and started tapping at it.

I made my way across the bar, typing on my phone before Matti had any other ideas.

Me: How is she?

I had to know. Carli hadn't come to any more ASL dinners. Val and Willow were tight-lipped as hell. A simple *she's alive* would have been sufficient. But nothing. Cut off like I was the bad guy here and not acting out of self-preservation.

Matti: You could have texted that from your date.

Me: Not really.

That would've been rude to everyone involved.

I stood in front of Matti. She must've said something to the group she was with, as they gave us some space. She eyed me carefully, mouth set in a thin line. She didn't often remind me of Carli, not with her hair and attitude. Now she did.

Either I hadn't been looking carefully enough, or I was a starved man.

Matti: If you really wanted to know, you could have texted her.

Me: She never responded to my last texts. Why would she respond to this one?

That awarded me a shocked look from Matti. I was tired of ignoring the obvious. I had one question I wanted answered.

Me: Is she still taking OxyContin?

Matti stared at her phone, and the little flame of hope I kept kindled—hope that Carli would open up her eyes and take care of herself—vanished.

Matti: I don't know.

I wasn't expecting that as an answer.

Me: What do you mean, you don't know? Carli was popping more pills than she needed to take in a day. She chose those damn pills over me. And you don't know if she's in trouble?

Matti read my message, then pushed me in the shoulder. Mouth flapping, hand flapping, neither making any sense.

Matti: You idiot. The Reynolds clan doesn't share shit like that. We keep things buried inside. Which means you should take a good long look at yourself in the mirror. YOU know this. What did you do with this information?

I ran a hand over the back of my neck. Damned either way I handled anything.

Me: How is she doing?

Matti: Good. Off but good.

That could be mean anything. I was about to respond when I noticed Matti typing more on her phone.

Matti: You have some nerve, you know that? You saw her after the attack. You stood by her side. You were there for her in ways the rest of us couldn't be, giving her everything she needed. And now you cut out, like she's the damaged goods she was beat into being. One day you were gone, and Carli is struggling on her own. You almost convinced her there was more to life and love than we were taught. But in the end, like everyone else in our lives, you failed.

I tried to swallow, but there was no longer any moisture left in my mouth. I had no excuse, and only one way to explain myself.

Me: My father overdosed on pills and killed himself.

Matti looked up at me after she read, the first hint of compassion in her face.

Matti: That's not Carli.

Me: You didn't see what I saw. She chose the pills. Not me.

Matti: She's hurting. She's struggling. And if I know that, that shows you just how much she's hurting and struggling. Every small piece of information she gave you about herself was and is huge. She opened up to you in ways none of us have with others.

I looked up at the wall, over Matti's head. Emotions battled and conflicted inside. Was Matti right? Was I right? Was there even a right answer here?

Matti: You gave me hope, after the attack, you know that? You showed me that not all men were like Dad, and some even had the balls to deal with the shit he left behind. But you don't have any balls at all.

By the time I finished reading, she had turned away from me, back to her friends, leaving me more confused than ever.

I returned to my date and unceremoniously called for its end. She pegged me on not being over the ex. Truth. I'd never be over Carli. She was still under my skin. Where she belonged. Where I didn't want her. I knew from Dad, from Juan, that time healed wounds.

There was no recovery from Carli.

In the outside air, I debated turning right instead of left and going to her dorm. I didn't. Not yet. Not until I dragged some information out of Val. Not until I had an actual plan for letting her deal with all this on her own.

Matti was right—I should have stuck by Carli. But watching her hurt herself was out of the question.

I stopped on the street and looked up at the sky. What would Dad say about this? I already knew Mom supported me even as she wanted to support Carli. But Dad was the culprit of both of our fears. He had initiated these thoughts, these feelings, when he took his own life.

What I would give for a little cosmic advice from a dead man.

I made it to my car and fiddled with my phone, thumbing through, not paying much attention to what I was doing. I ended up staring at the unplayed video message from Dad.

The two-year-old message from a dead man.

Did he really plan to crash into a tree fifteen minutes later?

Before I convinced myself otherwise, I hit Play.

Dad sat in the kitchen. The sight of him made my eyes tear. He looked...not good. Bags under his eyes, though it was late at night. His color off. A shiftiness to him. A look in his eyes that...

Crap. I'd seen that look in Carli's eyes. He'd already taken the pills.

"*Hi. I guess you're out. Or asleep. No, out, doing everything I told you not to do. So I'm going to come out and say it: I'm full of shit. You're an adult. A good man. Mom and*

I raised you well. But parental nurture is only part of the story. I've spent your life in fear of that nature, of what you would pick up from your friends. I should've been looking at you and who you are. But then I'd have nothing to fear, nothing to parent you on. I'd have to accept you as an adult, and I wasn't ready for that."

He ran a hand over his head. *"I'm not making sense. I haven't made sense for a long time. I failed. I taught you well, and I ignored it all myself. So I'm telling you this: fuck it all. Every last bit. Follow your gut. See where it takes you. Just remember one thing: I love you, and I'm proud of you. I'm sorry."*

I rubbed the heels of my hands over my eye sockets. Dad sent inspirational text after inspirational text and then told me to fuck it all.

What kind of closure was that?

It wasn't. But in some odd way, I did exactly as he asked in the past two years when I refused to watch the message. Hadn't I stepped out of my bounds with Carli? Not that it led anywhere good, but I had. Because at the end of it all, Dad didn't control me. He raised me. I respected his words. His words shaped me into the man I became.

Fuck it all. I looked up at the sky. *"Sorry, Dad. Maybe you needed to fuck it all for whatever demon plagued you. But I won't. I like the person you raised to me to be."*

Well, I used to like him. The past month I'd been a shadow, missing Carli. I scrolled through my phone until I got to her text message thread.

No. I wasn't ready. A month or two wasn't long enough. I didn't know when it would be long enough. She was poised to hurt herself more than her father had. Until I knew she wasn't a threat to herself, I couldn't risk any more of my heart. Dad, Juan, Elania, Beth...too many ghosts in my closet, even if I now had names for two of them.

I wouldn't let Carli be another ghost.

Chapter Thirty-Nine

Carli

THE AMBER BOTTLE sat on my nightstand, the same ten pills inside that I had recovered from my trash. For two months I'd kept them here. Not in case I needed them. Not as an easy way out of this hell of a life. As proof I didn't need them. I was stronger than the pills, stronger than anything my father did to me.

Each day that passed with ten pills was another day I survived.

It wasn't normal. But it was me. Hearing loss, brain injury, both hands made up Carli. If I wanted my future to be mine—and not what my father created—then I needed to continue forward. And somehow—somehow—I could do this. I could graduate and work. In my dark moments, I wasn't so sure. When the pain grew intense and my brain lost track of a thought, it was hard to imagine struggling for the rest of my life.

Regardless of my own inner demons, I needed to try.

The pills were step one. Amazingly the pills were the easy part. Reed was the hard part. I missed him more than the high of OxyContin, more than the loopy feeling making me forget my brain wasn't normal. I missed him more than I wanted to, more than I should.

This was as it should be. I proved time and again I wasn't good for him. I wasn't good for anyone. My plan was to live my life, teach, keep my few friends and sisters close by. That was all I needed. Nothing more. Nothing less.

I also needed to sever all ties from my parents. My sisters offered to collect the last of my belongings, but I refused. I wanted a few minutes alone in the house. Alone with my thoughts. Alone with the knowledge of what my youth had really been like. I could pack up what I wanted and leave my key behind, lest my parents thought I might darken their doorstep ever again.

I waited until my school was closed on a day my parents would be working. I gathered my luggage—and D's— and loaded up my car. As much as I wanted to do this, the thought of going "home" wasn't a pleasant one. In fact, the knot in my throat threatened to return my breakfast.

I pulled up to the house and sat in my car. In the exact spot I had parked the last time I was there. The house was the same, right down to the broken shutter. But it was forever tarnished in my memory.

It was the same, but different, just like me. I was the same Carli I'd always been, but my poor head had been abused more than it should. My father wasn't winning though—I was.

My hair was back in a ponytail, showing off my right hearing aid to the world. I had deposited my sisters' check and ordered new hearing aids. A more modern one for my right ear and one that could give my left ear a little power. Even if I just wore it for class, my audiologist felt it would help. My fingers were crossed it wouldn't hinder my head.

Today I suffered with a dull throb. No doubt due to being back where I had been injured in the first place.

And my thoughts were running away from me. Hard not to when visions of my father's fist rammed into my head with such force that I nearly felt the blows again.

I blew out a breath and stared at the house. The naked trees were still, the calm before the storm. I needed to get this done before the storm hit.

I took a deep breath and grabbed the first two bags from my trunk. If I did this correctly, it would take them months to realize I'd come and gone for the last time.

Inside the front door, I froze, not too far from the spot of attack. The house was dark and silent. Secrets were hidden behind the walls, dark secrets of parents who didn't know how to love, of daughters too scared to get help. Of hidden bruises, mysterious back pains, headaches, and sudden hearing loss. The floral furniture didn't fool me— this was a house of terror.

I made my way upstairs and opened the door to my bedroom. Left just the same as the last time I was here. My one small sanctuary in this house.

I opened my closet and pulled out my clothes, rolling them to pack as much into the bags as possible. Next came the drawers. I didn't stop to think; I took everything. Once my bags were full, I dragged them down to my car and took two more bags with me. This time I didn't pause. I went up to my room and rummaged through more drawers.

I gave each item a split-second decision, yes or no, either in the bag or back on the shelf. A half hour and two trips to the car later, I took in the sparse bedroom. Two twin beds, Matti's and mine, reminded me of the good sister moments we had shared in this room. The posters on the wall were remnants of old crushes.

I pulled the last item off the shelf, a snow globe I was given one Christmas. Inside the glass dome, a house similar to ours was coated in white flakes. I turned the snow globe upside down, then right side up. Snow fell in smooth, slow increments to cover the house. Each of my sisters had gotten the same gift that year. They were horrified. I was enthralled. Proof of our different childhoods.

As I was about to put the globe back on the shelf, with the snow still falling over the house-of-horror replica, a door slammed below. My heart leapt and I dropped the snow globe, glass shattering at my feet. Hands shaking, I rummaged into my pocket and pulled out my cell phone, thumbed in 9-1-1, and paused. Did I dare speak?

No. I swallowed, but the lump lodged in my throat didn't budge. I flipped to messaging and set up a text to my sisters.

Me: At house, cleaning out belongings. Dad just got home.

I clicked Send, muted my phone, and shoved it back in my pocket. My pulse raced; I didn't know what to do. To hide was my first instinct, but Dad already knew I was here. To protect was my second, but I wasn't sure how. On instinct, I locked the door.

Not my brightest move, but I knew I was dead meat anyways.

Why did I insist on doing this? Just when I was getting better, learning how to manage my disadvantages. Now I was a sitting duck with a bull's-eye on my chest. Or rather, my head.

My feet were rooted to the spot, too scared to move. Matti's face echoed in my mind. How many times had I seen her plastered to the door, face full of terror, waiting, waiting for something horrible to happen?

Or something horrible to finish happening?

Too many times. Why didn't I ask questions? Why didn't I get answers? How could I have let Matti freak out so many times and do nothing?

Because I had a good childhood.

I looked around the room, at the broken snow globe on the floor. Shards of glass were dispersed, the house angled into the now-soggy carpet with fake snow speckled around. No. I had a fake childhood—a better one than my sisters, but still a sucky-assed one, all thanks to the asshole downstairs.

The man had been allowed to win at everything in this house. His streak was over.

I glanced at the remaining box on the floor, the contents inside no longer worth the effort to save. I took a deep breath and opened my door, leaving the missing items, final box, and broken snow globe behind.

My heartbeat drummed in my ear, threatening to grow into a nasty headache, but I kept moving. Down the steps, one, two, three. Sounds of the television filtered up the stairs. Down more steps, four, five, six. I stopped counting and concentrated on one thing.

If he hit me again, it would probably kill me.

At the bottom of the steps, my father sat in his chair, giving me his back like he had for the past twenty-two years. "What do you think you're doing?" he bellowed.

"Just getting my stuff. I'm leaving now."

"You put the stuff back and get out of here." His eyes remained glued to the television.

"I'm getting out of here; don't you worry."

Bad timing, because a commercial had started. "I said, put the stuff back." My father's stone-cold face turned to me. Heavy bags weighed down his eyes, wrinkling at the corner, in need of a chisel to crease any farther.

"I'm leaving." I said a silent prayer and turned to leave the house for the last time. The only way out was to give the man my back. I wasn't about to back out like a coward.

"Put the damn stuff back, Carli," my father spoke loud enough for my left ear to ring.

Or maybe my tinnitus discerned the words' origin. Either way, I was scared. He'd always scared me. But I was sick and tired of being scared of this man. I turned to face him one last time.

"Ah, so you aren't pretending to be deaf today?"

I tightened one hand into a snug ball. "I'm not pretending. I've never pretended about my hearing loss. It's as real as you standing in front of me right now."

"You are. You always were. Anything to get out of listening, to get out of work. Manipulative little bitch is what you are."

To think I actually bought him a Father of the Year mug once upon a time. What a laugh. "My audiologist seems to think my hearing loss is real. My brain injury is real too. Want to take responsibility?"

"Stupid bitch. Put the stuff back, and get the hell out."

"I'm taking my stuff." A red haze worked into my vision as we continued to stare each other down.

"Anything under this roof is mine. Including you ungrateful little brats. Put the stuff back."

Someone should hit this man like he hit his so-called "ungrateful little brats." My fists itched to do just that. But my fists wouldn't be enough; I wasn't strong enough.

Without moving, I took in the room. Dad's snack tray was just out of reach. A single bowl of nuts graced the top of the worn wood. One step forward would change everything. One step would allow me to grab the tray. One step would put me into direct danger. I took the step, right under my Dad's nose. "No."

Something crossed his face, and it wasn't remotely warm. The veins bulged in his neck, and I knew from experience what came next. Only this time, I was prepared. As my father's arm pulled back, I reached for the snack tray. With a flick of my wrist, I snapped it closed and swung it toward his head.

Nuts spilled onto the floor, scattered as if they, too, ran from this horrible man. Everything moved as if in slow motion: the nuts, Dad's fist, and the tray. The wood burned in my hands, something eerily familiar about the motion.

We collided in the middle, his fist with the snack tray. A loud crack of a sound stopped the slow motion, and everything sped up to Dad's fist breaking through the wood to stare me in the face. Splintered shards poked out on all sides, but I held my ground.

Dad took a step back and pulled his arm with him. The tray split in two at the motion, the weight jerking my right hand at an awkward angle. I let go, and one mangled half of now-shredded wood thudded to the floor, speckled with blood from my father.

I'd seen a tray just like it speckled with blood before. My blood. In fact, every few months or so the tray would need to be replaced. I thought it was used too often, but I never realized *how* it was used.

The ever-present tray was responsible for my hearing loss, for my brain injury. A long-buried memory worked its way out of the darkness. Me, age four, at the table, drawing a happy family of six. My father said my name, but I needed to finish coloring in his pants first. Me, still coloring, tongue stuck out, when he whacked the side of my head with the snack tray, sending me flying out of my chair, my head crashing to the ground. Then the tray, and his fists, coming down on me over and over again finished the job.

The beating had gone on for so long, with me huddled into myself for protection. I must have blacked out at some point. How had I survived that? How had any of us survived?

Dad ripped the remaining tray half from my left hand and whacked into me, splintered wood scraping my palm. I pulled myself back to the present. He now had both parts of the tray and wore a sinister smile, complete with no warmth or humor.

"Let me explain what happens next," he said in a voice so controlled it made my skin crawl. I wanted the upper hand back and was desperately afraid it was too late. "You are going to put your crap back in your room and get the hell out of my house. I never want to see your ugly face here again."

Words meant to cause pain, to bring on tears. They didn't. Couldn't. How could they? I was staring at the ugliest man I'd ever seen, a heart full of tar. And I felt nothing.

"I'm leaving, with *my* belongings. And I'm never coming back." I backed away from him, but he made no move to come after me. He stood, tray ends poised for an attack. And leered until I slammed the door between us.

Outside the fresh air calmed the heat in my face, the rush of everything in my blood. I had no idea if he would come after me. I banked on not. The man was nothing except lazy. Therefore I sat down on the steps and pulled out my phone.

My text messages were ready to burst. I scrolled through my sisters' responses and knew the police were on their way. I rubbed my left hand down my jeans, from midthigh to knee, trying to work out the sting.

I repeated the palm-smoothing motion. The faint sounds of sirens occurred in the distance, then cut short. A few minutes later, a police cruiser pulled up to the house.

I wiped my palms on my thighs again and walked over as two uniformed officers approached me.

"You okay, miss?"

Yes? No? What kind of a question was that? "I think so."

"Whose blood is that?" the other officer said, looking at my left thigh.

I followed his gaze and saw streaks of blood on the worn path I had made. I turned my left hand over and picked a piece of fake wood out of my scraped, raw, and bleeding palm. "Mine."

In the end, neither of us pressed charges. Since Dad couldn't claim any of the belongings, I got to take them with me, so at least the trip wasn't rendered null and void. Not able to accept his defeat, Dad had the police escort me off the premises. I never thought I'd leave my childhood home for the last time with two police officers at my back. The last daughter leaving home. Unwanted daughter number four, the biggest disgrace. The most damaged.

The one who fought back.

As I drove away, I couldn't help but think of Reed. Of how he'd be proud of me. Of how I was proud of myself. He had faith in me when I had none. He gave me support even when I couldn't fully accept it. He gave me...everything.

Before I met Reed, I wasn't sure I had a heart. Now that heart struggled against her barred confines. I wasn't raised with love, but that didn't mean I couldn't know love. Brain injury and all, I could learn. It took a deaf guy to teach me what love meant.

My heart struggled further, and I took the barbed wire down. I didn't need to hide behind my awful childhood. I didn't need to hide my hearing loss or my brain injury. Not when a wonderful man like Reed loved me. As is.

Not when I loved him back. All his flaws, all his strengths. And it was high time I told him. The ship may have sailed; I had no idea if things between us could ever be as they were. He deserved my words, even if it didn't change our outcome.

Chapter Forty

Reed

CARLI: I WANT to see you. Can I stop by?

I stared at my phone in my hands, at the text. A thread sprung to life after lying dormant on my cell for two months. I took a deep breath. Carli was alive.

Me: Sure.

I had no idea what she wanted. For all I knew she wanted to call me on deserting her like her sister had. Or maybe…No. No maybe. No more thoughts until I saw what she had to say.

Carli: Good. I'm parked outside. Almost chickened out. Sorry, my nerves are a bit frazzled. It's been a long day.

My eyebrows drew together as I headed for my front door.

Me: What happened?

I didn't know why I let myself get sucked back in. But Carli in trouble always called to the caveman in me. Didn't matter that we were no longer an item. I still needed to protect her.

What an ass I'd been. I refused to protect her from herself, yet I was ready to get up in arms over some mysterious text. Matti was right to let me have it.

Carli: I went to my parents' house to get the rest of my stuff. Only Dad came home early, and we had a little talk that involved his fist and a snack tray.

I stopped moving. Stopped breathing. Jesus. Then I had no restraint. I raced outside and down the stairs to where Carli still sat in her car.

We looked at each other for some time. I couldn't tear away from her face. There was nothing troublesome in her eyes. Bruises all but a memory. She was more beautiful in the flesh than any image ping-ponging around in my head. My resolve to keep distance between us evaporated. It took everything I had not to scoop her into my arms and hold her close.

Instead I opened her door. Those brown eyes of hers, so clear, no trace of medication, seemed to read my face. "*I'm fine,*" she signed, only I barely saw the sign. I zeroed in on the white gauze wrapped around her hand.

I squatted before her. "*What happened?*" Not allowing her to answer, I took her hand into mine. Foolish to touch her, to tease myself with the feel of her skin. I couldn't help myself. No blood bled through, no indication of what it covered.

She let me hold her wrapped hand and signed with her other. "*S-N-A-C-K T-R-A-Y. Dad's worse.*"

I let go of her hand. "*You fought back?*"

Carli nodded.

"*Good.*" I backed up, and she got out of the car, following me into the kitchen. Only she didn't stop there; she kept going straight to my room. I was sure I missed something. When I joined her, she sat on my bed, the notebook in her lap, writing away.

I had a moment of déjà-vu. Carli, on my bed, writing, like it was the most normal thing. It hit me deep inside, a sight for sore eyes yet also a bit like a ghost sat in my room. I wanted to touch her, feel her body moving beneath mine, see her naked skin. Ensure she was real. I turned to the floor and worked on keeping myself in check.

She looked up, bottom lip tucked between her teeth, and handed over the notebook. I took it from her, careful not to touch her this time.

I'm sorry, and thank you. I haven't touched the Oxy-Contin since you left. I wanted to. Oh how I wanted to. But I couldn't. And I didn't. And as my head cleared, I realized it had been part of what held me back. If you hadn't challenged me…If you hadn't shared your father's story…I don't know where I'd be today. I owe my recovery to you.

I shook my head and picked up the pen.

But I pushed you away. I didn't stay to help you through the rest. I deserted you.

Her eyebrows pulled tight, and she looked up at me. "*You talk to M-A-T-T-I? Don't listen to her.*" She picked up the pen before I could respond.

You gave me what I needed. No one else would do that. D tries, but she doesn't know me like you do. No one does.

My chest ached at her words. She took the paper back and wrote. I studied her face, the curve of her cheek, wondering where we stood. Where I wanted us to stand.

She tore the paper off and folded it in half. She held up a finger and bent to her purse, pulling something out that she then held behind her back. Her eyes were wide. With her hair in a ponytail, a pulse point beat at the base of her neck. She nodded toward the letter.

I salvaged these from the trash. I haven't refilled. There's very little I can do to prove I haven't taken any. I kept this to prove to myself I could overcome. And, yeah, in case I failed. I don't want to fail. I want you. I know, I've prob-ably lost. Too little, too late. But you need to know, not everyone ends up like your dad. Sometimes the only crash is the pills going in the trash.

I looked up, and she held out the bottle, the date from months past. She walked over to my trash can and tossed them in. Shoulders back, shuddery breath aside, she turned to face me. Tears filled in her eyes, but she stood her ground. We stared at each other. Words floating back and forth, both of us trying to figure out the right thing to say.

"I like your beard."

Wasn't expecting that. I scratched my cheek as she collected the paper and pen.

I liked it on you the first time we met, and the random spots in between where you let it grow. I always wondered what it felt like.

Her cheeks were pink when I finished reading. Like when we first met, those two spots of color on her face. In fact, she resembled that woman, before the attack and the pills. Was Carli really back?

I took a step toward her and picked up her unbandaged hand, brought it to my cheek. Even through the hair, her fingers were cold, always cold. I held her to me as her fingers played with the bristles.

The wall between us crumbled. We stood still. One of us needed to make the first move. Did I trust her? Could I trust her again? Caution had been my way of life, taught to me by my father.

I thought of his last message, of his faith in me. He told me to go with my gut, to fuck it all. What I wouldn't give to do just that and take Carli back.

She slid her hand down my face, brushing her fingertips under my bottom lip. Then she was gone and back to writing.

I didn't know love until I met you. Sure, I love my sisters, and they love me. But we don't say those words. We don't know those words. We weren't raised with love. We were raised to survive. And be perfect. Only I was never perfect, and until you I truly believed that. Imperfect Carli, no one would want me.

I closed myself off. But you are stubborn. You told me you love me and kept signing it even when I never signed it back. You gave me all of you when I had nothing to give.

You must know you have my heart. You have all of me. I don't know where we stand, or where we can even stand after everything I put us through. But you deserve to know this much, to know what's been there and I've been afraid to acknowledge. So...

I blinked at her words for a moment, scarcely allowing myself to believe them. Was she about to tell me what I thought she was?

I looked up at her nervous face. She took in a breath and signed, "*I love you.*"

I smiled so wide it hurt. She loved me. I thought I lost her, either through my own behavior or her father's or the pills. Yet here she was, telling me she loved me.

I squatted in front of her. No longer holding back. This was what I wanted, what I needed. The only way to get it was to trust her words as truth. "*I love you too.*"

Carli's watery eyes nearly spilled over. "*Still?*"

I brushed at her cheek. It was dry, but I needed to touch her. "*Forever.*"

She grabbed my cheeks and pulled my face to hers, giving me an openmouthed kiss, one with the promise of longevity and future. The past two months faded away as I collected her into my arms and poured my heart into hers. Only this time, she poured right back. This was Carli, full and open and everything I'd ever wanted.

Mine. Truly mine.

I kissed down her neck, rubbing my beard against her skin. Her grip on me tightened, and something vibrated in her chest. I pulled back. "*You really like the beard?*"

She caressed my cheek. "*Keep it. Please?*"

I kissed her again, planning on never shaving it off again. "*Only if you stay. With me.*"

A flicker of worry crossed on her face. *"You want me, brain damaged?"*

She hadn't figured it out yet? I reclaimed her lips, giving her everything I had. *"Yes. I want you. As you are now."*

A warmth crossed her eyes, and I nearly kissed her again before waiting for her answer. *"I'm yours."*

I yanked her to me until we both fell backward on the bed. Our mouths devoured each other without reserve or resolve. Just her. Just me. Together.

Author's Note

SIGNS OF ATTRACTION began as a very simple concept for me: I wanted to write a story about my own hearing-loss journey. Once upon a time, I was very unhappy with my ears. I didn't like them. I didn't like wearing hearing aids. I wanted to be "normal." And yet in many ways, my ears have always been a part of me, as much as my hair color or the shape of my nose.

As a freshman in college, I took an ASL class. This class changed my life forever. I not only found a language, I found a home in the Deaf Community. I stopped calling myself "hearing impaired"—a negative term within the community—and began calling myself Hard of Hearing and sometimes even Deaf.

I transferred to Boston University, into the Deaf Studies program. One of those classes was a linguistics class. I had CART with me, and a grad student used interpreters. Now, *Signs* isn't a personal love story. Sure, he was cute, and we were friendly, but I was already dating my future husband.

Flash ahead years into the future, when an idea struck. I thought back to that linguistics class, with the mix of CART and ASL interpreters, and an idea was born. Carli began speaking her lines, replacing my actual linguistics professor with my macroeconomic professor I could *not* understand, and the rest really is history.

There are bits and pieces of truth in this novel from my own life, and many things that are not from my own experience. My hearing loss is genetic, though I did envision Carli as a mirror image of my ears. One thing that is true: I spent my first college party at BU in a corner, talking with another Hard of Hearing student. This was the first time I had a conversation with anyone who understood what it was like to wear hearing aids. This friend was so kind to spend the entire party with me. The experience affected me enough that I wanted to give Carli the same.

So, what are my ears like? I have what is considered mild to profound conductive and sensorineural hearing loss. What does this mean? I'll start with the second part: conductive sensorineural loss means my damage is from both nerves and bones. In fact, when I was nine, I had surgery on my right ear, resulting in a bone being removed from my body. As to the first part: my left ear has a mild hearing loss. I can hear spoken language even without my hearing aids on, though I do need the volume turned up.

My right ear is a bit more complex. When I was younger, this ear had a moderate hearing loss and missed some speech sounds without my hearing aids. The surgery didn't help, and two accidents later, my ear is now considered moderate to profound. Deaf. For me, this means I can still hear sound, but parts of speech are missing, and everything needs to be LOUD. I still wear a hearing aid, and it helps, even if listening solely with my right ear is a bit of an extreme sport in guessing games.

I sometimes describe myself as Deaf/Hard of Hearing, using both signs at the same time, much like Reed did in the novel.

As for Reed, I wanted to make him Deaf—he might hear a few extremely loud sounds like a lawn mower or airplane, but mostly he hears nothing—and show how much Deaf people *can*. We can drive. We can go to college. We can do just about anything, even play music and dance. Here I have an educated Deaf man, a teacher, a graduate student, who is very comfortable in his own skin. Is that true for every Deaf person? Sadly, no. It really boils down to language access. ASL is a full language and denial of it has hurt so many.

I always wanted to bring hearing loss into my stories. I find that many people know of hearing loss without really understanding it. Hearing aids don't fix hearing loss. They amplify sounds. That's all. Think of taking an old recording that is scratchy and turning the volume up. The sound becomes distorted and harder to hear. That's similar to hearing loss.

I hope to have spread a little awareness with Carli and Reed. But mostly I wanted to write stories about my world, my ears. And give these stories to others like me.

Hearing loss isn't something I've seen as an attractive trait I possessed, especially not hearing aids. It's been an uplifting personal challenge to write a heroine and hero with a hearing loss. These characters, these words, have helped alter my personal view of myself, removing those lingering traces of negativity related to my ears.

Thank you for stepping into this world with me. If you share my ears, I do hope you enjoyed. If you're hearing, I hope I showed you a little about what it's really like to have a hearing loss, from both Carli and Reed's POVs.

About the Author

LAURA BROWN lives in Massachusetts with her quirky, abnormal family. Her husband's put up with her since high school, her young son keeps her on her toes, and her three cats think they deserve more scratches. Hearing loss is a big part of who she is, from her own Hard of Hearing ears to the characters she creates.

Give in to your Impulses . . .
Continue reading for excerpts from
our newest Avon Impulse books.
Available now wherever ebooks are sold.

CHANGE OF HEART
by T.J. Kline

MONTANA HEARTS:
TRUE COUNTRY HERO
by Darlene Panzera

ONCE AND FOR ALL
AN AMERICAN VALOR NOVEL
by Cheryl Etchison

An Excerpt from

CHANGE OF HEART
By T.J. Kline

Bad luck has plagued Leah McCarran most
of her life, until the tide turns and she lands
her new dream job as a therapist at Heart Fire
Ranch. But when her car breaks down and
she finds herself stranded, the playboy who
shows up to her rescue makes Leah wonder
if her luck just went from bad to worse.

Leah McCarran couldn't believe her luck as she popped the hood of her classic GTO and glanced behind her, down the deserted stretch of highway in the Northern California foothills. Steam poured from her radiator, and there wasn't a single car in sight.

She blew back a strand of her caramel-colored hair as the curl fell into her eye and caught on her mascaraed eyelashes. Even those felt like they were melting into solid clumps on her eyes. It was sweltering for mid-May, and, of course, her car decided to take a dump on the side of the highway today. She fanned herself with one hand as she looked down at the overheated engine. It probably wouldn't have been nearly this big a deal if her cell phone hadn't just taken a crap, too. To top off her miserable day, she'd spilled her iced coffee all over the damn thing getting out of the car and likely destroyed it once and for all.

This wasn't the way she'd hoped to start her new job or her new life at Heart Fire Ranch.

Walking back to the driver's side of the car, Leah had no clue what to do now. Luckily, her boss wasn't expecting her until this evening, and she'd had the foresight, knowing her penchant for bad luck, to leave early. But until some Good Samaritan decided to drive by *and* stop for her, she was S.O.L. She kicked the tire as she walked by. As if trying to deny her even that small measure of satisfaction, the sole of her worn combat boot caught in the tread, nearly making her fall over.

"Son of a—"

Leah caught herself against the side of the car, willing the tears of frustration to subside, back into the vault where they belonged. That was one thing she'd learned as a child: tears meant weakness.

And showing weakness was asking for more pain.

She bent over into the car, looking for something to mop up the sticky mess the coffee was making on the restored leather interior of her car. She reached for the denim shirt she'd been wearing over her tank top before she'd left Chowchilla this morning, before the air had turned from chilled to hell-on-earth-hot.

"Shit," she muttered. Trying to sop up coffee with denim was like trying to mop a floor with a broom: it did absolutely no good.

"Hot damn! That is the most incredible thing I've seen all day."

The crunch of tires pulling off the asphalt of the highway was a welcome sound, but the awe she heard in the husky voice was enough to send a chill down her spine. Leah threw the shirt down onto the coffee-soaked floorboard. Standing up, she spun on the heel of her boot, her fists clenching at her sides as she tried to control the instinct to punch a man in the mouth.

"Excuse me? Do you really have so little class?"

"Oh, shit! No, that's not . . ." She watched as the man unfolded himself from a late model Challenger and shut the door, jogging across the empty two-lane highway to her side. "I'm sorry, I meant the car."

Leah crossed her arms under her breasts and arched a single, disbelieving brow. "Sure, you did."

A blush flooded his dark caramel skin. "I swear I meant the car. Not that you're not . . . I mean . . . crap." He cursed again. "Let me try this again. Do you need some help?"

An Excerpt from

MONTANA HEARTS: TRUE COUNTRY HERO

By Darlene Panzera

For Jace Aldridge, the chase is half the fun. The famous rodeo rider has spent most of life chasing down steers and championship rodeo belts, but after an accident in the arena, his career is put on temporary hold. When he's offered a chance to stay at Collins Country Cabins, Jace jumps at the opportunity to spend more time with the beautiful but wary Delaney Collins.

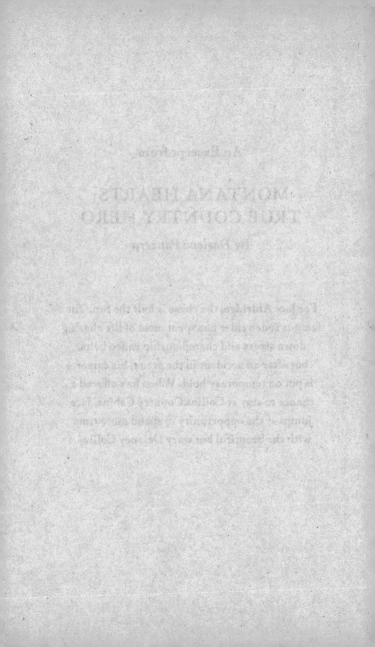

The cowboy winked at her. Delaney Collins lowered her camera lens and glanced around twice to make sure, but no one else behind the roping chute was looking his direction. Heat flooded her cheeks as he followed up the wink with a grin, and a multitude of wary warnings sounded off in her heart. The last thing she'd wanted was to catch the rodeo circuit star's interest. She pretended to adjust the settings, then raised the camera to her eye once again, determined to fulfill her duty and take the required photos of the handsome dark-haired devil.

Except he wouldn't stand still. He climbed off his buckskin horse, handed the reins to a nearby gatekeeper, gave a young kid in the stands a high five, and then walked straight toward her.

Delaney tightened her hold on the camera, wishing she could stay hidden behind the lens, and considered several different ways to slip away unnoticed. But she knew she couldn't avoid him forever. Not when it was her job to shadow the guy and capture the highlights from his steer-wrestling runs. Maybe he only wanted to check in to make sure she was getting the right shots?

Most cowboys like Jace Aldridge had large egos to match their championship-sized belt buckles, one reason she usually avoided these events and preferred capturing images of plants and animals. But when the lead photographer for *True Montana Magazine* called in sick before the event and they needed a fill-in, Delaney had been both honored and excited to accept the position. Perhaps after the magazine viewed her work, they'd hire her for more photo ops. Then she wouldn't have to rely solely on the profits from her share of her family's guest ranch to support herself.

She swallowed hard as the stocky, dark-haired figure, whose image continuously graced the cover of every western periodical, smiled, his eyes on her—yes, definitely her—as he drew near.

He stretched out his hand. "Jace Aldridge."

She stared at his chapped knuckles. Beside her, Sammy Jo gave her arm a discreet nudge, urging her to accept his handshake. After all, it would be impolite to refuse. Even if, in addition to riding rodeo, he was a hunter, an adversary of the animals she and her wildlife rescue group regularly sought to save.

Lifting her gaze to meet his, she replied, "Delaney Collins."

"Nice to meet you," Jace said, his rich, baritone voice smooth and . . . dangerously distracting. His hand gave hers a warm squeeze, and although he glanced toward Sammy Jo to include her in his greeting, it was clear who held his real interest. "Are you with the press?"

Delaney glanced down at the Canon EOS 7D with its high-definition 20.2 megapixel zoom lens hanging down from the strap around her neck. "Yes. I'm taking photos for *True Montana*."

The edges of his mouth curved into another smile. "I haven't seen you around before."

"I—I'm not around much, but Sammy Jo here," she said, motioning toward her friend to divert his attention, "used to race barrels. You must know her. Sammy Jo Macpherson?"

Jace gave her friend a brief nod. "I believe we've met."

"Del's a great photographer," Sammy Jo said, bouncing the attention back to her.

Jace grinned. "I bet."

"It's the lens," Delaney said, averting her gaze, and Sammy Jo shot her a disgruntled look as if to say, *Smarten up, this guy's in to you. Don't blow it!*

Except she had no desire to get involved in a relationship right now. And definitely not one *with a hunter*. She needed to focus on her two-and-a-half-year-old daughter, Meghan, and help her family's guest ranch bring in enough money to support them.

An Excerpt from

ONCE AND FOR ALL
An American Valor Novel
By Cheryl Etchison

Staff Sergeant Danny MacGregor has always said
military and matrimony don't mix, but if there's
one person he would break all his rules for, it's
Bree—his first friend, first love, first everything.

Bree Dunbar has battled cancer, twice. What
she wants most is a fresh start. By some
miracle her wish is granted, but it comes
with one major string attached—the man
who broke her heart ten years before.

The rules for this marriage of convenience are
simple: when she's ready to stand on her own two
feet, she'll walk away and he'll let her go. Only,
things don't always go according to plan . . .

An Excerpt from

ONCE AND FOR ALL

An American Valor Novel

by Chuck Hillman

She pulled into the garage of her parents' home and stared in the rearview mirror at the house across the street where Danny used to live. The same one where he was now staying. She had no idea how much longer he'd be in town, but odds weren't in her favor he would just leave her be. She'd thrown down the gauntlet and Daniel Patrick MacGregor had never been one to back down from a challenge.

Hitting the garage remote, the house slowly disappeared from view as the door lowered to the ground. Bree headed inside, her mother greeting her at the back door as she opened it.

"Can I help you carry some things in?" she asked while drying her hands on a dish towel.

"Nothing to bring in."

Bree scooted past her mother, not yet ready to rehash the morning's events.

"I thought you were going to the store?"

"I'll go back later."

She grabbed the ibuprofen from the cabinet by the sink, the dull ache behind her eyes now reaching epic proportions. After swallowing two small tablets with a single drink of water, she headed for her bedroom.

"Is everything okay, sweetheart? You look flushed."

"Fine," she said, ducking out of her mother's reach. Twenty-eight years old and her mother still wanted to check her temperature with the back of her hand.

"Are you sure? You're not running a fever, are you? Your immune system still isn't where it needs to be. You need to be careful—"

"I'm fine, Mom. I swear. Just going to lie down for a bit."

Bree darted upstairs, escaping to the relative peace and quiet of her bedroom. She closed the door behind her, sighing in relief to see her mother wasn't hot on her heels.

She loved her dearly and wouldn't have survived chemo treatments without her, but sometimes her mother's care and concern was too much. Suffocating. And despite her best intentions, she was always reminding Bree that she'd been very sick, when all Bree wanted to do was put it behind her.

For now, she'd settle for crawling into bed and trying to forget the morning ever happened. As she closed the blinds, a familiar old truck pulled into the driveway across the street. The door flung open, and booted feet hit the concrete. Instinctively she jumped back from the window, not wanting Danny to think she'd been standing there, watching, waiting all this time for him to return home.

Bree held her breath and with the tips of her fingers lifted a single wooden slat so she could peek out. The old truck's passenger door sat open wide, but there was no sign of either brother. The screen door swung open and Danny bounded down the porch steps, reaching the truck in four long strides. He grabbed the last few grocery bags from the floorboard and shoved the door closed with his elbow. On his way back into the house he suddenly stopped and turned to look across the street. At her house. At her bedroom window.

Despite peering through a tiny gap no wider than an inch, she knew he could somehow see her. She could feel his gaze locked on hers. But he didn't drop the grocery bags on the front porch or storm across the street toward her. Instead, he just stood there. His expression completely unreadable.

Surely he wouldn't march across the street and start things up again right now? He wouldn't dare.

Oh, but he would.

Maybe he expected her to do something. Wave. Stick out her tongue. Flip him the bird. Instead, like a deer caught in a hunter's sight, she stood frozen, unable to will herself away from the window. Then he did the very last thing she expected him to do.

He smiled.

A smile so wide, so bright, she hadn't seen the likes of one in over a decade. Although she didn't want to admit it, she'd missed that smile desperately and her heart squeezed painfully in her chest. Finally, Danny looked away, breaking eye contact, releasing her from his spell. As he turned to go inside, he shook his head, apparently unable to believe it himself.

For a long time after he went inside, Bree stood there looking out the window. And the more she replayed it in her mind, the more she began to wonder if she'd imagined the entire thing.

Only one thing was for certain—things between them were far from over.